"We're not hunting him yet."

"Stress the 'yet,' I presume."

"You'd be right. And it's official—we can't let them have him again. It's assumed that if they get another shot at him he'll crack," Bolan stated.

"I wouldn't bet my life on that," McCarter said.

"We're betting Katz's."

The Briton pictured Katz as they'd recently found him, then imagined himself sighting down the barrel of an automatic weapon at his old friend and comrade in arms, squeezing off a kill shot. Would it be a mercy in those circumstances, or a pure cold-blooded act of pragmatism?

"I'll do it if I have to," McCarter vowed.

"So will I," the Executioner told him.

"I guess that makes us heroes, then."

"It makes us soldiers—nothing more or nothing less."

MACK BOLAN ®
The Executioner

The Don Pendleton's
Executioner®
WARRIOR'S REQUIEM

A GOLD EAGLE BOOK FROM

W⊕RLDWIDE®

TORONTO • NEW YORK • LONDON
AMSTERDAM • PARIS • SYDNEY • HAMBURG
STOCKHOLM • ATHENS • TOKYO • MILAN
MADRID • WARSAW • BUDAPEST • AUCKLAND

First edition November 2003
ISBN 0-373-64300-4

Special thanks and acknowledgment to
Mike Newton for his contribution to this work.

WARRIOR'S REQUIEM

Printed in U.S.A.

That man travels the longest journey that undertakes it in search of a sincere friend.

—Ali Ibn Abi-Talib,
Sentences (7th century)

There's little consolation in revenge when a true friend is lost, but sometimes a little consolation is enough. And sometimes there's justice.

—Mack Bolan

For the victims and survivors of
September 11, 2001.
Justice.

Prologue

The terrorist camp lay forty arid miles northeast of Dar'a, Syria. The compound featured no-frills housing for 150 men, but fewer than one-third that number were currently in residence.

Mack Bolan, a.k.a. the Executioner, was concerned with only one of them, and that one was a friend. The hell of it was that he couldn't swear the man he sought was even really there. He wouldn't know for sure until he made his way into the camp and had a closer look.

By which time it would be light-years too late to change his mind.

"Ready," a male voice whispered from the earpiece Bolan wore.

"Roger," Bolan replied. He waited, counting heartbeats. He was coming up on seven when a female voice echoed the first: "Ready."

"On me," he said into the small stalk microphone that left his hands free for the MP-5 SD-3 submachine gun he carried, the grenades clipped to his combat webbing, the Beretta 93-R slung beneath his left arm and the mighty Desert Eagle semiautomatic pistol on his hip. Thus dressed to kill, he slithered forward on his belly, moving closer to the enemy.

And, Bolan hoped, a little closer to his friend.

It was a gamble, lacking any concrete proof, but the soldier couldn't let it go. He would've come alone, if need be, but his two companions were both equally committed to the quest.

Friendship and blood, respectively, had brought them here to do or die, seeking a kinsman who was worth the risk.

There was no fence around the camp, no roving sentries to prevent the Executioner from entering. He had their routine timed and memorized, worked out to let him reach the nearest Quonset hut while they were eighty yards away, backs turned. Because the compound's occupants relied on secrecy to keep them breathing, there were no floodlights to put him on display.

Perfect.

Bolan reached his preliminary destination, pausing for a moment there, pressing his ear against a corrugated metal wall that still held noonday's heat. Inside the hut, muffled voices spoke in Arabic, sounding relaxed, at ease.

But not for long.

The nearest window was around a corner, twenty feet away. It was propped open to allow the desert's cool night breeze inside. There was no screen in place, an error that the hut's occupants would rue—if they survived. Bolan selected a grenade, released its pin and tossed the bomb through the open window. There was no way to be subtle at a time like this. He heard it strike the wooden floor and start to roll, but only dim lights burned within the barracks, and it took a moment for his enemies to track the sound.

By then, it was too late.

Contained by roof and walls, the blast somehow seemed louder than it would have in the open air. Shrapnel punched through the hut's metal sides and shattered window glass, but other shards tore flesh and bone. He heard men cursing, crying out in pain, before the echo of the blast had ceased to ripple through the camp.

At once, all hell broke loose.

Bolan's two companions started firing from their places on the camp's perimeter, spotting targets where they could, strafing the huts if none was available.

The camp went wild, men rushing to and fro, some of them barely dressed. They all had weapons, though, and within moments the enemy guns were lighting up the desert night with muzzle-flashes, two heavy machine guns spraying emerald tracers through the darkness.

The Executioner was in the midst of it, moving, trusting in panic and confusion to disguise him. With his enemies in groggy disarray, no special uniform distinguished Bolan or betrayed him. Those who paused to give the man in black a second glance were leveled by short bursts from his SMG.

He moved from hut to hut, killing, searching. One face occupied his mind. One name was on his lips each time he crashed another door. Each time he pulled the trigger, Bolan hesitated long enough to make sure he wasn't about to kill a friend.

Nothing.

The battle closed around him like a straitjacket, as Bolan wondered whether he had risked three lives in vain.

DAVID MCCARTER knew whom he was looking for, but finding one man in the middle of a firefight could be bloody difficult, more so when the all the lights went out and he had no idea which corner of the killing ground concealed the bloke he sought. Not quite impossible—he never liked to use *that* word—but it was definitely touch-and-go.

The Briton was ready and waiting when Bolan kicked off the attack. He had his first three targets marked and took them down with short, precision bursts from his H&K submachine gun. Three or four rounds each, and that left him with nearly two-thirds of a 30-round magazine yet, before he was forced to reload. He didn't give the dead a second thought. They had been obstacles when they were breathing; they were simply cast-off rubbish now.

McCarter moved into the camp, taking advantage of the shadows and confusion as he sought the man he—all of them—had come to extricate. He'd come to terms with the idea that they might be too late, in which case there was nothing for it but a double portion of hellfire revenge. He'd come prepared for that, too, equipped with the silent MP-5, grenades, a SIG-Sauer P-220 semiauto pistol on his right hip, and a razor-honed Sykes-Fair-

bairn commando dagger sheathed on his left. Whether his enemies came at him from a distance or fought hand-to-hand, he was
prepared.

But he needed to avoid killing the man he sought, while he
was fighting for his own life.

Two members of the camp's defensive team were suddenly
in front of him, gaping at McCarter, yelling in Arabic as they
leveled Kalashnikov assault rifles. He took advantage of their
split-second confusion, noting that one was dressed only in
white boxer shorts, ignoring the rest as he raked them with a
stream of 9 mm Parabellum manglers from his SMG. The
shooters went down twitching, weapons tumbling from their
lifeless fingers, and McCarter instantly forgot them as he
pressed on with his quest.

The first two huts he checked were both deserted. In the third
he killed a young man who'd been slow responding to the general alarm, maybe embarrassed to be seen without his pants.
Whatever, he was grappling with a pair of baggy jeans when Mc-
Carter surprised him, both hands occupied, his rifle propped
against the wall beyond his reach.

McCarter didn't speak Arabic, so he tried it in English.
"Hostage! One-armed man! Where is he?"

The young Palestinian blinked at him, maybe confused,
maybe stalling. Whichever it was, he said nothing, but lunged for
the rifle. McCarter beat him to it with a rising burst that hacked
through ribs and vital organs, spinning the man in midair and
dumping him against the wall, the useless weapon pinned beneath his body.

Wasted effort, McCarter thought, biting back a curse. Instead
of venting, he used his slender microphone to ask the night,
"What news?"

"Nothing so far," Bolan replied.

"None here," the woman's voice came back to him.

He did curse then, but silently, inside his head. They'd come
so far and risked so much, for what? He couldn't see beyond the
killing moment, didn't have a clue where they'd look next if they
struck out on this attempt. They couldn't search the whole

damned country, much less scour the Middle East at large to find one man.

Not if his captors wanted him to disappear.

Try harder, then.

McCarter moved on to the next hut, and the next. He killed those he encountered, but he wasn't trigger-happy. Twice along the way, he asked young men to show him where the one-armed prisoner was kept. The first, blank-faced, uncomprehending, simply shook his head and died. The second answered back in broken English that he knew of no such man.

That one died, too.

Somebody knew, McCarter thought. Someone would talk.

But no one did.

Leaving the seventh hut he'd checked since entering the camp, two dead men sprawled inside, McCarter suddenly came under fire. At least two weapons by the sound of it, and the divergent impact of incoming rounds against the corrugated metal wall behind him. Dropping prone, he scanned the compound for a nearby muzzle-flash that would betray his enemies.

The nearer of them stood some ten or fifteen yards away, angling his weapon for a better shot. Behind and to his left, another six or seven paces farther back, a second shooter grappled with his rifle, as if trying to correct a jam.

McCarter took the closer gunman first, stitching him with a zigzag burst from groin to throat, spinning him around before he fell. The dead man went down firing, finger locked around his AK's trigger, and the wild rounds dropped his partner in a spray of crimson, before McCarter could correct his aim and do the job himself.

Up and at it!

He scrambled to his feet and pushed on past the two fresh corpses, trying not to think that he and his companions had arrived too late.

BOLAN WAS SWIFTLY running out of hiding places in his sector of the camp. The prisoner he sought was nowhere to be found, and confirmation from the others via radio told the soldier they were striking out, as well. He didn't want to think about the implications of that failure, but he had no choice.

They had the right group, he was clear on that from all reports, but Allah's Lance had other camps in Syria. The hostage could've been shipped out before they reached the site, assuming that his kidnappers hadn't conveyed him to another hideout in the first place.

Then again, he could be dead. It hadn't been a ransom job to start with. If they'd squeezed sufficient information out of him or failed to break him down, a close-range bullet and a shallow grave would clear the slate. It was impossible to guess how many corpses had been planted in the Middle East—mass graves or individuals—and finding one without directions from the gravediggers would be a hopeless task. If Katz was dead before they started looking for him…

But he had to think the prisoner was still alive, or every move he made became a futile exercise. They hadn't come equipped for scorched-earth vengeance, and the war wouldn't end here if it came down to that. This was a probe designed to locate and extract a living prisoner.

But they were striking out.

Bolan cut down a gunner who seemed barely old enough to shave. The automatic rifle in his adversary's hands made him a threat, though, rendering his date of birth irrelevant. The young man had picked his lifestyle and companions. He might've chosen martyrdom in other circumstances, but the shocked expression on his face told Bolan that he hadn't been expecting it this night.

"Report!" he rasped into the microphone.

"Nothing, dammit!" McCarter said.

"Nothing," Rebecca Mindel echoed.

"Roger. Fall back on the motor pool ASAP."

It was the plan they'd worked out in advance. Whatever happened, whether they made out or came up empty, exiting the camp would be a dicey proposition. If they'd found the prisoner, he might've been disabled. If they didn't, it was still a gamble, fleeing with the garrison's pissed-off survivors on their heels, perhaps with reinforcements coming from the next camp to the north.

They needed wheels, and since they'd hiked in from the drop site, that meant borrowing a ride from Allah's Lance. The compound's motor pool, as shown in aerial surveillance photographs, included several military-style jeeps and flatbed trucks, along with two dirt bikes and what appeared to be a homemade dune buggy.

A jeep would do, Bolan thought.

It would have to.

He hated leaving empty-handed, but it beat hell out of not leaving at all.

The motor pool was on the far side of the camp, due west, perhaps a hundred yards from where he stood. It was a straight shot through the middle of the killing ground, and Bolan didn't feel like wasting precious time. There'd been enough of that already, and the other members of his team were on the move.

He ran for it, head down, eyes tracking left and right by firelight, trying not to make himself conspicuous. He'd done his best and been found wanting. Now, the trick was to extract his team and try again.

Try what?

Another search, no doubt. But where?

He didn't know.

Priorities, he thought. Job one was getting out alive. They couldn't do Katz any good if they were dead or caged themselves.

Running, Bolan tried to guess how many terrorists were still alive inside the compound. From the random fire around him, he guessed that half or more of the original contingent were still fit to kill, if they could only find a target for their rage and bullets. Getting past them would require more nerve than skill. It also wouldn't hurt if they could score some luck along the way.

Luck had deserted them so far, but maybe they were overdue.

He found Rebecca Mindel waiting for him at the motor pool, crouched between the dusty flatbed trucks. McCarter hadn't made it yet, but since there'd been no squeal on Bolan's headset, he assumed the former SAS commando was en route.

"Pick a jeep," he told Mindel. "I'll see if I can slow them down on the pursuit."

"One jeep," Mindel replied and went to do her job, as Bolan

drew his Ka-Bar fighting knife and started down the line of vehicles, beginning with the nearest truck.

SALIM ZUHAYR WAS on the verge of panic as he moved about the camp, counting his dead, ordering the survivors to fall in behind him and stop wasting bullets on shadows. So far, he'd counted nineteen corpses, all of them his men and not a fallen enemy among them.

It was chaos in the camp, men racing here and there, without direction, firing blindly in the night. Zuhayr had already seen two of his men shoot each other, one killed outright, the other crippled by a gaping leg wound. If pressed to prove that there were enemies in camp, Zuhayr couldn't have offered anything resembling evidence.

And yet the first explosion had been caused by something. After that, the gunfire had spread rapidly from one side of the compound to the other. He had seen too many of his soldiers lying dead to think that all of them were accidental victims of chaotic friendly fire.

But if there *were* foes in the camp, who where they? Where had they come from and what did they want?

He thought first of Israeli commandos, then dismissed the notion, recalling their fondness for massed troops and aerial support. This near the Golan Heights, Zuhayr would've expected screaming jets, perhaps even an armored thrust across the border in defiance of Syrian sovereignty. Instead, they had small-unit engagement with light weapons and no air cover at all.

Who would do such a thing?

Leading his troop through battle smoke, collecting stragglers on the way, Zuhayr ran down a short list in his mind. He ruled out Syrian authorities, since they were friends of Allah's Lance and would've turned out in full force, should anything have altered that relationship.

Who else?

Perhaps one of the other Palestinian commando groups that trained in Syria. The bitterness between selected companies of freedom fighters was well-known, even notorious, and a primary reason their individual strikes against Israel hadn't been effective to date. Some who knew better preferred to trade insults among themselves. while allowing the common enemy to escape, and this wouldn't be the first time such animosity had spilled Arab blood.

The Sword of Truth, perhaps, or Mecca's Fire. Both groups had clashed with Allah's Lance before, and no doubt would again if they believed they had a shot at victory.

A runner found Zuhayr, wheezing as much from fright and pain as from exertion. He was bleeding freely from a scalp wound, and his right arm dangled uselessly at his side, a tattered crimson thing.

"The trucks," he gasped, pointing with his good arm to the west.

Zuhayr was in his face, demanding, "What of them?"

"Strangers," the young man said. "I tried to stop them, but..." In place of further words, he shrugged and flapped the ruined arm against his flank.

"Useless!" Zuhayr exclaimed, then turned to face his men.

"We must defend the vehicles," he told them. "Mark your targets well. Control your fire."

That said, he shoved the wounded man aside and set off for the motor pool, trusting the rest to follow him. He wasn't sure what they would find there, but he needed something—anything—to verify that the confusing firefight hadn't been initiated by his own soldiers. That much, at least, might save him from a court-martial and firing squad. If he could capture one of the raiders alive, so much the better for his case.

It was a short march to the motor pool and Zuhayr set the pace, double-timing past corpses and huts scarred by gunfire, a few bleeding smoke from their windows. He watched for enemies along the way, dead or alive, but still saw none. If they were gone before he reached the motor pool, or if his wounded soldier had imagined them, what would he do?

"Faster!" he commanded, picking up his pace. Speed might not solve the problem, but he had to try.

They were still thirty yards from the vehicle lineup when Zuhayr saw one of the jeeps come to life, headlights flaring, tires spitting sand as it surged out of line. He couldn't make out any details of the driver or passengers, except that they were armed and dressed in black. One of his soldiers tried to block the speeding vehicle and was cut down by silenced automatic fire.

"Go after them!" Zuhayr shouted. His troop of soldiers scrambled for the other vehicles. The fleeing jeep had barely reached the outer limits of the camp when one of them called back, "They've cut the tires!"

"And these!" another shouted to Salim.

"These, too!"

He cursed, watching the taillights fade, but they weren't completely without hope. "The motorcycles!" he commanded. "And the dune buggy! Hurry!"

Zuhayr was thankful now that he had parked the smaller vehicles beside his own quarters and kept them separate from the rest. With luck, they still might have a chance to overtake the raiders and discover who they were.

"Take one of them alive, if possible," he called after his running men. "And if not, bring me their heads!"

REBECCA MINDEL HAD expected to feel anguish if their mission failed, but in its place there was a cold, dead feeling in her chest. On balance, she preferred it to the pain she knew was bound to follow later, when she'd have more time to think. For now, the numbness met her needs.

"They're after us," McCarter said from the jeep's back seat.

Mindel saw Mike Blanski check the rearview mirror, as she swiveled in her seat. A mile or less behind them, gaining rapidly, she saw two sets of headlights. "Damn!" she said. "I thought we flattened tires on everything they had."

"Guess not," McCarter replied, half turning in his seat to cover their retreat.

Two of the chasing headlights picked that moment to divide and swerve apart, now running parallel with a distance of forty yards or so between them.

"Dirt bikes," McCarter stated. "They'll be faster than we are."

"So what's the other one?" Mindel inquired. "I counted off the jeeps and trucks."

"Maybe the dune buggy," Mack Bolan told her. "I didn't see it with the other vehicles."

Of course. Disgusted at the oversight, she checked her weapon, making sure the magazine was nearly full. A running fight on open ground wouldn't have been her first choice, but at least it beat being surrounded in the camp, or stranded somewhere on the desert flats with enemies on every side.

This way, at least, they had a fighting chance.

"We can't outrun them in this thing," Bolan said. "Be ready when they make their move."

"Ready," McCarter said. Mindel kept quiet, but she had her finger on the trigger of her SMG. On either side of them, the motorcycles still gained ground, their engines revved up to a high-pitched whine. The dune buggy held steady on their track, except when bumps or furrows in the desert hardpan made its headlights jump and sway.

How long before the hunters overtook them? Moments, Mindel thought, perhaps seconds. How many guns were after them? She knew the bikes seated no more than two riders apiece. As for the dune buggy, she reckoned two more passengers, then doubled it for safety's sake. Four guns, at least; more likely six, possibly eight.

"Incoming!" McCarter snapped, and ducked below the stiff back of his seat.

Mindel saw muzzle-flashes from the pillion seats of both dirt bikes and heard a bullet strike the jeep's rear end.

Bolan swerved the jeep to spoil the shooters' aims. He couldn't safely run a proper zigzag course at night, on unfamiliar ground, but anything was an improvement over running in a long straight line. This way, at least, the gunners had to work for every hit, while concentrating on control of their own vehicles.

It was working—to a point. The hunters on the dirt bikes still kept firing, but their rounds went high and wide. When Mindel and McCarter started to return their fire, the two-wheel trackers veered away and out of range, flanking the jeep and keeping it in sight. Bolan couldn't douse the headlights without crashing in record time, but he maintained the weaving course despite repeated jolts that sent a string of shock waves echoing through everyone's spine and skull.

The dune buggy commandos had a better time of it, coming along behind the jeep. It meant the hunters had to eat some dust, but they were keeping pace and laying down sporadic fire that made McCarter curse each time a round connected with the jeep. "There goes the jerrican!" he said, as one slug drilled their spare, rear-mounted fuel can.

Bolan raised his voice above the rush of wind. "Use it!"

"Roger!" McCarter flashed a grin and went to work, unfastening the punctured fuel can from its tailgate mount. A moment later, there was a flash of fire, as from a pocket lighter, and the jerrican was airborne, trailing flames.

It went up like a bomb, in the dune buggy's path, but their pursuers had steel nerves and quick reflexes. Swerving sharply to the left, they missed most of the leaping flames and charged ahead. Their left-rear tire was briefly lit and flaring, but the desert put it out in nothing flat.

"No joy," McCarter said, and raised his submachine gun once again. "Let's see if I can slow them some other way."

Just then, the dirt bike on Mindel's side adjusted course and veered closer, airborne for a moment as it cleared a gently rolling dune. The pillion rider fired again, his bullets hissing past her, one or more exploding through the jeep's windshield.

Bolan cursed and hit the brakes, twisting the steering wheel. He was already out and moving as they shuddered to a halt in rolling clouds of dust.

"Come on!" he barked. "We end it here!"

BOLAN HIT THE GROUND running, taking advantage of the dust cloud that momentarily screened his team from their pursuers. It wouldn't last, but it was something, anyway, and when it cleared, there'd be no cover from the hunters who encircled them.

Unless he acted swiftly to eliminate the threat.

The dirt bikes circled Bolan's jeep. The drivers had their hands full, but their passengers were busy firing compact automatic weapons. From behind him, eastward, Bolan felt as much as saw the dune buggy approaching, slowing now for caution's sake as it drew closer.

He hit a crouch and waited for the nearer dirt bike to complete its latest circuit, coming back around. At twenty yards or so it didn't qualify as being close, but it was near enough. Bolan was waiting when it passed, the pillion rider leaning out to aim another burst toward the jeep.

Bolan fired his SMG and watched the shooter spill from his precarious seat, tumbling head over heels in the dust as his ride raced away from him. The driver felt it instantly, the bike fishtailing as it suddenly lost weight. He glanced back for a heartbeat, giving Bolan all the time he needed for a second killing burst.

The MP-5 stuttered its muffled death message, Parabellum shockers cutting deep beneath the driver's left arm and flinging him off balance. He took the dirt bike with him when he fell, lying down almost gracefully, sliding for fifty-odd feet over sharp rocks and sand. The bike might rise again, if someone came along to salvage it, but the driver was finished.

That still left four guns, anyway, but even as the thought took shape in Bolan's mind another two were neutralized. He turned to face the sound of gunfire, just in time to see McCarter and Mindel open up in unison on the second dirt bike. Their silenced bursts cleared the saddle with near surgical precision, both shooters sprawled in the dirt before they knew what hit them. The bike ran on without them for some ten or fifteen yards, then stalled and toppled over on its side, the motor sputtering as it was starved for fuel.

Bolan turned back toward the dune buggy, parked now, some forty yards from where he'd brought the jeep to rest. The buggy's driver had already doused its headlights, but a three-quarter moon showed Bolan three figures fanned out on the flat ground, advancing swiftly toward the jeep. All three were clearly armed, and while he couldn't see what they were packing, Bolan put his money on Kalashnikov assault rifles.

His team would've been cornered and outgunned at longer

range—the AKs were capable of lethal hits at three hundred meters, compared to the MP-5's two hundred—but his adversaries had decided to close for point-blank kills. Thankful for the mental mechanism that subordinated logic to emotion, Bolan put the jeep between him and his human targets, feeling Mindel and McCarter join him seconds later. They were in a fair position now, but armor-piercing rounds could still pass through the jeep to cut them down. Their vehicle might also be disabled, leaving them afoot and vulnerable to pursuit while they were waiting for their pickup from the west.

Details.

Right now, he had to focus on survival, which, in turn, meant taking down the last three shooters without giving them a chance to score. Anything else would only amplify the failure of their mission, maybe turn it from a blunder to a wipeout.

He chose the nearest of the gunners, on the left of the advancing front, and framed the shadow figure in his sights. Bolan was on the mark and squeezing off a silent burst as the advancing man began to lay down a suppressing fire.

Too late.

His bullets cut the shooter from groin to chest, slamming the weapon from his hands before he toppled over backward, twitching in the dust.

The others had to have seen his muzzle flash, somehow. They swung around, unloading on the Executioner's position, bullets swarming through the air above his head, some of them striking metal, leaving scars and divots, chipping dusty paint to show bright metal underneath. It was enough diversion for Mindel and McCarter to rise and open fire at twenty yards, converging streams of fire taking down the last two gunners as one, leaving them crumpled on the sand.

When he was sure no more commandos were alive and waiting in the dark, Bolan got up and walked around the jeep, checking its tires, stooping to look for any fatal leaks beneath the engine block. As far as he could tell, the vehicle was fit to drive.

"Let's go," he said. "We've got a flight to catch."

"And work to do," Mindel added.

"And work to do," he echoed her. "That's right."

1

Yakov Katzenelenbogen woke to pain. It was a constant feature of his life these days, but this pain lacked the grim immediacy of an interrogation in progress. Even before his mind cleared from vague dreams, he recognized it as a residual pain—both recent memory and a preview of suffering to come.

It was a week today since he'd been lifted, and his captors hadn't broken him. Not yet. Katz didn't know if they had tried their hardest with him, so far. It was virtually impossible for a recipient of torture to decide such things, particularly if his tormentors were even moderately skilled at hiding their emotions while they worked.

In that respect, Katz ranked the men who'd handled him as consummate professionals. They gave nothing away, asked questions without dropping hints to prime the pump, and they were careful not to let him slip away from them, into the dream state that was sometimes nature's antidote to agony.

Professionals.

He'd made his mind up to annihilate them if he got the chance.

And **he** was working on that plan already, even as he banished tattered shreds of sleep to focus on the here and now. Survival was his first priority, and after that escape—but both seemed equally remote ideals, just then.

His captors didn't plan to let him go alive, that much was clear. They'd made no effort to conceal their faces when they picked him up or during questioning. Katz even knew approximately where he was, based on their travel time after the kidnapping and what he'd seen when he was herded—eyes uncovered—from the snatch car to his present quarters in a rundown warehouse.

Where wasn't the problem. If he could escape, survive the first half hour on his own, Katz reckoned he could make his way back to the city, dodge the hunters long enough to find some help. He wouldn't call Rebecca, but he still had friends in the Mossad who would remember him and help him if they could.

The trick was getting out—or, more precisely, getting out alive. That would require a mixture of ability, audacity and pure old-fashioned luck. Katz knew he had the nerve, and he was fairly confident—retirement notwithstanding—that he had the skills to back it up. His luck, though, that was something else again. It had gone sour on him, from all appearances. Katz wasn't sure that he could count on luck at all.

We make our own, he told himself. It was an old cliché—but, then, so what? There was a reason sayings became clichés: namely, because they'd been proved accurate over years or generations, until they were taken for granted.

But he still needed something to work with, a handle of sorts.

Katz took stock of his situation. He was hurt, but not disabled. Losing his prosthetic hand when he was captured was a setback, but it wasn't fatal. He was confined, but not restrained. Weakened by hunger, he still had sufficient energy to fight, if he could pick the time and fudge the odds a bit. A weapon would be useful.

Katz looked around his Spartan cell again. He'd had a week to study every detail of the room, when only seconds were required to list its furnishings. He had a worn-out mattress on the floor—no cot or bed frame he could take apart to improvise a makeshift blade or bludgeon—plus a threadbare blanket and a plastic pail that served him as a toilet. His abductors had relieved Katz of his belt, wristwatch and shoes; they'd turned his pockets out in search of weapons and left nothing but a handkerchief when they were done.

Maybe it wasn't hopeless, though.

Katz knew the only exit from his cell was guarded day and

night. A light burned in the corridor outside, around the clock, and he'd watched restless shadows pass beneath his door, a sentry marking time and wishing he was somewhere else. Katz knew the lookout was alone because he never spoke unless an officer approached him or he was relieved at the end of his shift. In either case, Katz heard the new arrival coming, footsteps audible as heels clicked on concrete.

He didn't know where the replacements came from, whether they were constantly on-site, or how many adversaries he'd be facing if he managed to escape his claustrophobic cell. He'd seen the corridor when his interrogators came to fetch him, at odd hours of the day and night. They led or dragged him to the left, no exit from the warehouse that way, so Katz knew he'd have to try the opposite direction.

If his plan worked and he got that far.

What was the plan again?

Simplicity itself, but that was still no guarantee that he'd succeed. The guard was younger, he was armed and Katz wasn't exactly at the pinnacle of fighting trim. Still, there were times when an old war dog could teach pups a thing or two.

Katz started with the bucket, standing over it, his rumpled slacks undone. He needed something for the guard, and someone had been in to dump the pail while he was grilled last time. It took several moments to relax and put his racing thoughts on hold, but finally he got it done. Katz noted crimson mixed with amber in the pail and mouthed a curse.

The guard would pay for that, in case he couldn't get his hand on anyone of higher rank before he fled. It would've pleased him to confront his two interrogators with a pistol in his hand, but Katz could always try for that another time.

But he would never have that chance unless he got away.

Katz took the blanket, drew its flimsy weight around his shoulders like a shawl, then knelt before the reeking plastic pail. One more glance at the door, and he began to moan.

THE DAMNED OLD JEW was making noise again. Abdel Tarafah checked his Timex watch and scowled. He didn't know when the interrogators would return to ask the Jew more questions, but Tarafah had three hours more to watch and wait before he was relieved. Abdel Tarafah was a warrior, young and strong, but he wasn't sure that he could stand three hours of caterwauling from behind the plain wood door.

He'd watched that door enough in the past week to recognize a range of sounds the prisoner was prone to make. Tarafah didn't count the screams that echoed from the drab interrogation room, a dozen paces farther down the hall. The old man was unconscious when they brought him back, or nearly so, and spent the best part of a silent hour coming back to life each time. There'd be some grunts and moaning after that, as he took stock of limbs and flesh, examining new injuries. Then, sometimes when he dozed, nightmares would bring the captive barking hoarsely back to consciousness, fighting some battle in his dreams that he would never win in waking life.

This noise was different, though. Tarafah hadn't heard the old man make these sounds before. They were the noises of a gravely wounded man—dying, perhaps— who understood that all was lost but still resisted the final draw of death.

The thought was troubling—not because Abdel Tarafah cared about the prisoner or what he felt, but from a personal perspective. What would happen if the old Jew died before he served his purpose, answered all the questions that were put to him? Would there be repercussions if he died alone and calling out for help, while Abdel Tarafah did nothing?

The young Arab's frown became a scowl. He despised Israelis in general, and their official agents in particular. The old man muttering and groaning on the far side of the door was an enemy who deserved no better than a screaming death. Tarafah would've gladly finished him, as he had finished others in his time. But he had been assigned to guard the prisoner, and it was possible that order covered more than simply making sure the old Jew didn't run away.

The more he thought about it now, Tarafah was convinced he might be called to answer for it if the captive died on his watch. Still, what could he do? He was a simple soldier, not a nurse. He knew no more of treating wounds or easing pain than any soldier learned in basic training. Less than most, perhaps, since he'd been taught to kill his wounded comrades rather than permit them to be captured by the enemy. They would accept it gladly, he'd been told, because God and Paradise waited for heroes just beyond the veil of death.

The prisoner wasn't a comrade, though, and mercy wasn't part of what Fate held in store for him. The plan—or what Abdel Tarafah knew of it—required that he survive until he'd answered every question, gave up every bit of information he possessed. And this one obviously couldn't talk if he was dead.

Tarafah considered alerting the captain of the guard, but that would mean leaving his post unattended to seek out Rashad Qasim. But what if Qasim came to check on him first, while Tarafah was gone? Tarafah could be executed for desertion if Qasim demanded it—or if he didn't wait to convene a field tribunal. Qasim was usually fair, but Tarafah didn't feel like gambling his life on the other man's mood, especially when the old Jew had defied Qasim for a week already, straining his patience to the limit. Tarafah had a key to the prisoner's room, passed from one guard to another during change of shift, held for emergencies. The key's existence and its presence in Tarafah's pocket implied permission to open the door if he deemed it essential, and who else was present to judge whether this was a true emergency?

Glowering, Tarafah fished inside his trouser pocket for the key, jingling coins before he found it and turned to face the door. Reaching down to the holster on his hip, he unsnapped the thumb-break retaining strap but stopped short of drawing his Czech CZ-100 semiautomatic pistol. There'd be time enough for weapons, he decided, if the old man turned on him.

The lock turned easily, and Tarafah left his key in the slot as he eased open the door. He was determined that the prisoner wouldn't surprise him. He would simply find out what was wrong, then decide for himself if he should call Qasim to have a look.

Tarafah found the Jew kneeling in the middle of his small room, hunched above the plastic bucket as if vomiting. He had a blanket wrapped around his shoulders and would've resembled an old peasant woman if his gray hair weren't so short, thinning to show his scalp on top. As Tarafah entered the cell, the prisoner gave out another gasping moan.

"What's wrong, old man?" Tarafah asked. He knew the prisoner spoke Arabic from overhearing him with the interrogators.

The old man said something, almost choking on it, but Tarafah couldn't understand him. Moving closer, Tarafah nudged the prisoner's hip with his boot. "Speak up, old fool!"

The captive slowly turned to face him, and before Tarafah realized he was smiling, the bucket was already rising, surging toward his face. The old man didn't hurl it at him, though—simply its contents, liquid filth splashing Tarafah's face, stinging his eyes.

The guard cursed, recoiling, one hand groping toward his pistol, but the prisoner was faster. Even one-handed—Tarafah remembered the old man's handicap now—he was quick enough to drop the bucket over Tarafah's head, then strike it hard enough to stun his guard. Strong fingers wrenched the pistol from Tarafah's holster, and a knee collided with his groin before the Arab could react.

Gagging from pain and the pervasive stench of urine in his nostrils, blinded, on the verge of losing consciousness, Abdel Tarafah slumped to his knees on the cold concrete floor. A foot slammed hard into the bucket, flattening his nose, then blessed darkness swallowed him alive.

THE SENTRY'S BOOTS were half a size too small, but they would do. Katz pulled the Arab's pockets inside out and scooped up everything he found: some coins and rumpled currency, a small bone-handled pocketknife, a ring with three brass keys. He tucked the pistol in his waistband long enough to close the door and lock it after him, then pocketed that key as well and drew the gun again.

The CZ-100 carried thirteen 9 mm Parabellum rounds in its magazine, with one in the chamber. Lacking spare magazines, the fourteen rounds would have to do. If it came down to using the penknife against armed opponents, Katz guessed he'd be dead before he had time to draw blood.

Katz hadn't checked the sentry's pulse and didn't waste the extra time required to make sure he was dead. So be it. If the man was still alive, he'd be unconscious long enough for Katz to make some headway and find new opponents down the hall, or maybe on the grounds outside the warehouse. Either way, he'd do his best to slip away unnoticed, but he couldn't count on getting past the other guards without a fight.

How many were there, altogether? Two interrogators and at least one man to call the shots, for starters, but Katz didn't know if they remained on-site between torture sessions. The guards outside his cell rotated every five or six hours, as best he could tell, but they wouldn't be needed while Katz was confined with his inquisitors, so he couldn't estimate their number with anything approaching accuracy. Call it half a dozen, anyway, to be on the safe side—and he could still take them all with one magazine, if they gave him clear shots.

If his time was up, Katz would rather die fighting than strapped to a table, writhing in helpless agony. He'd led a soldier's life from the time he was a teenager, spending the most of his years at war with one foe or another, somewhere in the world. He'd killed Nazis and Communists alike, slew enemies of Israel and America without regard to race or nationality, and he regretted none of it. Given a chance to do it all again, he'd have changed nothing but the accident that claimed his right forearm years ago, in combat not so very far from where he stood today.

But no one could reverse the clock, turn back the calendar. His only chance to see another sunrise was to come out fighting from the ground he occupied right now—and God help anyone who barred his path.

He moved along the hallway to his right, moving as quietly as possible in his liberated boots. Each sound he made along the way was a potential alarm for his captors, and Katz held the pistol ready in his left hand, finger on the trigger, with the hammer back and safety off. Katz wouldn't hesitate to use the weapon, but he also knew the first shot fired might open up a hornet's nest.

He didn't know if gunshots could be heard outside the building, but it was the unseen enemies lurking inside who worried him right now.

The hallway made a left-hand turn before it opened on the warehouse proper. Stacks of wooden crates and cardboard boxes, piled halfway to the twenty-foot ceiling in places, were arranged to create narrow aisles running the length of the cavernous building, east to west. One of the aisles might lead him out, but it could also be a death trap if his enemies spied Katz and blocked him in.

No choice, he thought. He had to try.

Katz was poised to break cover when a muffled voice distracted him. It was a man's voice, speaking Arabic, and emanated from his left. Katz crouched and risked a look around the corner, spotting a makeshift office, the partitions made of glass above waist height, some kind of dark plastic or fiberboard below. Two men were in the office, one behind a desk, conversing on the telephone, the other smoking while he paced.

Katz had a choice to make. He could go on, or turn and head back to his cell. In fact, when he considered it, that was no choice at all.

He sank to his stomach, stretched out on the floor. The move lit new flares of pain in his body, calling attention to injuries he'd either forgotten or didn't know he'd suffered. Everything hurt, but none of it was critical.

He wouldn't let pain slow him.

To falter was to die.

Katz checked the glassed-in office one more time, confirmed that neither of the men seemed on the verge of stepping out, then pushed off from his hiding place and started to slither across the floor. It made rough going on his knees and elbows, but the pain he felt with every move kept Katz alert. He glanced back every yard or so along the way, found no one coming after him and forged ahead.

When he was well inside one of the narrow aisles and hidden from a casual observer in the office, Katz stopped and scrambled to his feet. With cautious urgency he moved along the aisle, seeking an exit from the house of pain.

RASHAD QASIM ENJOYED surprising his men. It was a way to keep them on their toes, uncertain when or where he would appear to catch them slacking in their duties. Fear was instrumental to maintaining discipline in any military unit, all the more so when the soldiers were guerrillas, men who stood outside established law.

Qasim knew something was amiss as soon as he beheld the empty corridor. Abdel Tarafah was supposed to be guarding the prisoner, but he was nowhere to be seen. Qasim felt anger flare inside him, bringing heat and color to his cheeks. Moving along the corridor with long, swift strides, Qasim ran down the list of insults he intended to bestow upon Tarafah and his ancestors. That wouldn't be the limit of Tarafah's punishment, by any means, but rank humiliation was as good a place to start as any.

Qasim stopped on the threshold of the old Jew's cell. He glanced both ways along the corridor again, as if he could conjure Tarafah from thin air, by will alone. It didn't work, of course, and Qasim felt the first glimmer of concern as he stood there, alone in the silent hallway. Where had Tarafah gone? Perhaps the soldier needed to relieve himself. It wouldn't be so bad if he was in the rest room, two doors farther down. Qasim would still chastise him and concoct some penance for Tarafah to perform, but he understood that humans were slaves to their bodily functions. Scowling, he walked on to the rest room and stuck his head inside, crouching to look for feet that would betray an occupant in either of the stalls.

Nothing.

Qasim was worried now. He jogged back to the old Jew's door and used his master key to open it. He found Abdel Tarafah stretched out on the floor, unconscious, wearing the captive's slop bucket like a helmet. Qasim crouched beside him and removed it, grimacing at the smell and at Tarafah's slack countenance, smeared with blood and other things less savory.

Qasim would've slapped his soldier awake, but he recoiled from contact with Tarafah's filthy skin and hair. Instead, he found a dry spot on the soldier's shirt and poked him with an index finger, jabbing him between the ribs. It had no visible effect, so

Qasim rose and started kicking Tarafah's legs and buttocks, keeping it up until the man moaned and stirred.

"Wake up!" Qasim demanded, putting new, insistent force behind his kicks. Instead of sitting up or speaking to him though, Tarafah shuddered once and vomited.

"Son of a goat!"

Qasim stormed out to rouse the other guards. He didn't know how long ago the captive had escaped. Tarafah had been on watch for an hour and thirteen minutes, without supervision. Could the old man have been gone that long?

Impossible.

First, he would have to lure Tarafah from the hallway, trick him into opening the door. The contest would be brief, from that point on. The old man had been injured, drained by the interrogators. He would never last in a prolonged fight with a younger, stronger man. The slop bucket had helped him there, and he had grabbed Tarafah's pistol as he left.

Where would he go? Away from here, Qasim decided, but escaping from the warehouse proper was another challenge, and he didn't know if the old Jew was up to it. One contact with a guard along the way and he was finished—or he'd have to use Tarafah's gun, which would amount to the same thing. But if the others weren't expecting him and dropped their guard...

Qasim began shouting the alarm, picking up his pace from a jog to a sprint. His voice echoed through the warehouse, as if he were shouting in an underground cavern. It took a moment for the first of half dozen voices to respond, then his soldiers flocked around him, answering the call.

He told them what had happened, cursing Tarafah in the process, dismissing his condition as a matter of no concern. Qasim, in his fury, regretted not killing the guard where he lay, but there would be ample time for punishment later, after the court-martial.

After they recaptured the hostage.

If the old Jew got away, Qasim knew there would be a second court-martial. *His* life would be the price of failure to maintain security. He couldn't shift the blame, and there would be small consolation knowing that Abdel Tarafah had been shot before Qasim faced a firing squad of his own.

"Find him!" Qasim commanded, fairly barking out the words. Four soldiers and the two long-faced interrogators ran to do his bidding, fanning out through the warehouse. Qasim went after them. He didn't know what more to do. The place was large, replete with shadowed corners and a few small storage closets. If the prisoner was hiding, they would find him, root him out.

"Bring him back alive!" Qasim called after them, his loud voice echoing once more. He couldn't swear that any of the soldiers heard him, so he put more force behind it when he shouted, "Alive, I said!"

Qasim reached underneath his khaki jacket and withdrew the Walther P-5 pistol from its shoulder holster. He didn't intend to kill the runner, but he wouldn't move around the place defenseless, either. If it came to guns, Qasim had faith in his ability to wound the man and patch him up again, before he bled to death.

A sudden, chilling thought occurred to him. What if the old Jew was hysterical and chose to kill himself, in lieu of being taken back for punishment and more interrogation? One shot to the head and he was done, leaving Qasim to try to explain how the hostage had escaped and found a weapon in the first place.

They had to find him quickly and disarm him, before he ruined everything.

Rashad Qasim worried that they might already be too late.

KATZ CHECKED THE DOOR for an alarm, saw nothing to suggest it would alert his enemies if he stepped through, and took his chance. He had no way to guard against the risk of meeting unseen adversaries on the other side, but with the pistol in his hand, at least he had a fighting chance.

The steel door opened on a loading dock. Katz was surprised to find it dark outside. He'd lost all track of time under the rigors of interrogation, but the night could serve him now, helping him put some space between himself and his abductors.

First, though, he would have to move.

It was a five- or six-foot drop from the loading dock to ground level. Nothing drastic, but the very thought of jumping down sent spasms lancing through his legs and groin. Glancing to left and right, aware that he was wasting precious time, Katz spied a short flight of stairs at one end of the dock and made for them, jogging now despite his discomfort.

He nearly stumbled on the stairs, unable to use the handrail, but caught himself in time and reached the parking lot without mishap. Two vehicles were waiting there, a station wagon and a van, but both were locked. That told Katz he would find no keys in the ignition, even if he smashed a window to get in, and he had never learned the knack of hot-wiring cars with only one hand.

That left him afoot, but not hopeless. If his first impressions from the day of his kidnapping were correct, he was only a few miles outside Jericho. Katz doubted that his captors had crossed over into Jordan, since there'd been no stop or search of their vehicle in transit, characteristic of a border checkpoint.

He was still in Israel, then—or the West Bank, at any rate. In these unsettled times that didn't place him among friends, but it was a damn sight better than hiking back to the Israeli frontier from somewhere in Syria or Lebanon. As long as he made good use of the darkness and kept his wits about him, following the road but not revealing himself prematurely, he should be all right.

As if in answer to that thought, floodlights blazed on behind him, pinning Katz in the middle of the warehouse parking lot. It was another fifty yards to desert darkness, and he couldn't be assured of safety even there.

Katz turned in time to see men spilling through the same door he had used to reach the loading dock. He recognized his two interrogators, but the rest were strange to him. No matter, since they all had guns and all of them were glaring at him, several pointing at him while they spoke to their friends in Arabic. Katz got the gist of it, although he wasn't really listening.

This is the end, he thought, surprised at his own inner calm. He had always expected that death would enrage him, find him struggling for his last breath until it was squeezed from his laboring lungs. Incredibly, he wasn't angry now, but he could still put up a fight.

Katz smiled and raised his pistol, squeezing off two shots into the crowd assembled on the loading dock. He saw one Arab stagger, falling, and another raised his AK-47 to return fire, but a third man slapped the muzzle down and scolded him.

What's this?

It struck Katz then, how much his captors wanted him—or maybe needed him—alive. That knowledge gave him power over them, but only while his meager stock of ammunition lasted. Firing one more shot as his opponents scattered, Katz immediately turned his back on them and ran.

No one tried to shoot him, but he heard them running after him, calling for him to halt, as if he would obey them willingly. Katz was about to leave the lights behind, when he heard someone start the van. Its tires squealed briefly on asphalt, then headlights pinned him and the rolling bread box came for him, accelerating as it crossed the parking lot.

Katz spun and fired, cracking the windshield, putting out one of the headlights, scarring faded paint. The van bore down on him, relentless, like an elephant intent on punishing the hunter who has killed its mate. He fired twice more, trying to hit the tires, and knew both shots were wasted.

Run!

Katz turned and sprinted toward the open ground beyond the parking lot, pain jolting through his frame with every stride, but he couldn't outpace the juggernaut behind him. With a sudden surge of speed, the van raced up to strike him and he found himself airborne, tumbling head over heels.

Katz lost his pistol midway through the somersault, striking the ground with force enough to squeeze a gasp of bitter agony between clenched teeth. He tried to rise before the Arabs ran up to surround him, but he wasn't quick enough. A boot connected with his ribs as Katz was rising to all fours, the impact hard enough to flip him onto his back. At once, the others were around him, kicking and stomping in fury, desisting only when their leader fell upon them, dragging them away with slaps and curses.

Katz gazed up through blood as the scowling captain of the guard leaned over him, aiming a pistol at his face. He knew the

Arab wouldn't kill him now, a bit of knowledge that was simultaneously liberating and depressing. If they wanted him alive, it meant more questions and more suffering. Better, Katz thought, if they had ended it right here.

"You've got me, dammit," Katz remarked in Arabic. "Go on and do your worst, pig-fucker."

With a snarl of rage, the Arab brought his pistol slashing down on Katz's skull.

2

Five days before the raid in Syria, Bolan had caught a lift with Jack Grimaldi in a Bell LongRanger helicopter, east from Lexington, Kentucky, to the Blue Ridge Mountains of Virginia. He'd been wrapping up a short but not so sweet campaign against a group of neo-Nazis who thought they'd discovered a key to better dying through chemistry. They'd been startled to learn that the "Jew-specific" toxin a certain mad-scientist type had cooked up in his underground lab would kill Aryans, too. A final body count was waiting on the Hazmat team from the CDC, but Bolan marked it down as a clean sweep.

A final solution, in fact.

Grimaldi was humming to himself as he flew, holding the whirlybird close to its 133 mile per hour maximum cruising speed. Grimaldi had been flying for the Mafia when Bolan met him for the first time, in another life, but he hadn't liked the gig well enough to die for it. He ranked among Bolan's half-dozen oldest living friends, a survivor of Bolan's lonely war against the Mob who'd made the jump from private practice to Stony Man Farm, way back when. Unspoken was the fact that his first loyalty would always be to Bolan, rather than a program or a federal letterhead.

The flight to Stony Man hadn't been part of Bolan's plans, but he'd cleared his calendar in the wake of a terse phone call from Hal Brognola in Washington, D.C. "Katz is missing," Brognola had said. "Can you come?"

"Missing where?" Bolan had asked.

"I'll explain at the Farm."

"I'll be there."

The rendezvous with Grimaldi at Blue Grass Airport had been easily arranged and went without a hitch, just the way Bolan liked it. Ninety minutes in the air, and they were almost close enough for Bolan to make out the craggy stone face that had given the Farm its code name. Grimaldi held them close to treetop level, flying like a smuggler even though he was one of the certified good guys.

Bolan had tried to pump the pilot for details on Yakov Katzenelenbogen's disappearance, but the pilot had nothing to share. He'd been working a gig of his own in Missouri when the big Fed had reached out with a drop-everything plea for help, and Grimaldi had responded as Brognola knew he would.

"It's panic time," Grimaldi had suggested, and that sounded right to Bolan. Katz had been onboard with Stony Man from the beginning, first with Phoenix Force in the field, lately retired from frontline work to serve as a consultant and adviser at the Farm. His death would be a grievous loss to friends and family; his disappearance could be even worse.

The bottom line: Katz was a walking treasury of information on Stony Man Farm and its various covert operations, past and present. If he was kidnapped and cracked, the secrets stored in his brain could do untold damage on six continents—not counting the exposure of Stony Man itself, with the media shitstorm that was bound to follow revelation of a covert vigilante team directed from the White House.

It was obviously critical that Katz be found as soon as possible. Ideally, he'd be found alive and none the worse for wear, but failing that the Executioner would take what he could get. If it meant bringing home a body, he could do that too—and God help any man or woman still living who'd harmed his faithful friend.

"We're almost there," Grimaldi said. His voice snapped Bolan back to present-time reality.

The Farm had started out with 120 acres, lately expanded with the addition of forty-eight more adjacent to the original eastern boundary. The new plot, a fully functional tree farm, featured a wood chip mill and storage silo set atop a two-level subterranean facility secure against direct hits from most nonnuclear warheads. If it ever reached the point where nukes were falling on the Blue Ridge Mountains, Bolan reckoned that the Farm would be superfluous, in any case.

The approach to Stony Man was perilous. The Farm was invitation-only, and those invitations had to be confirmed before a new arrival set foot on the property. Most days, the airstrip was obstructed by a single-wide mobile home, manned around the clock by two blacksuits, equipped with quad-mount miniguns that could lay down a blizzard of 24,000 rounds per minute on command. Hinged walls and roof were made to fall away at need and give the two-man team an unobstructed field of fire. That kind of firepower was devastating to aircraft, not to mention the pilots and passengers.

A coded call received ten minutes in advance of landing brought another "farmhand" out to tow the mobile home with a John Deere tractor, clearing the runway but still leaving those miniguns close enough to wreak havoc on any surprise drop-ins. By the time an incoming plane touched down, the trailer team would've been reinforced by riflemen and blacksuits armed with Stinger missiles. Just in case.

Bolan and Grimaldi weren't braving the airstrip this evening, however. The pilot had clearance for a touchdown on the helipad behind the site's main building, ostensibly a two-story farmhouse, whose facade concealed state-of-the-art computers and communications gear, a well-stocked arsenal, and a basement War Room where Hal Brognola sometimes held court before missions. Since construction of the tree farm and mill, a thousand-foot tunnel had been dug, connecting the farmhouse to the wood chip mill, where vast new computers and satellite communications gear were concealed underground. More antiaircraft weapons were positioned to defend the mill and its secrets, ready for anything.

"Two minutes," Grimaldi announced, handling the Bell's controls with his usual deft touch. They passed over the tree farm first, the chopper's shadow printed on the flat roof of the mill below, then they were skimming over open fields, a man on horseback who glanced up at them without concern, another on a tractor who seemed to ignore them completely.

The house came into view, and Bolan felt his stomach lurch as Grimaldi throttled back. He recalled the sensation from landings in hot LZs where the jungle itself was a seductive enemy, beautiful and lethal. There were no traps waiting for him here, today, as far as Bolan knew.

Why was it then, he wondered, that he felt as if emerging from the helicopter was his first step into hell?

"YOU MADE GOOD TIME," Brognola said, as they were shaking hands.

"That's Jack," Bolan replied. "I'd still be somewhere on the highway, otherwise."

"We caught a lucky tailwind," Grimaldi said, as if that explained his quick response to Brognola's alert.

David McCarter, on hand for Phoenix Force, was next in the receiving line. No words were needed between him and Bolan, both long familiar with the dread that came from learning one of your best friends was MIA. The mystery was worse, sometimes, than news of violent death. Until it was resolved, one way or another, the doubts could be oppressive—debilitating, in some cases. Bolan and McCarter were too professional to lose it that way, but the solemn mood they shared was written on their faces, plain to see in the way they clasped hands.

Brognola caught the look that passed between Bolan and Barbara Price, the Farm's mission controller, but he did his best to ignore it. Strong feelings there, beneath the surface, but they kept it under wraps. Whatever happened when they were alone, it hadn't interfered with business so far—and that made it none of his. Despite a lifetime spent accumulating and assessing covert information, there were some things the man from Justice simply didn't need to know.

A little ignorance was beneficial, now and then.

"Bear's waiting for us in the War Room," Brognola remarked. "Unless you need to freshen up, or—"

"No," Bolan interrupted him. "Let's get it done."

"Okay."

The War Room was a work in progress, constantly evolving to accommodate advances in technology. It hadn't been transplanted to the new facility because it was essentially a briefing area, not a command post in the standard sense, and cables laid inside the access tunnel linked it to the Farm's expanded AV library and commo net. Weeks had elapsed since Brognola last sat down at the War Room's conference table for a full-dress briefing, and he wished he could've skipped this one. If he'd possessed a magic lamp, Brognola would've rubbed it to a gleaming shine and wished the whole damned mess away, but there was no bright magic in his world.

Just death and darkness.

Aaron Kurtzman, nicknamed "The Bear," was waiting for them in the War Room. He had coffee poured, projectors ready, and the hidden screen deployed. A gunshot to the spine kept him from rising as his friends entered the room, but Kurtzman wheeled around to greet them, shaking hands with Bolan and Grimaldi. Years of manhandling the chair had given him a grip most power lifters would've envied, but he only made a point of crunching knuckles with selected persons who displeased him.

"Right," the big Fed said, when they were seated. "I was cryptic on the phone because we still don't know how bad this is. God's honest truth, we don't know very much at all."

"Share what you have," Bolan replied.

"You know Katz still has family in Israel," Brognola began. "Not much, but some. An older brother and his wife on a kibbutz outside Be'er Sheva and their daughter, Katz's niece."

The final word was on his lips when Kurtzman keyed a hidden slide projector and the big screen brightened with a photo of a woman in her thirties. It was difficult to guess her age behind the aviator's shades she wore, hair pulled back from her face and tied off in a ponytail. The next shot was in color, plainly lifted from some kind of ID card.

"Rebecca Mindel," Brognola said, introducing her as if she were among them in the room. "We don't know if it matters yet, but she's a field agent for the Mossad with eight years on the job. Her specialty is counterterrorism, so they keep her hopping over there."

"Does the Mossad have anyone who's not a terrorism expert?" Grimaldi asked.

"One or two, I think," Brognola said, "but this one's special. She took down Mahmoud Hazred last year, all by herself."

"The Uganda embassy bomber?" McCarter asked.

"One and the same. Word has it he wasn't the first."

Something dawned on Bolan. "Katz was over there?" he asked.

Brognola nodded. "He was getting desk rash, missing fieldwork. I persuaded him to take a month at home and lose the blues." Brognola felt his sour mood reflected on his face. "That was the plan, at least," he added.

"What went wrong?" McCarter asked.

"We can't be sure. My guess is, Katz missed the field too much to let it go, and being in the old home neighborhood with all his cronies from Mossad and military intelligence got him revved up. I believe he went looking for trouble and found it—or trouble found him."

"Same result, either way," Bolan said.

"So it seems."

"He's been missing how long?"

"Two days and counting," Brognola stated. "We gave him twenty-four hours in case there'd been some kind of accident. Maybe he went on a binge with his buddies. Who knows?"

"That's not Katz," McCarter said. "He's never been one for lost weekends."

The big Fed nodded his agreement. "Anyway, we sat on the call for one day—"

"Call from who?" Grimaldi asked.

"The niece. Here's where it gets peculiar. A few days before he dropped out of sight, Katz takes Rebecca aside and slips her a phone number. Mine. He tells her that he's looking into something, but he won't say what it is until he's done connecting all the dots. It's no big deal, he says, but just in case something should happen to him, she's supposed to call me and report."

"Instead of talking to Mossad?" Grimaldi asked.

"She did that too, of course. From what I understand, they started looking right away but came up empty." Brognola surveyed the faces ranged around him, looking for a hint of condemnation, finding none. He should've felt relief, but their acceptance of his comments had no impact on the sense of guilt he'd carried for the past two days.

"And we have no idea what he was working on?" Bolan asked.

"There's a hint. The niece went through his things, looking for clues, and found a dime-store spiral notebook. It was new, as far as she could tell. No pages missing, and he'd only written on the first one."

Kurtzman keyed another slide. Rebecca Mindel's photo was replaced by a facsimile of a magnified notebook page. It was ragged at the top, torn free of metal rings. Four words were printed on the page in neat letters: Allah's Lance, Jabbar, Zuhayr.

"I recognize the group," McCarter said. "It spun off from Hezbollah, back around 2001. Members have been linked to a number of suicide bombings in Israel and Gaza, along with threats or attacks against European embassies."

"That's the gang," Brognola confirmed, as a mug shot of a bearded Arab filled the screen. "It's led by Wasim Jabbar, once cozy with the Abu Nidal Organization. Today, he claims the ANO is corrupt, and diverted from the sacred goal of holy war against Israel and the West."

"He thinks the ANO is soft on Israel?"

"That's about the size of it," Brognola said. Another full-face photo blossomed on the screen, a slightly younger man this time. "His second in command is Salim Zuhayr, another fundamentalist hard case. The Israelis convicted him of a fatal school bus bombing, back in '97, but he broke out of prison and went back to work. They still won't say how he got out—if they know."

"That's some pair to draw to," Grimaldi remarked. "They've got Katz?"

"We don't know, but we need to find out."

LOGISTIC DETAILS ate up the rest of the briefing: times and places, flight schedules, connections on the other side. David McCarter sat and listened, asking questions when he thought of something, staying focused for the most part on his private sense of dread.

He didn't hold with self-defeating pessimism, but he had a hard time picturing a happy ending to their present difficulty. Yakov Katzenelenbogen was a veteran soldier and a seasoned covert agent. He had enemies at large—particularly in the Middle East—and contrary to popular belief, he hadn't killed them all. Toss in their brothers, cousins, sons and cohorts in several dozen radical organizations, and the suspect list revealed a small army, any one of whom would gladly murder Katz if given half a chance.

But would they kidnap him?

Why not? McCarter asked himself. Kidnapping without ransom demands was a means to some other felonious end, perhaps a way to make the body disappear and thus divert attention from the killers. Add the fact that Katz had seemingly been on the trail of a terrorist group known for pitiless mayhem, and his outward prospects for survival ranged from slim to none.

I'd know if he were dead, McCarter thought, but that was hocus-pocus, instantly dismissed. Katz was among his closest friends on Earth, granted, but they had fallen out of touch since Katz retired to desk work at the Farm. A phone call now and then, a trip to the farm for a briefing. He'd known about the visit home, had even joked with Katz about the need to keep his nose clean in the not-so-Holy Land, but that's all it had been: a joke. McCarter knew his friend was restless, but he hadn't thought Katz would pursue some private mission of his own.

Assume it wasn't planned, then. Maybe Katz had stumbled onto something, spotted a face in the crowd and run with it, seeing where the business led. He could've tipped Israeli officers if there were terrorists about, of course, but Katz would yearn to pin the details down, do something for himself, instead of standing back and watching others work.

"Damned fool."

"Say what?" The question from Grimaldi tipped McCarter that he had begun to think aloud.

"Nothing. Sorry."

Brognola cut it short to keep another date in Washington. He had an hour's flying time, and it would be a squeaker even if his pilot set him down on Pennsylvania Avenue. He said goodbye and shook hands all around, leaving a stack of files on Allah's Lance and its main players for review. McCarter knew the basics, but he had ten hours to absorb the rest, before they flew.

He had Wasim Jabbar's file open on the table when Bolan approached him, grim-faced. "We'll find him," the soldier stated.

"Maybe."

"I won't give up until we do."

"There may be nothing left to find," McCarter said. It startled him a little, even though the voice was his. Thinking Katz dead and saying it aloud were very different things, apparently.

"I don't see anyone he's tangled with before caring enough to make him disappear," Bolan replied. "They'd shoot him on the street or bomb his car, but why a kidnapping?"

McCarter answered with a question of his own. "Payback?"

Bolan could only frown at that. He plainly didn't like to think of Katz confined and kept alive by terrorists, the butt of their sadistic fantasies.

"It's possible," he grudgingly admitted, "but they have to know it puts the wheels in motion. Terrorists don't relish that kind of attention."

McCarter acknowledged the point with a nod. "Allah's Lance, then? He's never gone up against them before. They wouldn't have known who he was."

"But they'd want to find out," Bolan said, completing the thought.

Two days and counting, thought McCarter. It was too damned long. "They may have broken him by now."

"He won't break easily," Bolan stated, but he didn't sound convinced.

"You want the files?"

"I'll read them over when you're done," Bolan replied. "We have some time."

Too much. McCarter wished they were already airborne, winging toward the last place Katz was seen alive. He hoped to see his friend that way again, but hope was fragile. It had trouble living in the real world.

"Right," McCarter said. "I won't be long. An hour or so."

"Sounds good."

Bolan moved off to speak with Barbara Price and Aaron Kurtzman, huddling at the far end of the table. When they left, McCarter barely noticed. He was studying Wasim Jabbar, a man whose life was seemingly consumed by hate. He hated Jews— or Zionists, at least—because his grandparents were driven from their homes in Palestine, in 1948. He hated the United States and Britain for supporting Israel through decades of struggle to survive. He hated rival Palestinian commando groups for their "betrayal" of jihad, the holy war that had defined his life.

McCarter wondered what it felt like to be ruled by hate, each waking hour of the day and night. His thoughts turned back to Katz then, seeing him alive, tormented by his captors, and McCarter got a taste of what it had to be like. He would've given damned near anything, just then, for one shot at the kidnappers, no matter what it cost.

Obsession.

McCarter knew the feeling, but it didn't rule his life. When a mission consumed him, he gave it his all, but he'd always been able to walk away in the end, clear his mind and move on.

This time, though...

It wouldn't be the first time Phoenix Force had lost a member to violence, and Katz was already retired from the team. Still, he'd been a fixture from the day the program started, his dogged persistence and gruff common sense stiffening the outfit's collective spine in times of crisis. McCarter had felt better knowing Katz was still around, if only in a modified advisory capacity. Now he was gone, and McCarter feared the worst.

Or was he?

The worst, he realized, might not be Katzenelenbogen's death. McCarter had seen other warriors maimed, sidelined with crippling injuries, some left in vegetative states that made Kurtzman's spinal wound seem like a slap on the wrist. If Katz was still alive, determined captors working on him day and night, would rescue be a blessing or a curse?

Like every other fighting man, McCarter had considered death and its alternatives. The men of Phoenix Force were pledged to leave no living comrade for their enemies to cage and torture, knowing even as they made the promise that rescue might not be possible. The vow was understood among them, never spelled out in detail.

If it came to that, McCarter owed Katz the release of death.

I promise you, he thought, and turned back to the open file.

"I'M SORRY, Mack."

Bolan saw tears in Barbara's eyes and resisted the impulse to draw her from her chair, into his arms. "It's not your fault," he said.

"I know that, but it doesn't help."

"Trust Katz to go off hunting terrorists on his vacation time. I wish he'd told the niece—"

"Rebecca," she reminded him.

"Okay. I wish he'd told Rebecca more about his plans before he went ahead."

"If he was here," Price told him, "I'd have to chew him out for violating protocol."

"As if he'd listen." Bolan knew how Katz's mind worked. Even when he'd worn his homeland's uniform, there'd been a strain of insubordination just below the surface, waiting to erupt whenever Katz thought he'd devised a quicker, cleaner way to solve a military problem. He'd fight to the death against hopeless odds for an arid acre of ground, but send him out on patrol with a prearranged route of travel and he might surprise all concerned by ad-libbing his way through the mission.

Bolan brought his mind back to the plan Brognola had devised. He was determined not to follow Katz's rebel lead—not yet, at least. "Okay," he said. "We meet Rebecca in Jerusalem tomorrow afternoon. By then, with any luck, she ought to have some leads on Allah's Lance and where to track them down."

"With any luck," Price echoed.

"I don't know about her helping out beyond that point," he said. "I'd rather not have relatives onboard. Pain messes with priorities."

"Who else is there?" Price asked.

"Mossad must have somebody they can spare who isn't next of kin."

"Hal talked it over with the brass in Tel Aviv. They count Rebecca Mindel as one of their best field agents, and they seem to think her personal involvement will provide extra incentive."

"That's what I'm afraid of."

"She's a professional."

"No argument. But there's a reason doctors don't operate on their kids, and detectives don't investigate the deaths of family members."

"Right," Price said. "Because they might go overboard. The cop might kill a man who harmed his relatives. The perpetrator might not go to trial. This situation, though, she may just have the extra measure of determination that you need."

"I guess we'll see."

"Where's Jack?" she asked.

"Catching some sack time. He wanted to be fresh and frisky for the flight tomorrow."

"There's a mental image for you." Price smiled.

"I've never seen him down that I recall."

"He's got that kind of personality."

"So, how's yours holding up?"

"I'll live."

"I hope so," she replied. "You've got as much invested in this mission as the niece."

"You mean Rebecca."

"Smart-ass."

"That's my middle name."

"You need to work on that," Price said. "I'm thinking something more like *Cautious,* for the job at hand."

"Well, that's my other middle name."

"I wish." Her tone turned serious. "Do me a favor, will you?"

"If I can."

"Don't take too many chances over there."

"No more than usual."

"I mean it, Mack."

"I see that."

"Chances are, he's dead already. They just haven't found the body yet."

"Is that what you believe?"

"I don't know what to think," Price said. "But if I had to play the odds, I'd say he's gone."

"Katz never put much stock in odds," Bolan reminded her.

"You mean he liked to push his luck." The past tense sounded harsh to Bolan's ears. "This time, I think he pushed too hard, too far."

"I have a job to do, regardless."

"I know that. But if there's nobody to rescue, you don't have to push *your* luck too far."

"You mean it's just another job?"

"I didn't say that—but somebody should. We all love Katz, but there's a point beyond which sacrifice stops making sense. You have a problem with that concept, Mack, in case you haven't noticed."

"Problem? Me?"

"It isn't funny, dammit! A response is called for, obviously, but I don't see sacrificing three lives for the sake of one. This isn't *Saving Private Ryan.*"

"Damn, there goes my Oscar."

"Just watch yourself, okay? That's all I ask."

"No problem."

"Right."

Bolan tried to distract her with details. "You say Mossad's cooperating?"

"Within limits," Price replied. "You've got Rebecca Mindel,

and she has a pipeline to their files if anything comes up, but they're walking a tightrope these days, between shaky peace and another all-out war."

"Meaning?"

"Meaning they'd love to fall on Allah's Lance like the proverbial ton of bricks, but they need something more than a vanishing tourist to flash the green light."

"He's one of theirs," Bolan said.

"*Was* one of theirs," she replied. "The new brass doesn't know him from Adam, and they don't appreciate a U.S. agent snooping around on their patch. We're already looking at the next worst thing to an international incident. We shouldn't try to make it any worse."

"For Katz, or for the politicians?" Bolan asked.

"You know what I mean. It's all politics or religion with that crowd, however you slice it. We all want Katz back—"

"But the White House doesn't want him bad enough to poke a hornet's nest," Bolan suggested.

"No. They really don't. Maybe, if he'd been on a mission..."

"Who's to say he wasn't?"

"An official mission," she amended.

Bolan shrugged. "If he'd reported back, it might've been official. I won't have a take on that until we've looked around a bit."

"The job description's search and rescue, not search and destroy."

"You're assuming there's a difference," Bolan said.

"Call it wishful thinking."

"I don't have much time for that, lately."

"Sometimes," she said, "things are just as they seem. Katz would've known Jabbar and his people are hot. They're on everybody's most wanted list from Tel Aviv to Washington. A chance encounter in the city, and he'd go from there."

"Why not report it?" Bolan asked.

"And let somebody else have all the fun? That's never been his style."

She had a point, of course, but Bolan still wasn't convinced. "Just think about it. He's retired and on vacation with his family, presumably unarmed—"

"I wouldn't count on that," Price interjected.

"Anyway, if all he did was spot a fugitive, why not tip the authorities? Why risk his life against a team of hard-core shooters when he wasn't on the job? Unless..."

"Unless he figured they were up to something more than hiding out?" she asked.

"It's possible."

"I'll buy that, but it makes no difference. Hal isn't asking you to take on Allah's Lance or mop up every heavy in the Middle East. It's basically a missing-person case."

"And the best way to find a missing person is to learn what he was doing when he disappeared. Jabbar may be behind this, or it may be someone else."

"I'm not liking the sound of this."

"Don't worry," Bolan said, smiling. "I'll ask them in my best, most reasonable style."

3

"You're sure about this lead?" McCarter asked.

Rebecca Mindel frowned at him. "You've asked me that five times, already. It's a bit late to be getting cold feet now."

She was right on that score, Bolan thought. They were ten minutes short of jumping off and well beyond the point of no return.

"I haven't got cold feet," McCarter said. "I simply want to know—"

"I trust my source, all right?" Mindel stood facing him, defiant, even though the Englishman was easily twelve inches taller, carrying an extra hundred pounds of muscle. "If you're asking me to guarantee the information is correct, it's bloody stupid!"

"That's enough," Bolan growled. "We need focus, or we may as well forget this thing and write Katz off."

That silenced them, as Bolan hoped it would. He kept his eyes glued to the night glasses and felt the others move in closer, flanking him. He had their full attention now, where it belonged.

The target—fingered on a tip from an informant to Mossad, and on from there to Mindel—was a warehouse three miles outside Anha. The town was also known as Jericho, and once upon an ancient time a famous battle had been waged there, centuries before Israel or Jordan or the West Bank were imagined. God had lent a hand that time around, the legends claimed, but Bolan didn't have His number on speed dial. He didn't have a magic trumpet in his pack tonight; in fact, he didn't even need the warehouse walls to tumble down.

He simply had to get inside.

Mindel's report claimed that the place was owned by Allah's Lance, and that a certain hostage might be hidden there. It sounded like a long shot, but they'd already tried Syria and come back empty-handed. Bolan would try damn near anything at this point, and be grateful if the wildest lead paid off.

A dusty Fiat van and an old model Citroën sedan were parked outside the warehouse, but Bolan saw no trace of lookouts or roof-mounted cameras. That didn't mean they weren't there, of course, simply that he couldn't pick them out with his night glasses. They'd know more about the facility's defenses when they got closer, and the time to make that move was now.

"All set?" he asked the others.

"Ready," Mindel said.

"Let's go," McCarter urged.

They went, black-clad, their hands and faces darkened with combat cosmetics, to guard against exposure by an errant moonbeam. They were armed as on the raid in Syria, trusting the silenced MP-5s to deal with any threat encountered here. If there was killing to be done, the battle would be won or lost at point-blank range.

It angered Bolan to think they'd wasted precious time and risked their lives on a raid in the wrong damned country, but he'd played the only cards they held at the time, and after-action reports from Mossad confirmed that the camp they'd raided belonged to Allah's Lance. It simply wasn't the target they'd hoped for.

But maybe this one was.

Maybe.

"Let's go," he said, an echo of McCarter's words. His two companions followed him through darkness toward the warehouse, crossing open ground.

The warehouse occupants—if they existed—were apparently more conscious of their power bill than physical security. A single light burned on the loading dock, reflected in the windshields of the Fiat and the Citroën, but otherwise the place was dark. Without night glasses, Bolan might've worried about snipers in the shadows, but he'd picked out nothing with the infrared or thermal register. He couldn't see inside the place, of course, but one full circuit had revealed nothing to slow them.

Except locked doors.

They gave the lighted loading dock a pass and tried a door positioned at the southwest corner of the warehouse. Bolan made an up-close visual examination and saw nothing to suggest the door was wired with an alarm. He risked it, tried the knob and found it locked. When no alert brought shooters rushing to the scene, he palmed a set of picks and went to work.

It was a simple lock. Bolan defeated it in fifteen seconds flat and put his picks away. He paused and glanced at each of his companions, one hand on the doorknob now, the other on his SMG. If anything went sour on the entry, it was most likely to happen as they crossed the threshold.

He turned the knob and pushed his way inside. The door was silent, either well maintained or rust-free thanks to the prevailing desert climate. Either way, it let them pass without a squeal of protest and McCarter closed it gently, leaving it unlocked.

They stood between a metal wall and ranks of wooden crates, piled higher than their heads. Above them, half a dozen fixtures lit the warehouse dimly, showing them a long, straight aisle ahead. Bolan heard voices at the other end and started moving toward their source.

KATZ HUDDLED in his cell, arms bound behind his back, and waited for the two inquisitors to come for him again. They'd punished him for his escape attempt, no questions this time as they strapped him down and went to work. It had been payback, plain and simple, with the sentry he'd humiliated joining in to get his licks. Katz had lost track of time and finally lost consciousness, waking to misery in every fiber of his being, thin cords biting deep into his biceps.

They had bound his upper arms, because the absence of a right hand frustrated attempts to tie his wrists. It was effective, painful and potentially destructive if it cut off circulation to his one remaining hand.

But Katz was still alive.

That fact alone confirmed his supposition that they wouldn't let him die until he answered the persistent questions that they posed to him. Who were his contacts? His superiors? Who'd sent him snooping into matters that were none of his affair? What had he learned so far and who now shared that knowledge?

Katz almost smiled, imagining the fury of his captors if he simply told the truth—that he was on his own, acting without authority, and had reported them to no one on God's Earth. It would've vexed them terribly at first, knowing they'd wasted so much time and energy on him, and that alone was almost worth the risk.

Except that it would surely get him killed.

Which might not be the worst scenario, Katz thought, if there was no hope of escape or rescue. He was on the edge, uncertain how much more abuse he could absorb before he cracked and told his captors things he shouldn't share. If scum like this knew anything of Phoenix Force or Stony Man...

Katz might have imagined the first shot, distant and muffled as it was, but it still snapped his mind into focus, every sense straining for input. When startled voices sounded, seconds later, they were closer at hand and included the sentry stationed outside his cell. Katz tracked the man by sound, moving, then heard an order barked that sent him back to guard the prisoner.

What was happening? Katz wondered. Could it be—?

A flurry of gunfire erupted, closer this time, and no mistake about it. Katz struggled to his feet, leaning against the wall for support, grimacing as that contact sent pain jolting through him. The thorough bastards didn't miss a trick. He wouldn't put it past the guard to execute him, if the Arabs thought a rescue effort was in progress, and Katz meant to face death on his feet, not cringing on a filthy mattress.

Rescue.

Was it even possible? Of course. How would a rescue party track him here—wherever "here" was? Katz had no idea.

He didn't care, in fact, if there was any chance of getting out alive. Failing escape, perhaps he could live long enough to share his information with the raiders, tip them off to what he'd learned and what he thought it meant. Katz strained against his bonds, feeling the cords bite deeper, warm blood spilling down his forearms. Every lurching move made him unsteady on his feet. He slumped against the wall again and focused on the twisting, tugging effort to free his arms.

One of the cords felt looser now, or was that simply blood and tattered flesh? Katz didn't know; he couldn't stop. He flexed his biceps, then relaxed them. Straightening his arms, he rubbed against the wall, trying to roll the cord down past his elbows. Blood smears left a record of his struggle on the wall's beige paint, Katz cursing bitterly between clenched teeth. He wouldn't, couldn't stop until—

The blood-wet cord slipped lower. He could feel it moving. No more than a fraction of an inch, at first, but it was progress. It was something. With more effort and a bit more blood, he still might have a fighting chance. Katz pressed himself closer against the wall and went to work. The pain redoubled and he welcomed it, an old, familiar friend.

It told him he was still alive.

REBECCA MINDEL KILLED the first guard to surprise them, but she wasn't quick enough to do it silently. The Arab had a pistol drawn before she saw him, and he squeezed the trigger as a stream of bullets from her silenced SMG tore through his chest. One shot was all he managed, wasted on the ceiling as he fell, but it was still enough to put the others on alert.

"Dammit!" McCarter wasn't looking at her as he swore.

I know, she thought. Don't rub it in.

They heard the others coming—some of them, at least—and from the number of voices, there were obviously more men in the warehouse than she had expected. She couldn't tell how many, but she guessed at half a dozen and supposed there might be others who were smart enough to keep their mouths shut.

They had a choice to make. The shooter had been waiting for them where a north-south aisle connected with their east-west course of travel. They could move north, past the corpse, or keep on heading east and hope they weren't penned in by the approaching enemy. She waited, watching Mike Blanski as he pondered it for something like a second and a half.

"This way," he said, and stepped across the man Mindel had killed. McCarter followed, the woman bringing up the rear and pausing long enough to claim the dead man's pistol. Slipping it inside her belt, she satisfied herself that no one else would come along to use the piece against them while their backs were turned.

And she would have a few more rounds to fire if they were cornered, maybe holding one back for herself. Capture was unacceptable, less for the pain that would inevitably follow than because she couldn't guarantee her own silence. There were too many secrets she might spill, if tested to her limit and beyond.

No risk of that, she thought. Their adversaries in the warehouse were too agitated to think of taking prisoners, even if they had been given the chance. She could hear them rushing up and down the narrow aisles between stacks of cartons and crates, calling back and forth to one another in excited Arabic. Blanski was on point when the next one showed himself, and a short burst from his MP-5 sheared off the left side of the startled Arab's face.

A gun went off behind them, and she flinched involuntarily. The bullet whispered past her face as Mindel turned to see the gunman lining up another shot. She squeezed the trigger of her SMG without aiming, waggling the fat muzzle to rake her target with a rising zigzag burst of Parabellum shockers. The man died on his feet but spent a moment zombie-dancing as the slugs ripped into him, spinning him awkwardly about and slamming him against the nearest stack of crates.

Mindel was no stranger to violence, but she'd never taken pleasure in it, never joined the bragging sessions that some of her comrades held after missions against Black September, Hezbollah, or al-Qaeda. She felt no guilt at killing terrorists, particularly when she thought they might have abducted her uncle—but she saw no cause for celebration in it, either.

No balls, a young man in her boot camp graduating class had once remarked, sneering, before she dropped him with a roundhouse punch, but maybe he'd been right, in one respect. She lacked whatever made men glory in a kill, whatever made the human male responsible for ninety-odd percent of senseless murders in the world. And if the missing ingredient was testosterone, Mindel thought she could live quite nicely without it.

Assuming she survived the night.

Two more gunmen stepped into the aisle, ducking back out of sight as she chased them with gunfire. Her bullets gouged splinters from a row of crates labeled Machine Parts in Arabic, but something sparked and flared inside one of the crates, igniting with a rush of flame and thick white smoke.

McCarter was beside her in an instant, asking, "What the hell is that?"

"Some kind of incendiary," she suggested. "The crates are mislabeled."

"And we're in the middle of a bloody arsenal," McCarter said.

The flames and smoke were spreading rapidly, the wooden crates and cardboard boxes perfect fuel. Mindel saw no trace of the two gunners she'd fired on moments earlier; in fact, she couldn't make out much of anything down toward the west end of the aisle they occupied. She knew they had a problem when a case of ammunition started cooking off, full-metal-jacket rounds spraying the warehouse walls and ceilings.

"Jesus! Let's get out of here!" McCarter said.

She turned to follow him and saw Blanski already ahead of them, moving swiftly along the aisle, eastbound. Mindel cursed and double-timed along behind him.

They still didn't know if her uncle was inside the warehouse, but it seemed she was about to burn the damned place down or blow it up, before they could find out or even save themselves.

RASHAD QASIM WAS ANGRY and frightened, a lethal combination for anyone who crossed his path. He shouted orders at his men, cursing when some of them stood gaping at him, trembling like rabbits trapped in the headlights of an oncoming car. He slapped one of them viciously and saw the others wince in sympathetic pain, but they got moving then, dispersing in accordance with his orders to surround the enemy.

But even as he spoke, Qasim feared it might be a hopeless task.

He still didn't know who his enemies were, or how many had entered the warehouse. He had no idea what they wanted, although the Jew hostage came quickly to mind. It was all too much for coincidence—first his attempted escape, and now this.

The damned warehouse was burning now, Qasim saw, or at least the precious merchandise contained within its metal walls. Some of the items wouldn't burn, though he suspected they might melt in the face of such heat. Other items were already gone, ammunition exploding as if a hundred machine guns were firing together, smoke and incendiary grenades filling the place with clouds of vapor that could blind a man or starve his lungs for oxygen.

Trailing the slowest, most reluctant of his soldiers, Qasim tried to guess who the raiders might be. Israeli commandos were the most likely suspects, but they could also be Palestinian police, even guerrillas from a rival army sent to capture arms. The old Jew might have nothing in the world to do with it, but Qasim doubted that very much.

Crossing a smoky aisle, he noted movement to his left and glimpsed a man he didn't recognize. He was dressed all in black, with his face painted to match. Qasim thought the stranger's weapon might be fitted with a sound suppressor, but he couldn't be sure in the midst of so much racket from exploding cartridges. Qasim saved himself by dropping prone and feigning death, holding the pose for a long ten count before he raised his head.

The man in black was gone.

One of Qasim's soldiers came up behind him, scanning the aisle before he knelt to help his captain. "Are you all right?" he asked. "Where is your injury?"

"I'm fine," Qasim told him. "There is no wound."

The young man's face screwed up, as if that concept was too abstract for his mind to grasp. Qasim was on his feet and moving cautiously into the smoke before the other said, "A trick! I see."

Qasim ignored him, keeping low as burning ammunition cracked and popped behind him, bullets whining all around the warehouse. He thanked God that they were located well away from town, but even that was no guarantee of privacy. A passing motorist might hear the racket anytime and summon the authorities. Qasim had work to do—protect the hostage, save what arms he could before the fire claimed everything—but nothing could be done until his enemies were killed or driven from the warehouse.

The young guerrilla who had tried to help him trailed Qasim along the smoky aisle, lurking within a yard of him, as if afraid to lose his master in the swirling smoke. It grated on Qasim's nerves, made him feel as if he were a larger target with the soldier on his heels. At last he turned to face the other man. "You must—"

The soldier gasped and lurched against Qasim, as if embracing him. His rifle clattered to the floor. Reflexively, Qasim reached out to catch him, braced himself to keep from falling backward with the young man in his arms. The soldier's deadweight nearly dragged him down regardless, and he felt warm blood on his hands where they were clasped behind the other's back.

He dropped the body and recoiled, crouching. Were they behind him now, his enemies, or was the fatal round but one of hundreds crackling in the nearby fire? Qasim took no chances. Dropping prone once more, below the pall of smoke, he put the corpse behind him and began to crawl along the aisle, southward. His course would take him right across the warehouse at its midpoint, if he wasn't intercepted by an enemy or hit by flying slugs and shrapnel from the fire.

Qasim no longer had duty in mind. Survival took priority. If he couldn't protect the hostage or the arms, at least he could escape to tell his masters what had happened, warn them of a new, tenacious enemy. If he was eloquent enough and had a bit of luck, Wasim Jabbar might even spare his life.

Qasim crawled onward, toward the nearest exit, praying that his luck wouldn't desert him now.

THEY HAD AGREED to separate and search for Katz, thus saving time. The warehouse had been filling up with smoke and fumes, bullets and shrapnel cutting through the haze, and they'd agreed the probe was going sour in a hurry. Ten more minutes, maximum, and they were set to rendezvous outside the same door that they'd used to get inside.

McCarter reckoned he could find it, if he didn't get cut off. It didn't really matter, though. As long as he could make his way outside, it was a short jog to the building's southwest corner. Bolan and Mindel would meet him there, if they were still alive.

The corridor he'd found was relatively smoke-free at the moment, but that wouldn't last for long. The fire was spreading quickly, fueled as much by gunpowder and chemicals as by cardboard and wood. It pleased McCarter that the weapons stashed there would be left inoperable. Even if they didn't find Katz on the premises, it would be an achievement of sorts. Allah's Lance would have fewer munitions to use on its next sneak attack into Israel, perhaps sparing innocent lives.

McCarter's ears picked up a rhythmic banging sound. It emanated from somewhere ahead of him, around a sharp turn in the corridor. Advancing cautiously, he hesitated at the corner, then leaned out to risk a look around. Halfway down the hall in front of him, two Palestinians took turns kicking a door, pausing to try the knob from time to time, as if they thought their kicks would cause the lock to change its mind and open automatically.

They wanted in the room, that much was obvious. But why? What mattered so much to them in the midst of crisis, and why didn't they have keys to fit the lock?

McCarter edged around the corner, closed the gap between them while the shooters were distracted. Under other circumstances he'd have found it comic, watching them, but he was swiftly running out of time and something told the Briton that the locked room just might hold the answer to his quest.

When he was fifteen feet away, McCarter spoke to the distracted terrorists. "Hello, boys. Can I help with that?" They turned on him, startled, both fumbling for the automatic rifles they had slung across their shoulders. It was too little and much too late, McCarter's SMG spraying the pair with silenced Parabellum rounds at something close to point-blank range. The two men went down twitching, dead before they hit the floor. McCarter watched them for another moment, making sure, and saw their blood track crimson lines across concrete.

He stepped up to the door and knocked. "Is someone inside there?"

A gruff, familiar voice came back at him, squeezing his heart. "You know damn well I am!"

"Stand well back from the door," he said, and gave Katz time to move before he blew the lock apart. McCarter shouldered through and found his old friend standing slumped against the far wall, arms tethered behind his back.

"I thought you'd be here yesterday," Katz told him, smiling cheerfully through split and swollen lips.

"I had a previous engagement," McCarter replied. "Turn around and let me see those ropes."

The cords had lacerated Katz's arms, but it was nothing that some first-aid treatment wouldn't fix. As for the rest of him, they'd have to wait until the team was well away and safe. If Katz could walk, though, there was still a chance they'd both get out alive.

McCarter cut the cords with his commando dagger, sheathed it and went back to check the outer hall as Katz shook circulation back into his arms. "You wouldn't have an extra gun, by any chance?" he asked.

McCarter took a rifle from the nearer of the two men he had killed and handed it to Katz. "You still remember how to use it?"

The former Phoenix Force warrior flashed another painful smile. "Line up some targets, and we'll see if it comes back to me."

"That shouldn't be a problem," McCarter told him. "But we've got a rendezvous to keep. No time to lurk around for sport."

"Who else is here?" Katz asked, hefting the rifle and suppressing another grimace of pain.

"You'll see them soon," McCarter said. "I wouldn't want to ruin the surprise."

"Nobody likes a smart-ass," the Israeli said.

"Somebody must. There wouldn't be so many of them, otherwise. Ready?"

"I'm right behind you."

"Don't get lost. We have a bit of smoke," McCarter said.

"I warned them not to play with matches," Katz replied, and trailed his friend into the corridor.

That's done, at least, McCarter thought. *Whatever happens now, we'll be together.*

Even as the thought took form, he hoped they wouldn't be together in a shallow desert grave.

BOLAN EMERGED onto the loading dock, smoke trailing on his heels. Two silenced Parabellum rounds put out the lights that bathed the platform in illumination, making him a target for whatever enemies had managed to escape ahead of him. He crouched and waited, half expecting gunfire from the outer darkness, but none was forthcoming. If any guerrillas had fled by this route, they had to have kept running and vanished from sight.

Behind him, the warehouse still echoed with sounds of exploding munitions. He wasn't concerned about plastic explosives, which wouldn't detonate from heat, requiring instead a primary explosion, but he thought there might be rockets or grenades stored in the warehouse, and if so, he wanted to be clear before they blew.

A quick glance at his watch showed three minutes remaining to his scheduled meet with Mindel and McCarter at the point where they'd first entered the warehouse. It galled him to leave empty-handed, but he'd found no trace of Katz or any other hostage in the sector he'd scoured before smoke and shrapnel drove him out. He hoped McCarter and Mindel could make it out, regretting their decision to split up, but it was done and there was nothing he could do about it now.

He hopped down from the loading dock and paused beside the two vehicles parked there. Bolan didn't know if there were any terrorists still living in the warehouse, but he thought it couldn't hurt to hamper their escape, if so. He checked his submachine gun's magazine—half-full—and turned the weapon on the Citroën first, raking its engine through the rust-flecked hood and flattening the two front tires. That done, he turned to face the Fiat van and fired off the rest of his magazine, shredding both tires on the left-hand side, cracking the radiator, leaving gasoline to dribble from the ruptured fuel tank.

Bolan left the two disabled rides and circled toward the southeast corner of the warehouse. When he looked around the corner, it appeared that someone had switched on a bank of lights he hadn't seen before, their thin beams lancing through the night at odd angles, but then he understood. Wild rounds exploding from within had drilled erratic patterns in the wall, and he saw firelight shining through. It made an abstract light show in the desert darkness, but revealed no snipers waiting for him on that side.

He moved out from the shadows, feeding his MP-5 a fresh magazine as he paced off the yard, staying well out of range from stray rounds. The echoes of gunfire were dying as the flames ran out of ammo to consume. That didn't make the warehouse safe, by any means, but it was easier to listen for the sounds of anyone approaching in the night. He waited, kneeling in the sand to make himself less obvious, ready to answer any challenge with his silenced MP-5.

Rebecca Mindel was the first to show, jogging around the west end of the warehouse, scanning for some sign of her companions. Bolan whistled to her, waving as she sought him out, rising to greet her as she closed the gap.

"McCarter?" she asked him, the one word saying everything.

"Not yet."

Another ninety seconds remained before the Phoenix Force warrior missed their deadline. Bolan didn't mind delaying if they had no opposition on the ground, but every minute wasted raised the odds against a clean getaway. There was no sound of distant sirens yet, but Bolan knew it was only a matter of time. How much time? He couldn't predict, but the less they spent waiting, the better he'd like it.

"There!" Mindel said, pointing off to his right. "Someone's coming."

Bolan saw two shadow-shapes approaching on the same route he had followed, from the east end of the warehouse. Both were armed with rifles, he could see that much by moonlight, and he reckoned two meant trouble on the hoof. He raised his SMG and sighted down its barrel in the darkness, focused on the man out front.

"Hold fire!" McCarter called out as he crossed the open ground.

"Is that—?" Mindel gasped and broke from Bolan's side, running to meet the man who trailed McCarter at a slower pace. Bolan moved out behind her, still on guard, until he saw Katz let his rifle drop and sweep his niece into a hug that stole her breath away.

"Where was he?" Bolan asked McCarter.

"Lounging in a private room, of course," McCarter said, grinning.

"My ass!" Katz growled, releasing Mindel long enough to reach for Bolan's hand. They shook left-handed, Bolan taking in some of the damage suffered by his friend, grateful that darkness hid the rest for now.

"You ready to get out of here?" he asked.

"Ready, and then some," Katz replied. He glanced back toward the warehouse, as a loud explosion shook the walls. "But I'm not finished with these bastards yet!"

4

Al Mazrá'ah, Jordan

Wasim Jabbar wasn't a patient man. He hated to receive bad news, particularly when it meant one of his master plans had gone awry or had been sabotaged by enemies. Under those circumstances, he'd been known to rave, smash glassware, topple furniture—and sometimes, if the news was very bad indeed, to kill the messenger.

It came as no surprise, therefore, that Rashad was nervous as he stood before his master, flanked by soldiers armed with automatic weapons. He had nothing but the very worst of news to share— destruction of his men and the facility at Jericho, loss of the arsenal stored there, the likely rescue of their prisoner by enemies unknown—and it was highly possible that he would never leave Jabbar's safehouse alive.

Qasim seemed puzzled, therefore, when he finished laying out his tale of woe and stood before Jabbar, waiting for the explosion that was sure to follow. After several moments, standing with his eyes downcast, Qasim glanced up and frowned, confused.

It pleased Jabbar to keep his pitiful lieutenant guessing. True, his first impulse had been to seize a weapon from one of his bodyguards and fire point-blank into Qasim until the gun ran out of bullets or Qasim quit twitching on the floor. On second thought, however, it seemed wise to wait and bide his time.

Qasim was his, to do with as he liked. Jabbar could kill him now, next week, next year—the time and place were immaterial.

There was a chance, however, that for all his evident incompetence, Qasim might still be useful in the search for those who had defied Wasim Jabbar. *That* was important. It persuaded him to forgo vengeance for the moment and enjoy it icy cold, another day.

"You saw one of these men?" he asked Qasim at last.

"Yes, sir! I did see one."

"Describe him, please." The courtesy fell from Jabbar's lips like a drop of rain on thirsty ground. He saw Qasim draw courage from it, thinking hard before he answered.

"He was tall, sir. Large, not fat. He had an athlete's body."

"And his face?"

"All painted black," Qasim replied.

"Painted?"

"As when the Jews attack our camps, sir. Painted black for fighting after nightfall."

"He was not in truth an African?"

"No, sir. The nose and lips were...different."

"How was he dressed, again?" Qasim had told this part before, but Jabbar reasoned that it couldn't hurt to double-check.

"All black, sir, as I said. He carried a machine pistol and wore suspenders, with a belt..." Qasim was demonstrating with his hands, a childlike pantomime. "There was a pistol on his belt, I think. Perhaps—"

"You only saw one man?" Jabbar asked, interrupting him.

"Yes, sir. One only."

"But you think there were more?"

"If there was only one," Qasim replied, "we would have killed him."

"Yet, you faced this one and killed him not."

The wheels turning inside Qasim's head seemed to slip, making his face go blank for two or three heartbeats. "No, sir," he said, recovering. "The smoke... He fired at me. When I looked up..."

"You fired on him, at least?"

"Well, I—"

"One shot, perhaps?"

Qasim's eyes filled with frightened tears. "No, sir. It all happened so quickly."

"Never mind." Jabbar dismissed the blunder with an open-handed gesture. "You may have another chance, if luck is with us."

"Sir?"

"These nameless enemies destroyed a major cache of weapons in your charge and liberated he whom you had orders to maintain in custody at any cost. Is that correct?"

"Yes, sir." Almost a whisper, hopeless now.

"I have no doubt you're anxious to repay them for the losses we have suffered and regain a place of honor in my eyes."

"Yes, sir! I will do anything you say."

"I know you will." The very prospect brought a smile to Jabbar's narrow face. "Let us consider what must be achieved."

"Identify the enemy!" Qasim suggested, sounding like a child in school, trying his best to make a good impression on the headmaster.

Too late.

"Indeed," Jabbar replied. "Unless we know the men responsible, all else is wasted time and energy. How would you go about it, then?"

The question stalled Qasim. "I'm not—"

"Our men in Tel Aviv? Of course. We'll let them earn their pay, for once."

"Yes, sir!"

"The old Jew was Mossad or worse," Jabbar continued. "I could smell it on him. Someone knows who sent him out to spy on us. Someone will share that information, if you pose the question properly."

"Yes, sir."

"Don't be afraid to ask the question forcefully."

"No, sir. I won't."

"Too much depends on this for a faint heart to intercede."

"You have my word, sir."

"And I trust you absolutely," Jabbar lied. "I know you'd never let me down a second time."

"As God is my witness!"

"So He is, Qasim. And so am I. What else?"

"Sir?"

"What else have you planned, after our foes have been identified?"

"Determine where they are and wipe them out!"

"Before you question them?"

The question stopped Qasim again. He frowned and shook his head emphatically. "No, sir! I would determine who they serve and why they interfere with Allah's Lance."

"What else?"

"And...and..."

"And where they've put the prisoner, perhaps?"

"Yes, sir! I won't lose him a second time."

"I hope not. That would be a disappointment. You don't want to disappoint me twice, do you, Qasim?"

"No, sir! I shall not fail!"

"You have my every confidence." Another blatant lie. "Be on your way, then, and report back when you have good news."

"Yes, sir! Immediately, sir!"

Salim Zuhayr was smiling when Jabbar glanced over at him. "What amuses you?"

"You let him live," Zuhayr replied.

"For now. It's a reprieve, best not mistaken for a pardon."

"It's still mercy. You surprise me."

"Mercy with a purpose. Don't presume to question me."

Zuhayr's smile disappeared. "I'd never think of it."

"I don't mind what you think, Salim, but only what you do."

"I stand corrected, sir."

"You're sitting down, in fact. We have no time for that."

"What would you have me do?"

"Qasim's a bungler. Let him try to find out what he can. If he succeeds, I may reward him with a swift death. In the meantime, do your very best to find out who these people are and where they've taken the old man."

"I'll see to it."

"Yourself, Salim. No substitutes."

"Of course. And you, Wasim?"

Jabbar suppressed a sudden urge to scowl. "For my part, I must reassure our partners that we've only had a setback, not a tragedy."

Jabbar dreaded the phone call he had to make, but he wouldn't allow Salim to see it on his face. He would be strong and do his part.

He would survive.

Riyadh, Saudi Arabia

ARNOLD NAPIER LIT a fat cigar—one of his treasured Monte Cristos from Havana—using the moment to collect his thoughts. Across the spacious desk, Sterling Holbrook studied him with ill-concealed uneasiness.

"You still think he can handle it?" Holbrook asked.

"If he can't," Napier replied, "who will?"

Holbrook could only shake his head. "I don't like this," he said. "I don't like this at all."

"We've hit a rough patch on the highway," Napier stated. "That doesn't mean we turn around and run back home."

"It might not be a bad idea."

"For God's sake, Sterl, you can't go yellow on me now."

"It isn't that," Holbrook replied stiffly.

"Okay, then, what? You knew we'd have to break some eggs before we got this omelette done."

"So far, the only eggs I see broken are ours."

"Jabbar's," Napier corrected him. "We haven't lost a thing."

"Nothing except a fortune, if this thing falls through."

"You worry too damn much."

"It's what you pay me for," Holbrook reminded him.

"Then earn your money. Think of some way we can help Jabbar, if it turns out he needs a hand."

"You want to get involved?"

Napier grinned at his second in command through floating smoke. "You make it sound like we'll be swapping spit with him, next thing you know. We *are* involved, in case you missed the memo. Right up to our necks."

"I meant the physical dimension," Holbrook said. "No one advised me we'd be fighting grubby little wars out in the desert, somewhere."

"And it may not come to that. It probably won't happen. But

if so, it wouldn't be the first time things got physical. You *do* remember Singapore?"

"That was an isolated incident."

"And so will this be, isolated, if we're called on to do anything at all."

"It stinks, is what I'm telling you."

"Relax. Just wait until you smell the money."

"Have you told the others yet?"

Napier shook his head. "Not yet. I thought we'd take a moment, first."

"They won't be happy."

"They're pragmatic men. They know you have to take great risks for great rewards."

"I hope it's worth it," Holbrook said.

"What's wrong, Sterl? Don't you want to be a billionaire?"

"A billion dollars doesn't help me if I'm sitting in a prison cell—or dead."

"You're turning into an alarmist," Napier said. "That time of month?"

"Funny. Suppose Mak's people get cold feet and pull the plug?"

"No way. They're sitting safe at home and thinking we take all the chances—"

"Which we do."

"—and counting all that money in their future Swiss accounts. You know the big thing now in China is to Westernize. They'd love to be us if they could, round eyes and all. They won't blow off this kind of money, trust me."

"That's my weakness," Holbrook said.

"Say what?"

"I trust you, Arnie. Always have."

"Hell, that's your strength, Sterl. That's exactly why we make the perfect team. Your heart, my balls."

"We need to use our brains right now," Holbrook replied.

"I'm on it. If Jabbar can't do the job, we'll put some backup on it and make sure there's no loose ends."

"Like Washington? Like Tel Aviv?"

"They'll never know what hit 'em, partner."

"Right. The question is, will we?"

"You'll give yourself an ulcer, if you think like that."

"Too late."

"Then have a glass of milk. Get laid. Do something to relax before you blow a fuse."

"I'm with you, Arn. You know that, right?"

"I'm glad you cleared that up."

"But we can never take it lightly," Holbrook said. "We can't take anything for granted."

"Wouldn't dream of it," Napier replied. "Hell, that's the first thing that you ever taught me, thirty-something years ago."

"If you want me to, I'll call Andrastus. Mak's all yours, though."

"Thanks, but no. I'll do 'em both. We get along all right. They'll see it my way."

"I hope so."

"No sweat."

"It's late, then. I could use some sleep."

"If you have any trouble dozing off, try counting bars of gold—or maybe showgirls."

"I'll keep that in mind. Good night, Arn."

"Later, Sterl."

In truth, Napier was dreading the two phone calls that he had to make. His partners would be troubled, maybe even angry, but he hoped they wouldn't fall apart.

Pragmatic men.

That much was true, at least—but they were also ruthless men. Cold-blooded men. Dangerous men.

He couldn't come off cheerful or sarcastic when he spoke to them; it might be fatal. Condescension definitely wouldn't play, either. Any slip at all would be a critical mistake.

No slips, then, Napier told himself, drawing deeply on his cigar. Smooth sailing, all the way.

Or they were sunk, and he could take that to the bank.

Hell, he could take it to the grave.

HAL BROGNOLA PICKED UP on the second ring, already wide-awake despite the hour. It was a trick no lawman ever really lost once he was trained, waking to news of trouble in the middle of the night.

"Hello."

"It's me." The strong, familiar voice.

Brognola pushed up on one elbow. "How'd it go?"

"We've got him. Alive."

Brognola felt a sweet rush of relief, tempered by caution. "And in one piece?" he asked.

"He's had a hard few days," Bolan replied. "I'd feel better if he was in the hospital, but it's like talking to a wall."

"Tell me about it. What's the damage?"

"Hard to say, without a full examination, but he's mobile, on his own steam."

"Well, that's something, anyway."

"It might be better if he wasn't," Bolan added.

"What's the problem?"

"Basically, he wants a rematch. Says we won't get anywhere without him."

"Will you?" Brognola asked.

"If he opens up."

"So, it's like that?"

"He wants a piece of somebody. Figures they owe him."

Brognola had trouble faulting Katz's logic, but he saw the problem. "Try reminding him that he's retired," he said.

"Been there, done that."

"No good?"

"We've got two problems," Bolan told him. "The first is that they roughed him up and hurt his pride. The other is, he misses fieldwork."

"We've been over that," Brognola said.

"I'd say he's having second thoughts about those golden years."

"You have him handy?"

"Not right now. He needed some first aid."

"I'll talk to him myself. Call back as soon as he's patched up, all right?"

"Will do."

"How was the other?"

"Inconclusive. We took out some hardware, more or less by accident. Ran up a body count. I'd be surprised if any major players were involved."

"So, what's your feeling? Is it anything beyond a wrong-place, wrong-time kind of thing?"

"He thinks it has potential, but I can't assess that while he's holding back."

"Okay," Brognola said. "I'll see what I can do to smooth that out for you. I want him out of there ASAP. Debrief him first, but get him on a plane."

"He won't like that," Bolan replied.

"I don't like sending people out to chase his ass around the desert, either."

"That'll need to come from you."

"Count on it. One way or another, he gets on that plane. I want to see him at the Farm no later than tomorrow night."

"I'll put the niece on it. She's motivated, and it may sit better with him if it comes from blood."

"Whatever works," the big Fed said. "Hog-tie him if you have to. Throw him in the baggage hold."

"I'd like to see somebody try."

Bolan was laughing as he broke the link, and Brognola cradled the telephone. He glanced at his wife and found her still asleep, conditioned to his wake-up calls from long years as a federal agent's spouse. Aware that he'd have trouble getting back to sleep, he rolled out of bed and picked up a robe on his way to the kitchen for coffee.

He was troubled by Bolan's report, though it didn't surprise him. He'd known, at some level, that Katzenelenbogen wouldn't take abduction lying down. The old warhorse was pleading for another term in harness, maybe just a chance to pay back those who had abused him in captivity, but the big Fed wasn't prepared to make that wish come true. Katz was retired from fieldwork, dammit! He'd agreed to terms, and Brognola wasn't about to start from scratch on those negotiations, just because Katz got himself in trouble on what was supposed to be a quiet visit with his family.

Brognola knew how the gruff Israeli's mind worked. It was not unlike his own, in fact, though tempered by an early lifetime in a nation under siege. Katz was a warrior and a patriot. Brognola would no more ask him to turn his back on that than he would ask a fish to sunbathe on dry land. But every warrior has his limits, and they had agreed that Katz was past his prime for fieldwork. He was still valued as a tactician and adviser—always would be—but the basic facts of life were unavoidable. Brognola himself had only dodged the FBI's mandatory retirement age by shifting to an upper-echelon slot in the Justice Department where he served at the President's pleasure.

And one sure way to jeopardize that pleasure was to unleash a revenge-happy wild man in the midst of the Middle Eastern tinderbox.

As far as security went, Brognola was covered. He'd maxed out his federal pension already, income and benefits guaranteed for life unless he stepped in something unexpected and was sent up on a major felony conviction. His concern, right now, was for the team he had created—both at Stony Man and in the field. It was a finely tuned machine, and any single worn or damaged part might cause irreparable damage if it was ignored.

Brognola didn't micromanage Stony Man, but he made sure to keep a finger on the operation's pulse and move with all dispatch if anything went wrong. Right now, Katz was a damaged cog, but he could be repaired—at least in theory. While that patch-up work was underway, Brognola had a duty to protect the rest of the machine from Katz himself. If that meant riding herd and pulling rank, it wouldn't be the first time.

He would do what had to be done.

That didn't mean he would be looking forward to it, though.

He hoped Katz wouldn't turn the operation into a fiasco with some wild-ass game plan of his own, but Brognola would leap from that bridge when he came to it. Overt defiance would mean using Bolan and McCarter to retrieve Katz before he could harm himself or Stony Man, and that, Brognola knew, might prove to be impossible.

He put the coffee on, reflecting as he did so that he didn't need caffeine right then to make his gut twitch with a sour feeling. He already had that covered, thanks to Katzenelenbogen's private quest.

Brognola kept his fingers crossed, hoping it wouldn't lead him to another funeral—or two, or three...

Kalámai, Greece

CHRISTOS ANDRASTUS took the phone call over breakfast, on the sun-drenched terrace of his villa, facing the Mediterranean Sea. It spoiled his appetite, but he refused to leave the table without finishing his meal. Andrastus valued discipline above all else—well, nearly all—and he refused to let a group of Third World peasants spoil his morning mood.

There was a problem with the Palestinians, of course. He'd seen enough of them in recent months to know that there was always something wrong, some glitch that tossed their best-laid plans into a cocked hat every time. It troubled him, but he had confidence that Mak and Napier could chart a course around such obstacles as they arose, or plow them under with strategic force, if it came to that. As long as Mak and Napier did their jobs, it ought to be smooth sailing all the way.

Andrastus automatically thought of his problems and progress in nautical terms. He'd begun life as a fisherman's son and followed his father to sea, grasping opportunities as they came—or creating them—until he ruled a global fleet of tankers, cargo ships and cruise liners at age sixty-one. Friends and enemies alike called it a miracle, and who was he to argue, in the circumstances?

Mopping up the remnants of eggs Benedict with whole wheat toast, Andrastus thought about the trouble that was brewing even now in Palestine. Violence had been expected, it was part and parcel of the plan, in fact, an absolute necessity, but he was concerned by the introduction of an unknown quantity, this interloper who had managed to escape from Wasim Jabbar before he was even identified. Jabbar seemed to think he was linked to Israeli intelligence, but who could say? And what would it mean to their joint enterprise, if he was?

Tel Aviv's interference was taken for granted, though Andrastus had been pleased to find it minimized thus far, in the early stages of their plan. He understood Israeli ruthlessness—even admired it, from afar—but they could ill afford a full-scale offensive at this stage, much less exposure on a global scale before their plans were finalized.

After the trap was sprung, well, that would be another story, for another time. It wouldn't matter what the Jews did, then. Too late by then, Andrastus thought, and smiled. A few more weeks were all they needed, less than that, perhaps. The game pieces were all in place. Only a few deft moves remained. But they could still lose everything, if some gate-crasher tipped the board and sent it tumbling into ruin.

Sometimes Andrastus rued the day he'd cast his lot with Mak and Napier, but the deed was done. He couldn't back out now, unless his partners caused some difficulty so egregious that options remained. The loss he bore in that case would be painful, granted, but it might not cripple him.

With luck, he might survive.

It was too early for such thoughts, Andrastus told himself. Jabbar would likely find the prisoner who'd slipped away from him, and even if he didn't, there was still no reason to suppose that loss foretold catastrophe. Suppose the old man *was* a spy. What, then? He couldn't have learned much or traveled far along their road, if he'd been caught by Allah's Lance in Israel.

Andrastus didn't want to think about the plan unraveling at this stage, when he'd already invested so much money, time and energy. He wanted to succeed and profit from the scheme beyond his wildest fantasies. Already someone to be reckoned with, one of the richest men in Greece, Christos Andrastus wanted to he huge. He longed to dwarf Onassis, watch the competition shrivel in his shadow as it stretched from Athens to the Far East and America.

He yearned to be a power on a global scale, not limited to shipping manifests and schedules, crude oil prices and the latest trends in tourism.

He wanted nothing less than everything.

It galled him to suppose that some old man he'd never even met could spoil it for him with a cheap stunt in the desert waste of Palestine. It was a bitter pill to swallow, almost more than he could bear.

Andrastus was a fighter, though, a born survivor. He wouldn't throw in the towel without exerting every effort to defeat his enemies and profit from their ruin. Better men than this elusive stranger had gone up against him in the past.

Where were they now?

All gone, most of them dead. A few had died by his own hand. Andrastus hadn't done his own wet work in many years, but he hadn't forgotten what it felt like, either. Any man who tried to injure him or meddle in his plans was risking life and limb with no great hope of victory.

Andrastus knew his partners were both formidable men. He thought they underestimated him to some extent, and that was good. It gave him the advantage of surprise and might be useful someday, when their backs were turned.

For now, though, he required their services. Both Mak and Napier had their uses, serving as his bridge to different worlds of politics, intrigue and industry. As long as they were useful, he was pleased to let them serve him.

But if either one of them should ever let him down...

Christos Andrastus smiled.

It might turn out to be a good day, after all.

Hong Kong

LIN YUAN MAK LIT his third unfiltered cigarette of the past hour, drawing smoke deeply into his lungs. It was a habit that would likely kill him someday, but he clung to it for all that, perversely relishing the power he held to affect his own future, however adversely.

Lin Mak's adult life had revolved around the pursuit of personal power in a society that championed communal achievement over all else, disdaining heroes unless they served the state, guarding against the rise of titans with a hive mentality that discouraged—even punished—individual initiative.

That was the theory, at least, in the People's Republic of China, but Lin Mak understood the reality behind the Bamboo Curtain. He'd grown up in a family of loyal party stalwarts—grandson of an old guerrilla fighter who had joined Mao on the historic Long March, son of a martyr in the war against America's invasion of North Korea—and he knew all the fine points of manipulating Communist theory for personal profit. To that end he had climbed the ladder of bureaucracy in Beijing, first as a military officer and now as a civilian minister assigned to supervise commerce in the former British colony of Hong Kong.

The manipulation was easier now, in this time and place, with the atmosphere of improved relations between China and the West—especially America—but Mak still had to exercise caution. China wasn't a free society by any means, no matter how much power he had managed to accumulate for himself. There were limits, even now, and overstepping certain boundaries could still produce catastrophic results.

If certain people in Beijing had known of the previous night's phone call, for example...

Mak lit a fresh cigarette from the dwindling ember of his last and surveyed his small office through a veil of curling smoke. His business quarters weren't exactly Spartan, but they offered no suggestion of his true net worth, much less his personal ambition. There would come a day, Mak promised himself, when he would leave cramped rooms like this behind forever.

But today wasn't that day.

Not after what Napier had told him on the telephone.

It wasn't a disaster *yet*. Napier had emphasized that point repeatedly. It might not even be a major problem, if their comrades on the scene could recover in time to correct their mistake, prevent unfortunate events from spinning irredeemably out of control.

If it wasn't already too late.

That was Mak's fear, that events occurring halfway around the world might betray him now. He could lose everything if some peasant fool he'd never met allowed mistakes to go unremedied. Napier appeared to have a handle on the situation, but Mak knew the oilman well enough by now to wonder how much of his voluble self-confidence was bluff, and how much could be trusted.

The Middle East was a quagmire, worse than Southeast Asia with its tribal conflicts and endless guerrilla warfare, but it was also a source of unlimited wealth, and wealth meant power. Whatever the regime or jurisdiction, money talked—and in sufficient quantities, it normally had the last word.

Mak recognized the irony of his mistrust where Palestinian guerrillas were concerned. Ostensibly, the People's Republic of China supported their fight against Zionist aggression in spirit, if not with infusions of money and weapons. In practice, though, he found them generally suspect and untrustworthy, too heavily influenced by religion and the sort of blood-feud mentality that bred martyrs and filled cemeteries to no result. Mak didn't voice those opinions publicly—in fact, he generally kept them secret even from his covert partners, Napier and Andrastus—but he knew that many others of his rank and station felt the same. Elitism was contrary to Marxist theory, but it still existed in the Worker's Paradise.

And why not?

What was the point of striving to excel, if all men ended up on the same level?

Some of Mak's countrymen and fellow party members would have called him a traitor for harboring such thoughts, but he knew the truth of it. There was no such thing on Earth as a functional "Communist" state, in the sense intended by Marx and Engels. Lenin and company had moved directly from revolution to personal aggrandizement in Russia, as had Mao in China, Kim Il Sung in North Korea, and Castro in Cuba. In Mak's experience, no one served the human race unfailingly without some profit for himself. It was a rule of human nature and perhaps a law of Nature itself.

The day would come when he would leave China forever, if the climate didn't change. Or maybe he could help to change it from within, using the power he'd accumulated and the even greater influence he meant to have in the near future.

Then again, he might decide to buy his own country and reign in the style of an old-fashioned emperor. Lin Mak the First.

Before that happened, though, he had to make sure that no more stumbling blocks were thrown across his path. If his associates couldn't control their hirelings, he might have to take a more personal interest in the details, perhaps hammer some of them out on his own.

But not yet.

He would trust Napier a bit further, before it came to that. As far as he could see the glib American, in fact—but no further.

It was that kind of world, and Lin Mak meant to make it his own. If Napier wasn't careful with his Arabs, he might find himself cut out of the game altogether.

No man was irreplaceable. Mak had learned that as a child.

It was a lesson he'd be more than glad to share.

5

Tel Aviv

Yakov Katzenelenbogen clenched his fist beneath the table, squeezing hard enough to make the knuckles crack if they hadn't already done so moments earlier. He tried to keep his face impassive, check his temper, but it wasn't easy with the anger roiling in his gut and coloring his cheeks.

"You can't just cut me out of this," he said tersely. "I deserve a piece of this. *They* had a piece of *me*."

"All the more reason for you to stay clear," McCarter said between sips of Coke.

"I can carry my weight," Katz replied heatedly.

"No one's saying you can't." McCarter took another sip to punctuate his comment. "But you're blown, old friend. They know you now. They'll see you coming from a mile away."

"I'll take my chances with the rest of you," Katz said.

"That's just the point," Bolan told him, speaking for the first time since they'd taken seats around the dining table in the small safehouse. "It's not just you at risk. Because they know you, you'd be jeopardizing all of us."

"You don't think I can do the job?"

"Uncle—"

Katz rounded on Rebecca, catching himself as he was about to snap at her. Restraining himself with an effort, he said, "I never should've taken on a desk job. That was a mistake. I'm as fit as ever."

"And again, that's not the point," Bolan replied. "You came here on vacation and you stumbled into something. We're still not sure what it is, but—"

"Give me time," Katz interjected. "I can put it all together."

"No, you can't," Bolan stated. "David already hit the only point that matters now. They know you by sight, and they may have had time to work out your ID. Bottom line—you're a risk to the mission from this moment on."

"*My* mission," Katz insisted. "You'd have nothing without me."

"And it's appreciated," Bolan said, "but let's backtrack a minute. You came out here on vacation, to spend time with family. You spotted a familiar face."

"The chief of Allah's Lance," Katz said. "Wasim Jabbar, no less, showing his face in Israel!"

"Right. And you've connected him to Arnold Napier, the CEO of Global Oil."

"Global Petroleum," Katz said, correcting his old friend. "The first meeting I shadowed put Jabbar in touch with Sterling Holbrook, Napier's number two."

"So there's a link we need to look at," Bolan said. "But none of that changes the fact that you were captured."

"And interrogated," Katz reminded him. "Don't leave that out."

Bolan leaned back and took a beat before responding. "I don't need to ask about that. I assume you didn't crack."

"Thank you for that, at least."

"It's understood, and it's beside the point."

"I'm out of it because they saw my face? Is *that* the point?"

"You're out of it because you have a desk job now, which you agreed to," Bolan said. "You're out of it because this whole thing was a fluke, an accident. You're out of it because the man says so."

"Brognola."

"He still calls the shots," Bolan replied. "On this one, I agree with him."

"So it's like that," Katz said.

"You knew the way I felt before I called him. It's official now. Hal wants you back at Stony Man, ASAP."

"He thinks I've lost my touch," Katz said. And even as he

spoke the words, he thought of recent times when he'd thought much the same about himself. The adjectives that came to mind in those dark moments were disheartening.

Redundant.

Obsolete.

Useless.

"Nobody thinks you've lost the touch," Bolan told him. "By the same token, no one fights forever. Smart warriors know when to step back."

"Remember Stonewall Jackson," McCarter pointed out.

"He was shot by his own men in combat," Katz observed.

"All right, then. Not the best example. General Patton?"

"Car crash," Bolan told McCarter.

"I'll be quiet now."

"I won't," Katz said. "I still have something to contribute, dammit! Just because Hal thinks I'm past it, there's no reason why I can't participate. I'm not much older than Brognola, for God's sake!"

"He isn't active in the field and hasn't been for years," Bolan replied. "He still contributes, so do you. On this team, though, Hal calls the shots. You knew that coming in."

Katz scanned the faces ranged about the table. They belonged to two of his best friends on Earth and the niece whom he loved more than life itself—and yet, for a moment, it seemed to Katz that they were enemies, conspiring against him in his moment of weakness. The thought smacked of paranoia, and he wondered if maybe the time *had* come for him to bow out—not merely from fieldwork, but out of the game altogether.

Why should he spend his so-called golden years behind a desk at Stony Man, living vicariously through reports and photographs of battles fought by younger men? Katz reckoned he'd be better off on some kibbutz or deep-sea fishing off the coast of Florida than dwelling in the shadows cast by younger, stronger men.

Men with two hands.

Katz caught himself and shrugged off that notion, discarding it. The amputation hadn't held him back, once he'd been through a course of therapy and learned to cope with it. He'd held his own in combat countless times, with weapons and bare-handed, always coming out on top.

Until this time.

That was the problem in a nutshell—part of it, at least. He was a desk jockey these days, but he was also an old warhorse prone to charging after shadows if he didn't keep a tight grip on the reins. This time the targets had been real enough, but Katz had bungled the approach and others had been called to pull his fat out of the fire.

If one of them had died...

He scanned the ring of faces one more time and then made his decision. "I'm outvoted," he declared, letting his shoulders slump a bit to signal resignation. "If I could rest up here a day or two—"

"Rest up at Stony Man," Bolan suggested. "Take whatever time you need."

"It's that urgent?"

"Long flight, jet lag," the Executioner replied. "They'll set you up with anything you need."

Katz forced himself to smile. It felt as if his face was slit, the smile an open wound. "Such generosity," he told his friends. "I'd be a madman to refuse."

REBECCA MINDEL WATCHED her uncle rise and leave the table, moving slowly in deference to the pain from his recent injuries. At first she thought he was headed for the kitchen, but he passed it by and started down the hallway leading to his room.

"Uncle? Are you all right?" she asked.

"I'm fine, Rebecca. I should rest up for my flight, in case we hit a patch of turbulence."

The three of them sat waiting for the soft click of his closing door, before they spoke again. It felt as if they were betraying him, keeping their secrets, but she knew more talk about the mission would unsettle him, perhaps provoke a new outburst of pleas to be included in the action.

And since that had been ruled out, for reasons Mindel understood and heartily approved, she saw no point in making matters any worse.

The tall American she knew as Mike Blanski put his elbows on the table, leaning forward as he spoke, his voice pitched low. "He takes it hard."

"I'd be relieved to have the bastards off my neck," McCarter said.

"It's the embarrassment, as much as anything," Mindel suggested. "He hates getting older, being left behind."

"He hasn't, though," McCarter said. "Been left behind, I mean. We've traveled halfway round the bloody world to save his life, for pity's sake."

"Pity's the last thing that he needs from you right now, I'd say."

McCarter crushed the Coke can in his fist. "It's a figure of speech," the commando replied. "I'd have said, 'For Christ's sake,' but He hasn't got much of a flock in these parts."

"No one pities your uncle," Bolan stated. "We respect him. We've fought alongside him. I owe him my life."

"That goes triple for me," McCarter said. "But still, there's a time to stand down."

"He knows that," Mindel stated. "It's still a bitter pill to swallow."

"Better than Parabellum pill between the eyes," McCarter said. "He cut it too damned close this time."

"He knows that, really. But..."

"But what?" Bolan asked.

"I think he'd like to go out on a better note, with more respect," she said.

"That's just the point," Bolan stated. "I don't want him going out at all. I want him fit and breathing on the job, where he can do some good."

"I understand, of course."

"You'll take him to the airport, then?"

She hesitated, slowly nodding. "Yes, I will."

"Okay, that's settled, then," McCarter said. "What do we know about Global Petroleum?"

"The name's no euphemism," Mindel said. "The firm is a

true multinational, with oil and natural-gas holdings on five continents, plus drilling fields in Indonesia. Petrochemical business is the company's mainstay, but they also dabble lucratively in prescription drugs and computer software—the marvels of diversification. Cash-wise, Global is worth more than most small countries and some larger ones. They've virtually handpicked presidents in two Third World nations, while their covert veto has scuttled environmental protection laws in half a dozen others."

"And Napier runs it all?" Bolan asked.

"More or less. He's theoretically responsible to a board of directors, naturally, and beyond that to his various investors. In practical terms, the board's a rubber stamp for his decisions. The investors don't care what Global does, who they bribe or bulldoze, as long as the dividend rates keep increasing."

"We could say as much for any one of several thousand other firms," McCarter noted.

"But the others don't have CEOs meeting with terrorists in Tel Aviv," Bolan pointed out.

"Let's hope not," McCarter answered, frowning. "What's this Napier's angle, then?"

"If we knew that," Mindel replied, "we'd have a lock on what comes next. Wasim Jabbar's a hunted fugitive in Israel, already convicted in absentia for multiple murders and other acts of terrorism. Anyone who harbors him or aids his cause is subject to arrest. If we can prove a link, Napier would be deported at the very least."

"And Global?" Blanski asked.

"We're not a major oil-producing country, as you know," Mindel said. "Global has investments here, but mainly real estate—some office buildings and the like. In order to expel the company itself, we'd have to prove Napier's collusion with Jabbar was a matter of corporate policy, not just some personal whim. Even then, expulsion wouldn't cost them much—thirty million or so."

"Pocket change," McCarter said, shaking his head ruefully.

"It is, when we're talking in billions," Bolan stated. "Still, why risk it by meeting with Jabbar in Tel Aviv, or anywhere in Israel, for that matter, when Global has property and offices all over the Mideast?"

"Unless they have specific business here," Mindel suggested.

Bolan frowned and said, "Go on."

"It's obviously nothing I can put my finger on, without more information," she replied. "Jabbar's a terrorist. He lives for one thing only—the destruction of Israel and her committed allies. Nothing else means anything to him."

"Not even cash?" McCarter asked.

"If he could use it for the cause, of course. We know he's carried out contracts for other factions in the past, including some from Europe and the Japanese Red Army. He'd take Global's money for a mercenary job as quickly as he would from anybody else."

"Which brings us back to square one," Bolan said.

"The job," McCarter said, nodding. "It's too bad no one let the details slip in front of Katz."

"They were too busy torturing him," Mindel said.

McCarter raised his hands. "Easy, old girl. No criticism meant."

"We're all on edge," Bolan stated, though in fact he sounded calm enough to Mindel. "Maybe you should see if Katz is ready for his flight?"

"Perhaps you're right. And while I'm gone..."

"We won't commit to anything," Bolan said.

"Right, then." Mindel rose and left them, moving toward her uncle's temporary quarters at the rear of the safehouse.

And at the moment, she felt anything but safe.

"I DIDN'T MEAN to set her off," McCarter said after Mindel had left the room.

"It's not your fault," Bolan replied. "She's known Katz twice as long as either one of us. He's family. She nearly lost him."

"Still, we've got the whole Mossad thing going on, as well."

"We're on their turf. It's only natural."

"I'm not complaining, mind you."

Bolan smiled at that. "I didn't think you were."

"All right, maybe I was," McCarter admitted. "I just can't help thinking she may leave us hanging, if push comes to shove. I've had dealings with this crew before, don't forget. Their motto's 'All for One'—and they're always the one. It's Israel *über alles* when the chips are down."

"You blame them?" Bolan asked. "Their country has been under siege for close to sixty years. They were invaded by six different armies on the day their government was founded, and they haven't known a moment's peace since then."

"I've heard all that from Katz a thousand times," McCarter said, "and I agree with most of it. I've dropped my share of Palestinians and then some, long before this job came up."

"What, then?"

That was the question, and McCarter had some difficulty pinning it down in his mind. When he tried to verbalize his misgivings, they grew even more vague. Still, he gave it a shot.

"I think the lady has three interests here," he said. "We've covered one of them, retrieving Katz."

"Let's hear the others," Bolan urged.

"Payback for what he's been through would be second on the list, if she decides to make it personal," McCarter said. "The last point—orders from the brass in Tel Aviv—may override the other, if they jerk her leash."

"It's hard to picture that one being called to heel," Bolan remarked.

"Mossad's funny that way," McCarter said. "They're hell on insubordination in the ranks."

"It didn't take so well with Katz." The Executioner produced an almost wistful smile.

"You're worried that he'll try something."

"I hope not," Bolan said. "He knows Hal's serious."

"But will it make a difference?" McCarter asked.

Bolan shrugged and said, "It's not the kind of thing we've had to think about before."

McCarter thought about it then, for the first time. What would Brognola do if Katzenelenbogen flouted orders and refused to leave Israel? What *could* he do, without resorting to brute force? And if it came to that, who would be called upon to crack the whip?

He didn't like the general direction where that train of thought was taking him. Katz was a longtime friend who'd saved McCarter's life on more than one occasion, under fire. There'd never been a formal officer in charge of Phoenix Force, when they were in the field, but Katz had come as close as anyone, with his advanced combat experience and longer time in the harness. Anyone who viewed the one-handed warrior as disabled was in for a rude surprise, and age had only slowed Katz a fraction. Just enough to get him caged and nearly killed.

McCarter knew they couldn't use that event as a basis for judgment though, if Katz went rogue and they were ordered to hunt him down. Tracking Katz around Israel would be hard enough; extracting him without serious injury might be impossible.

Which way would his niece jump, if it came to that? Would she protect her uncle or help bring him in? Would the Mossad have some obscure game plan of its own, working at cross purposes to Bolan and McCarter?

"We should try to wrap this up as soon as possible," he said.

"Agreed." The thoughtful look on Bolan's face stopped short of worry, but he plainly wasn't happy with the situation, either.

"What if we put Napier through the ringer?" McCarter asked.

"It's a thought," Bolan replied. "It could get ugly if we come up empty, though. A company like Global will have friends all over Washington and who knows where else."

"I can't see them publicly defending any kind of deal with Allah's Lance. Can you?"

"We'd have to make that case somewhere besides the Farm. Even if Hal authorized a hit, the repercussions could be fatal. Two or three loud voices in the Senate, say, and you've got oversight committees checking up on Stony Man."

"No worries there," McCarter said. "Give me a day to think about it and I'll set the bastard up."

"For what? We can't stage a convincing scene unless we find out what he's up to with Wasim Jabbar. So far, all we've got is one alleged meeting."

"Alleged?" McCarter cocked a curious eyebrow. "You think Katz was mistaken, after all that happened?"

Bolan shook his head. "I mean we've got no film and nothing else to back up any accusations. If Katz goes public with the story, he'll be opening a can of worms that won't win any friends for him in Washington or Tel Aviv."

"Napier could have an accident," McCarter said. "He might just disappear."

"Let's put that thought on hold until we find out what his game is and whether he's playing alone."

"You have some means in mind to work that out?" McCarter asked.

"I might," Bolan said. And his narrow smile was as cold as steel.

BOLAN PASSED Rebecca Mindel in the hallway, coming back from Katz's room. Her attitude stopped short of bald resentment, but he recognized that she was on the edge. Bolan hoped her professional demeanor would win out this time and forestall any pointless incidents.

"How is he?" Bolan asked.

"How do you think?"

"I understand he doesn't want to leave a job undone."

"*You* understand? I don't think so."

"We're not exactly strangers," Bolan said.

"I wonder. First he's forced into retirement, now he's virtually being sent home under guard."

"You sound as if you'd rather see him in the field," Bolan replied. "It makes me wonder why."

Angry color flushed her cheeks. "Of course I wouldn't. I'm

not blind. Still, with a man like this it's best to let him keep a bit of dignity."

"Let's clear this up right now," Bolan said. "First, your uncle wasn't 'forced' into retirement, any more than he was forced to run a one-man game on Arnold Napier and the crew from Allah's Lance. He should've passed it off, instead of charging in alone. He made the wrong choice and it almost got him killed. It could've cost *your* life to bring him out."

"We're all alive," she said.

"This time. As for respect, I've never shown him any less than he deserved."

"Tonight—"

"Tonight he made me go over his head because he wouldn't stop and think. You talk about his dignity? There's none in going off half-cocked and getting killed for no good reason."

Mindel stared at Bolan for a moment. He could see the muscles clench along her jaw. At last she said, "I know he can't pursue this. Honestly, I know it. But you can't just spit out orders and expect him to obey."

"That's where we differ," Bolan said. "I look at Katz and see a soldier who's been taking orders all his life."

"This time may be too much."

"I hope not," Bolan said, "for all our sakes."

He left her standing in the hall and moved along to Katz's door, rapping lightly and waiting for the muffled come-ahead. He found Katz packing a well-traveled suitcase, its leather nearly as battered as the old soldier himself.

"Come to make sure I'm leaving?" Katz asked.

"You're a big boy," Bolan said. "You know your own mind."

"But you had to pull rank," the Israeli accused him.

"What else is rank for?" He tried a smile for size, but couldn't make it fit. "We can't afford to lose you," he went on. "Hal and the Bear need help around the office."

"You don't have to sugarcoat it," Katz replied. "I'm following my orders as instructed."

"And with such good grace."

Bright anger flared behind the one-armed warrior's light-blue eyes. "You want me to be *happy* now?"

"I wouldn't call it inappropriate," Bolan replied. "You weren't exactly taking them by storm when we found you. In fact, I'd say you were about a day or two from being dead."

"Some things are worse than death," Katz said.

"I'm with you there, but coming home to family that loves you isn't one of them. If you're about to tell me you'd prefer the hospitality of Allah's Lance, we need to fit you for a straitjacket."

"You still don't understand Israel," Katz said.

"Explain it to me, then."

"We live surrounded by a multitude who want us dead. Not merely *gone,* you understand? I mean wiped off the earth, as if we never were. The czar's Black Hundred tried it once, and then the Reich. We've lost our millions, but the remnant still holds on. We fight because we must. Because we *can.*"

"You *left* because you could," Bolan reminded him.

"I left the land, but not the fight," his friend replied. "Never the fight. Israel is always in my heart. Her enemies are always in my sights."

"It works out better when you have a gun," Bolan said.

"So I've noticed. You could lend me one of yours."

"Not this time."

Katzenelenbogen's shoulder slumped a little, as if he were giving up. "I'm sorry you don't trust me."

"On the contrary," Bolan replied. "I trust you absolutely to be smart and do what's right."

"Right for the team, you mean."

"That's what it's always been about."

"I trust you, too," Katz said. "You mustn't let them slip away. They're far too dangerous."

"We're on it," the Executioner told him. "And you'll be on it too, as soon as you get back to Stony Man."

"The desk," Katz said. "I know it well."

"It's not a cage, you know."

"Wasim Jabbar reminded me of that, just recently."

"Some guys in your place might think they were lucky," Bolan said.

"I'm one of them, believe me. Still..."

"It's never easy standing down," Bolan said.

"Have you ever, really?" Katzenelenbogen asked him.

Bolan thought about it. He'd been lucky, so far, but pure logic told him that it couldn't last forever. He'd lost friends and casual acquaintances, seen hapless bystanders cut down by bullets meant for him, and he'd sustained more wounds than any soldier had a right to walk away from. Someday, Bolan knew, it would be his turn on the desk—unless one of his adversaries killed him first. And for a fleeting moment, Bolan wondered which he would prefer.

"We all get there," he said, "in our own time."

"My luck to lead the way then, eh?" This time Katz smiled, but there was bitterness behind it, thinly veiled.

"There's no one else I'd rather have on point."

They shook left-handed, Bolan leaving then and heading back to join McCarter in the kitchen. They had moves to plan, starting from scratch, and little more to go on at the moment than suspicion.

Bolan hoped that it would be enough.

He hoped it wouldn't get them killed.

KATZ FINISHED packing in a rush, anxious to get the chore behind him. He had been dismissed, with gratitude of course, for whatever that might be worth, and told to go about his business like a good soldier.

Why did that gall him so? He'd been exactly that—a fighting man who followed orders—for most of his life, beginning as a teenager when Israel needed him to stand in her defense. He'd waged relentless war against her enemies and never let his country down.

Not until today.

Katz knew it was ridiculous, the gnawing sense of guilt he felt inside. He'd uncovered a plot against his homeland, even if he didn't know the details yet, and he had done his best to crack the mystery. In that pursuit he'd run afoul of Allah's Lance and very nearly lost his life. If he were still in uniform, Katz might've been rewarded with a decoration for his bravery, instead of being sent to bed without his supper like a child.

But in his heart and in his gut, Katz knew what he'd done wrong. It was the solo act that put him in harm's way. Brognola and the rest of them were right on that score, anyway. He should've asked for help, at least—or better yet, let others do the dirty work after he put them on the scent.

The truth was that he hadn't wanted any help. A part of him was bent on proving that he still had what it took to face determined enemies and take them out, leave all their best-laid plans in shambles. Looking back on his decision, Katz couldn't say if he'd been trying to convince Brognola and the rest or prove it to himself.

In any case, he'd blown it. Captured, tortured, nearly killed. Bolan was right in his description of events. Katz had allowed the enemy to take him by surprise, and it had very nearly cost his life. He thought again of his Rebecca and the others, risking everything to set him free. It was embarrassing to need their help, and when Katz thought of losing them he felt a deeper flush of shame.

But nothing had gone wrong. They were alive and well, he was at liberty—albeit under marching orders that would send him back to the United States. The only sour note lay in his failure to unmask the plotters and determine what nefarious design they had in store for Israel. It defied imagination that a terrorist like Wasim Jabbar would meet with Global's money men in Tel Aviv for any reason short of devilry.

But Katz was no closer to the answer now than when he'd started in pursuit of Napier and Jabbar nearly a week earlier. He had bruises to show for it, and little more beyond determination that his quest was not in vain.

Unless he left the job unfinished.

I have orders, Katz recalled, and added grimly, in another mental voice, So what?

Brognola spent so much time at his desk in Washington these days, he had begun to think that wars were won from swivel chairs. Katz knew the man from Justice was mistaken on that score, and he could prove it to the lot of them, if given half a chance. He could redeem his early failure and roll on to victory.

He only needed time, the proper tools—and luck.

"Strike three," Katz muttered to himself, closing the suitcase and securing its locks. By any reckoning, he'd stretched his luck so thin already that it had to have the consistency of tissue paper in a rainstorm. He had no equipment other than his wits and one good hand. And he was swiftly running out of time.

It was a bitter thing to leave Israel in need. He'd walked away before, as Bolan had so aptly pointed out, and while the state was ever short of heroes, some times seemed more opportune than others for a fighting man to strike out on his own. This morning, after coming through his longest night alive and more or less intact, Katz felt as if it would be nothing short of treason to withdraw and leave his mission unfulfilled.

It wasn't his mission.

He was clear on that point, having heard it hammered home nonstop since he was rescued from the snares of Allah's Lance. Mossad, Brognola and the rest appreciated his assistance but they'd carry it from here, meaning they wished he would stop meddling in their business and go play a rousing game of badminton.

It *was* his mission, though. Who had a better right to see it through than a devoted warrior who'd exposed the plot to start with? Granted, Katz had gotten off to an uneven start, but he was primed to try again.

Rebecca meant to put him on a plane, but there were ways around that problem. He could arm himself without much difficulty, and he'd held back certain information on his enemies once he had seen the way things stood with Bolan and McCarter. If he managed to elude them, Katz thought he would have a chance to show them he was still a man who pulled his weight in battle.

One step at a time.

He didn't want to harm Rebecca, but Katz knew he couldn't slip away without subjecting her to some embarrassment. Katz didn't like it, but he saw no other way. If he was on that plane when it took off, his last hope of redemption would be left behind in Tel Aviv.

Step one: Escape.

Katz hadn't done so well in that respect, with Allah's Lance, but he had an advantage with his niece. All matters being equal, he was reasonably sure she wouldn't shoot him in the back.

6

The basic plan was simple. Bolan and McCarter would start rattling cages and hope it produced some result, while Mindel drove Katz to Ben Gurion Airport and put him aboard the next El Al flight to New York. There was a layover in Paris, but Brognola had arranged for someone from the U.S. Embassy to greet Katz on arrival and keep track of him for the five hours he was on French soil.

The old war dog was on his way—not going home, but rather leaving it behind. Bolan knew how that felt, from personal experience, but there was no sense dwelling on it now, when he had other pressing matters on his mind.

Katz had reported a connection between oilman Arnold Napier and Wasim Jabbar, the terrorist in charge of Allah's Lance. He hadn't nailed down any details before he was captured, but it still gave Bolan a starting point for the hit-and-run blitz. They would begin in Tel Aviv, rocking Global Petroleum's world.

One drawback of working in Israel was the prospect of colliding with the nation's crack antiterrorist troops and police. Fifty-odd years of bombing, sniping and random massacres made every veteran cop and soldier a de facto expert on terrorism, trained in countermeasures that kicked in on instinct. They preferred forceful action to chitchat, neutralizing threats without regard to their ID or choice of targets. It could make for dicey close encounters in a combat zone.

Especially in light of Bolan's private vow that he would never drop the hammer on a cop.

Their first target was Global's suite of corporate offices on Ben Yehuda, near the marina. The place was guarded, uniforms on the street and armed suits in the lobby. Combined with civilian foot traffic, that made a hard probe on the premises too dangerous for Bolan's taste. He would go with long-distance instead.

The Executioner was about to reach out and touch someone.

His vantage point was a rooftop across the street, another commercial building two stories taller than the high-rise where Global occupied most of the nineteenth floor. Bolan made the ascent in a service elevator. As long as no one spoke to him in Hebrew he'd be fine.

At least until all hell broke loose upstairs.

He had the sun-baked rooftop to himself, already simmering despite the fact that it was barely half-past nine a.m. A dozen air-conditioning units, each one the size of a compact car, clicked and whirred at apparent cross-purposes, enslaved by thermostats on the floors below. Bolan checked out each row as he moved toward the bird's-eye view of Ben Yehuda, confirming that he was indeed alone.

Spotting the target high rise and Global Petroleum's floor, he removed his light jacket and lifted the components of his weapon from his waistband. He'd chosen a Galil sniper rifle because it was manufactured in Israel and would lead searchers nowhere if Bolan had to leave it behind at some point. He assembled the weapon, seating its magazine with twenty rounds of 7.62 mm NATO Match grade rounds, and double-checked the settings on its Nimrod 6-power telescopic sight. His target lay some eighty yards to the northwest, no challenge for the Galil with its seven-hundred-meter effective killing range.

Bolan was thankful that his target windows weren't heavily tinted or coated in reflective film. He had a clear view of the office he'd selected and the man who called it home. Seated behind a modernistic desk, the stocky figure rocked his high-backed chair and made expansive gestures as he lectured three men ranged in smaller chairs before him.

He sighted through the scope, gauging the distance, calculating drop and probable deflection of his first round as it drilled through glass. As a professional, he didn't like mistakes and didn't want to kill by accident. Timing was critical, a cool head indispensable.

He took a deep breath, let part of it go and held the rest. His index finger curled around the rifle's trigger lightly, almost lovingly, as he took up the slack. Downrange, his target leaned across the desktop, reaching for a telephone.

BEN GURION AIRPORT LIES twelve miles southeast of Tel Aviv and thirty-one miles northwest of Jerusalem. Rebecca Mindel made the drive in nineteen minutes, with her uncle brooding silently beside her in the shotgun seat. She parked as close as possible to international departures, but he wouldn't let her take his single suitcase as they hiked off toward the terminal.

Security around Ben Gurion was always tight, doubly so since terrorist attacks in New York and Washington were echoed by a new spate of suicide bombings in Israel. No one had targeted the airport lately, but precautions established in Israel were seldom relaxed. Mindel had grown up in a state of siege, accepting it as normal, and those circumstances showed no sign of changing in her lifetime.

There were armored vehicles outside the terminal, soldiers inside with pistols on their hips and Uzi submachine guns slung on shoulder straps. They eyed apparent Muslims with suspicion verging on outright hostility and got brooding resentment in return. It was a vicious cycle, rooted in the years before Mindel was born.

Her uncle's time.

She walked him through customs, flashing her credentials in place of a ticket to get past the checkpoint herself. The soldier who examined her ID blinked once, but otherwise concealed his evident surprise behind a practiced poker face.

Mindel had long since grown accustomed to the double-takes and thinly veiled disbelief that sometimes accompanied her introduction to strangers as a Mossad field agent. She didn't fit the stereotype of a female commando—stocky and muscular, plain of face with short-cropped hair, her sexuality in doubt. A new acquaintance would be hard-pressed to believe that she had killed nearly a dozen men with firearms and her own bare hands.

The things we do for love, she thought, in this case, love for Israel and her uncle. She had killed to rescue him, and those she slew had been her nation's enemies. Weary of violence now, she hoped no force would be required to put him on his scheduled flight.

"They're making a mistake, you know," he said, as they drew near to the departure gate.

"How so?"

"By sending me away."

"Uncle—"

"What could it hurt to let me stay?"

"What could it hurt? You almost died last night."

"I didn't, though, and that's my worry."

"Not when others risk their lives to rescue you, it isn't. You put everyone at risk."

"I didn't ask for help, Rebecca," he said petulantly.

"Wonderful. And if we hadn't found you, you'd be dead now. How would that contribute to your precious mission?"

"All I'm saying is—"

"I know exactly what you're saying," Mindel interrupted him. "You don't like being set aside. You'd rather throw your life away than see a younger man step in to finish what you've started."

"I'm as strong now as I ever was," he said.

"But maybe not as quick. Would they have captured you five years ago? Or even two?"

"It was bad luck," he answered, scowling.

"You've always told me that we make our own luck. Preparation, practice, perseverance. You remember that?" He glowered at her for a moment, then seemed to relax a bit, one corner of his mouth lifting in the suggestion of a smile. "Who knew you'd listen and remember, dammit?"

"I remember the important things."

"Maybe you're right." He shifted in his seat, apparently uncomfortable. At last he said, "I need to visit the men's room."

She felt a sudden stab of apprehension, instantly embarrassed by it. How could she refuse to let him use the toilet?

"No problem. I'll go with you."

"They won't let you in," he said, winking.

"I didn't mean inside, for heaven's sake!"

"You don't think I can use the pissoir by myself?"

"It isn't that," she said.

"You think I'll slip away from you?" He looked around the terminal and made a face. "Where would I go, Rebecca? We're surrounded by at least a full brigade of the Israeli army."

"Let's just say I need the exercise, all right?"

He lost the teasing smile. "So please yourself. I can't wait any longer. If you're coming, let's get on with it."

Embarrassed now, but stubbornly unwilling to back down, she rose and trailed her uncle toward rest rooms on the far side of the busy terminal.

STERLING HOLBROOK enjoyed holding court, watching subordinates hang on his every word as if he were some anointed Old Testament prophet. Spell it *profit* and the comparison would have been closer to the mark, though, since the men and women working under him were concerned primarily with cash.

Much like Holbrook himself.

"It doesn't matter what the Saudis think," he told his captive audience, smiling, "as long as they keep holding out their hands and signing on the bottom line. I've just flown back from there, and you can take my word on it."

"It can't go on forever," Eric Wolter said.

"Oh, no?" The smile on Holbrook's oval face was fierce. "They may have more money than God Himself, but there's no such thing as enough. Remember that, gentlemen. It's the first law of human nature."

"I thought that was sex," Jules Marquand offered, smiling.

"Get the money first," Holbrook advised. "You'll have more sex than you can handle in a lifetime. Hell, two lifetimes."

"Money first, of course," offered Kenji Shibura, the yes-man from Japan.

"Now, about that little disagreement with the prince," Holbrook pressed on. "I think you'll find what put him in a snit was that the bribe you offered him was on the puny side."

"Three million dollars, puny?" Wolter had to scowl at that. "I could live on that for the rest of my life."

"Not if you're living like the prince. Three million wouldn't get him once around the Med in that new yacht of his. He drops that much at Monte Carlo in a weekend."

"Still..."

"You need to think bigger," Holbrook said. "And while you're at it, bear in mind that when the prince's family signs off on this contract, Global stands to make two billion dollars yearly for the next ten years, with options to renew. What's your commission on a deal like that, again?"

The German's frown had managed to invert itself. "I understand, sir. Thank you."

"Not a problem. In fact, I'll go one better. Let me get that little devil on the horn right now and grease him up for you a little." Holbrook reached for the receiver, lifting it. "It never hurts to kiss a little ass, if we can come out smelling like a bunch of roses on the other side."

A sudden popping sound made Holbrook swivel to his right, facing the eastward-facing window, where a small hole had appeared, cracks branching outward from it in a pattern reminiscent of a spider's web. Before Holbrook could analyze the strange phenomenon, a crystal paperweight next to the phone set exploded, bursting as if a cherry bomb had detonated at its heart, cruel slivers spraying Hoolbrook's face and scalp. Bifocals saved his eyes, and he was diving for the floor behind his desk, even as Wolter hit the carpet, shouting, "Sniper!"

The others bolted then, Shibura lunging for the door, while Marquand went to ground behind a filing cabinet. The massive window shivered from repeated impacts, then imploded like a frozen waterfall. Holbrook rolled underneath his desk, trusting the heavy teak to shield him, even though he didn't know the first thing about firearms. He shivered in a fetal curl and waited for the storm to pass him by.

And somewhere in the midst of it, he heard security burst through the doorway to his office, shouting to be heard above the gunfire, amateurs pretending they were in control. He didn't see the bullets find them, but he heard their shouts turn into gasps and cries of pain before they fell. And later, when he finally emerged from hiding, he would find the walls and carpet of his inner sanctum stained with blood.

But for the moment, Sterling Holbrook was of no mind to desert his makeshift cave. Not while the crack of bullets overhead beat out a steady rhythm of destruction, each round causing him to jump as if he had been jabbed with an electric prod. And somewhere in the midst of it, the oilman understood his critical mistake.

The first law of human nature wasn't money, after all. It was self-preservation, the plain act of staying alive.

KATZENELENBOGEN left Rebecca at a newsstand near the entrance to the men's room in the international departures terminal. It irked him that she'd followed him that far, but he couldn't fault her logic, since he planned to slip away the moment that her back was turned, if he could find a means of doing so.

Her proximity to the rest room would make his task more difficult, of course. Katz couldn't simply wander off and lose himself in the milling crowd, as he might have with Rebecca lounging back at the departure gate. He needed a diversion now, perhaps some kind of a disguise, and even then it might not work. Katz wasn't sure he could outrun her, and he didn't want to use brute force against his niece, particularly since a chase or public brawl would bring troops on the run to club him down and hold him at gunpoint as a potential terrorist.

They would be right, at that, in one respect. Katz meant to terrorize the men who'd tortured him and those who ordered it, but Israel had nothing to fear from his wrath. Sadly, there'd be no time or opportunity for Katz to plead his case with the authorities. Mossad no doubt agreed that he should leave the country with all possible dispatch. Its leaders would regard him as a meddler, not an asset. His record meant nothing to those who would cast him aside.

Not this time.

Katz locked himself inside a toilet stall and tried to come up with a plan for slipping past his niece, out of the terminal, to reach the parking lot and bag himself a vehicle. It would've been too obvious to steal Rebecca's car, but there were hundreds more outside, if he could only get that far.

Katz was checking his watch, wondering how long he could dawdle before Rebecca sent someone to find him—or came in herself, as bold as she was—when he heard the door *whoosh* open and shut, footsteps crossing the polished tile floor. Katz tracked the new arrival by his sounds, bending to peer through the crack of the door on his stall as the man took his place before one of the wall-mounted urinals.

The stranger was an inch or two taller than Katz, perhaps a few pounds lighter, though his baggy pants and jacket made it difficult to tell. His outfit was an eye-catcher, verging on flamboyant: a pink jacket over maroon slacks, topped off with a wide-brimmed Panama hat in pale yellow. He looked like something from a cartoon strip, but being obvious wasn't always a bad thing.

Even when you were trying to hide.

Katz emerged from the toilet stall, stepping up behind the stranger as Panama finished his business and zipped up his trousers. *"Shalom,"* he said.

The gaudy stranger turned to face him with a curious expression on his soft, round countenance. *"Shalom."*

"I need your help with something," Katz informed the other man. "In point of fact, I need your clothes."

"Excuse me?"

"Certainly."

Katz smiled and slammed his right forearm into the stranger's face with stunning force. He took care not to strike the nose or lips, which might've showered blood across the garish clothes he coveted. The stranger staggered backward toward the urinals, arms flailing. He was on the verge of crying out for help, but Katz moved in and jabbed the man's throat with his right-arm stump. Katz pulled the punch, employing force enough to silence his opponent without crushing his larynx. One more crack on the temple to put him out, and Katz caught the stranger as he fell, dragging him back into the toilet and placing him on the commode.

Katz took the stranger's hat and put it on, pleased that it was a bit too large and drooped to hide the upper portion of his face. So far, so good.

"All right," he told the slack form balanced on the toilet seat, "it's nothing personal, but let's have those trousers off, shall we?"

"WHICH ONE is Napier's yacht?" McCarter asked.

"The big white one," Bolan replied.

McCarter squinted into the Mediterranean glare, his shades barely helping. There seemed to be no end of yachts moored at the Tel Aviv marina, making him wonder if there was a scheduled regatta this weekend. "When you say big..."

"I mean that monster at the far end of the line, blue trim."

"Of course. Conspicuous consumption."

"If we're splitting hairs, it's Global's yacht. A first-rate tax write-off for corporate travel and entertainment. Take a sheikh out on the briny blue, feed him a lobster and a showgirl, maybe cut a deal."

"Your cynicism shocks me," McCarter said with a smile.

"Too much for virgin ears?" Bolan asked.

"No, but from the look of things on Napier's floating bachelor pad, we may be overmatched on the security."

"Which would explain the uniforms."

McCarter glanced down at his outfit, frowned and said, "I wonder what the prison term is for impersonating customs officers?"

"It only matters if they catch us," Bolan told him.

"That's encouraging."

Rebecca Mindel had supplied the customs uniforms and some official-looking paperwork, via her bosses at Mossad HQ. McCarter knew Bolan was right. The scam should stand at least a cursory inspection, and it wouldn't matter after that—unless they found themselves outgunned and suddenly devoid of choices other than a bullet or the deep blue sea.

The great yacht's motor launch was plainly visible as they approached on foot, which made McCarter feel a little more at ease. If they survived to board it, they should have an easy time returning to the mainland, anyway. If not, well, then the bloody launch would be irrelevant in any case.

They moved along the waterfront, McCarter leading, wearing captain's bars that glittered in the sunshine. They were armed with pistols, which was normal in surprise customs inspections, but their uniforms allowed no hiding place for heavier artillery. McCarter hoped that if the Global crew had any bigger guns aboard their vessel, he'd be able to appropriate one when it hit the fan.

The yacht was labeled *Global III,* painted in navy blue across the stern. McCarter didn't know if that meant there were more afloat somewhere, or whether *Global I* and *Global II* had simply gone to their reward in bygone days. Whatever had become of them, McCarter reckoned that the vessel moored in front of him had to be the largest yacht he'd ever seen. It wasn't the *Titanic,* granted, but it was better than a hundred feet from bow to stern, more reminiscent of a cruise ship than a private yacht.

A well-groomed crewman met them as they climbed the gangplank, blocking access to the deck. "How can I help you gentlemen?" he asked, not bothering to fake a smile.

"By standing back and letting us perform our duty without hindrance," McCarter told him.

"And what duty would that be?"

"Customs inspection." The commando raised a hand and tapped his badge for emphasis.

"We were inspected on arrival," the crewman said. "Passed with flying colors, I might add."

"Nothing to fear then, I expect, if we just have another look?"

"I'll need the captain's word on that." The burly sailor had lost any trace of friendliness he'd once possessed.

"Quite right. Take us along to see him, will you?"

"That's not necessary." As he spoke, the crewman took a compact walkie-talkie from his belt and spoke into the mouthpiece. "Captain Donovan, you're needed on the pier, sir. We have unexpected company."

A disembodied voice came back to say, "I'll be right down."

The captain had a full head of dark hair, with silver highlights showing through to match the buttons on his uniform. McCarter wondered if he went around in full-dress every day, or if he was a quick-change artist seeking to impress his uninvited visitors. He seemed pleasant enough, although a chill crept in as he reviewed McCarter's warrant for the search.

"I'm sorry, I don't understand this, gentlemen."

"I've no details to share," McCarter said, "just orders for the search."

"Perhaps," the captain replied, "if I had some idea what you were looking for..."

"That's all right, sir. Let's just get on with it, shall we?"

"Of course," the captain answered stiffly, handing back McCarter's paperwork. "Where would you like to start?"

"Let's try the bridge," McCarter said. "We may as well start at the top."

BOLAN FOLLOWED McCarter and the yacht's captain up to the bridge, after the seaman from the gangplank was dismissed with thanks by his superior. The sailor left them with a frown, as if reluctant to leave his captain alone with them. Bolan restrained an urge to watch the crewman go, recalling that a certain measure of disdain would make him more believable in his portrayal of a civil servant.

The *Global III*'s bridge was state-of-the-art, from radar and communications gear to a GPS satellite feed. A younger officer was waiting for them, but he held his tongue. A glance around the bridge revealed no weapons, but Bolan felt sure they'd be somewhere aboard, perhaps stashed belowdecks.

"How many crew aboard, just now?" McCarter asked.

"Eleven," Donovan replied. "Twelve, if I count myself."

"By all means, do. No passengers?"

"We're not expecting anyone today."

"The cruise should be no problem then," Bolan said, speaking for the first time since he'd come aboard.

"Excuse me?" Captain Donovan appeared confused.

"We're going on a run," the Executioner replied. "Give orders to cast off and fire the engines up, then make for open sea."

"You must be—"

"Mad?" McCarter asked him, leveling his P-220 autoloader at the captain's face. "You may be right. Why take the chance?"

Casting off took five minutes or so, Bolan watching the younger crewman while McCarter covered Captain Donovan. When they were clear of the marina, he replaced his pistol in its holster, with the thumb-break strap unsnapped for a quick draw. They were a good mile out from shore and making headway when the sailor from the gangplank appeared. He wore a lightweight jacket now, over his crisp white shirt.

"Permission to enter the bridge, sir?" he asked.

"Granted," Donovan said before McCarter could respond. "What is it, Wilson?"

"Sir, the other men and I were wondering if everything's all right."

"It's fine," McCarter replied before the captain could respond.

"I'd like to hear that from my captain, *sir.*"

"There's nothing wrong, Wilson," Donovan said. "Go on about your duties now."

"Yes, sir."

Wilson was backing out when Bolan saw him start the move, reaching inside his jacket. Bolan's draw was faster, clearing the Beretta on his hip and firing once into the seaman's chest at nearly point-blank range before Wilson could pull his hidden piece.

The close-range shot blew Wilson backward, out the door and down a narrow flight of metal stairs serving the bridge. An outcry from below told Bolan more men were waiting at the bottom, and he risked a glance around the bulkhead, ducking backward as a bullet struck the frame above his head and ricocheted.

"My God!" the captain blurted out.

McCarter grabbed him by the collar of his dress blues and propelled him toward the open doorway. Pausing just inside it, he called out, "You men below should hold your fire. Your captain has a word for you."

"What word?" Donovan demanded.

"Your choice," McCarter said, pressing his SIG-Sauer pistol to the captain's rib cage. "You can either have them throw their guns over the side, or you can say goodbye and meet them on the other side."

Donovan blanched at that and called out through the open door, "Hold fire a moment, men! I'm stepping out."

No bullets flew as he emerged, McCarter close behind him with the pistol to his back. "Be careful, Captain," he admonished. "It's a long way down."

"I want you men to take your guns and throw them overboard," the captain called down to his crew.

"Like hell!" a gruff voice answered. "They killed Tommy!"

"And I'm next," Donovan said, "unless you all cooperate."

"Who says they won't keep shooting anyway?" the rough voice challenged from below.

"I don't know how to answer that," the captain told McCarter.

"Right. Your crew can swim, I take it?"

"Certainly. They're seamen."

"That's your answer, then. They can go over with the hardware and start swimming back to shore right now. If no one tries to play it cute, you join them. Otherwise, you're shark bait."

Donovan explained the terms and shouted down a couple of the men who answered with complaints about the swim. When they'd agreed, Bolan followed McCarter and the captain out on deck to watch the crew abandon ship. He counted twice to make sure ten went overboard, then asked McCarter, "Can you drive this thing?"

"No sweat," McCarter told him, grinning.

"Great. In that case, Captain, hit the drink."

They didn't have to tell him twice. Stepping around the body of his fallen crewman, Donovan proceeded to the nearest rail, took off his shoes and jacket, then dived gracefully into the sea.

"Ready?" McCarter asked.

"If you are."

"Born ready, mate." He flashed another grin.

They took the yacht another half-mile out from shore, then killed the engines. After lowering the motor launch, they went below and found the engine room, with fuel tanks close at hand. The short incendiary sticks they carried in their pockets were positioned for maximum effect, fuses snapped to start the two-minute countdown.

"Time to go," McCarter said, but Bolan was already moving. They scrambled into the launch and got its motor started on the first try, veering away from the yacht, back toward shore. At a hundred yards out, Bolan set the motor to idle, watching and waiting.

When it blew, the *Global III* was consumed from within, a fireball bursting through the afterdeck, liquid flames spilling out to race in all directions. Within moments, the great boat was sinking and the sea itself was on fire, fuel riding the surface, trailing black smoke downwind.

Bolan steered the launch back toward the specks that were Captain Donovan and his crew, stroking toward shore. He slowed as they caught up with the captain, waiting until Donovan rolled over to float on his back.

"I've got a message for Napier," Bolan said.

"I'm listening," the captain answered, slightly out of breath.

"Tell him this is what happens when he plays with fire."

"SO," THE TWENTY-something soldier asked, "you're here with your grandfather?"

Mindel smiled at the self-conscious pickup line. "He's my uncle," she said. "He'll be back in a moment."

"You're not flying with him?"

"Just seeing him off," she replied.

The soldier smiled and said, "Good news for me, perhaps."

He had approached her moments earlier, while she was studying headlines in the wall-mounted newspaper dispensers. At first

Mindel thought he would ask for her ticket and boarding pass, back-stopping security at the terminal's final checkpoint, but it seemed he only wanted to flirt with her, passing time.

"I'm afraid I don't follow," she told him, not playing along.

"If you're not flying out, then you're free to have dinner with me," he replied. "I'm off duty within the half hour."

"No, thank you," she said. "I already have plans."

"You could change them, I think." His smile had begun to irritate her. There was too much confidence behind it, verging on arrogance.

"I think not, Sergeant." Rebecca glanced back toward the men's room, in time to see the flamboyantly dressed man who had entered moments earlier retreating back along the concourse, toward the security checkpoint and exits beyond. He moved briskly, with purpose, as if he were late for a crucial appointment.

"You don't like soldiers?" the pest asked from her left. His tone told her the thought was incomprehensible.

"It depends on the soldier," she said, removing all levity from her tone and expression as she glanced at her watch. Too long, she thought. "Are you in charge of this concourse?"

"In charge? Dear lady, I—"

She palmed her credentials and held them six inches from his startled face. "I need your help. Do you agree?"

"You are Mossad?"

"Do you agree, Sergeant?"

His mind was clicking over now, examining the various alternatives. "I do!" he said.

"Good. I need you check the men's room and find out what's become of my uncle."

"The men's room?"

"At once!"

The young sergeant frowned, but thankfully stopped short of scratching his head. Mindel followed him as far as the door, waiting impatiently as his brisk footsteps echoed from within. A moment later she heard voices—no, a single voice—but she couldn't make out the words.

"Sergeant? Is he all right?"

The soldier barged out past her, reaching for the two-way radio on his left hip. She stopped him with a firm hand on his shoulder, before he could make the call.

"What is it?" she demanded.

"I think your uncle's been attacked," he said. "And yet, he doesn't quite resemble—"

She missed the rest of it, shoving by him and into the forbidden sanctuary of the men's room. Mindel moved straight to the toilet stall where bare legs and stockinged feet protruded, looking pitifully defenseless. Even before she glimpsed the man's mottled face and turned back, she knew it wasn't Uncle Yakov in the stall.

"Damn him!"

She charged into the concourse, searching for the Panama hat and pink jacket. They were nowhere to be seen, but she had the general direction, running from the sergeant, brandishing her ID at the checkpoint without slowing. She paused in flight to scan the ticket counters and their milling crowds, feeling the breath catch in her throat at sight of this or that pink garment.

All in vain.

She moved outside, knowing he'd want to put as much distance between himself and the airport as possible, without delay. He wouldn't trust the ruse to keep her guessing long.

Passing the trash can nearest to the exit, Mindel hesitated, doubling back, and peered inside. The Panama was there, atop a crumpled jacket.

Gone, she thought. Already gone.

How long would it take him to steal a car? From where she stood, Mindel saw half a dozen cars pulling out and leaving the airport. They were trailed by a bus and two taxis. She had no hope of remembering the license numbers, even if she'd been able to see them all.

"Goddamn it!"

Two policemen passing on the sidewalk paused to glance at her, then went about their business. It was best for them that they did so.

She had to find the others, quickly, and report her failure at a very simple task.

Before it was too late.

7

Riyadh, Saudi Arabia

"Calm down," Arnold Napier ordered. "I can barely understand what you're saying."

He had Sterling Holbrook on the speaker, to spare his own ear, and even with the volume lowered, his aide's excited jabber seemed to fill Napier's office with a sound like fingernails scraping a chalkboard.

"Calm down? *Calm down!*" Holbrook was working up another head of steam. "I guess you didn't hear me when I said they shot the fucking hell out of my office! Calm down, you said?"

"I understand there was an incident, Sterling."

"An incident? Two of our people from security are dead, Arnold. Israeli cops are asking questions."

"Which I'm sure you've answered honestly," Napier replied, "within the limits of your knowledge."

"What?"

Napier was glad that Holbrook couldn't see him roll his eyes. "We're working in a region fraught with terroristic violence," he said, as if explaining to a child. "Because of our longtime support for Israel, we've become a target for those terrorists. I'm sure they grasped that point as soon as you explained it, Sterling. Yes?"

"Explained it? Oh! Exactly right. Of course!"

"And that we naturally have no connection to the individuals responsible for this atrocity."

"Atrocities," Holbrook corrected him.

"Excuse me? Say again."

"There was a second incident. I've only just got word of it from the authorities."

"And that would be…?" Napier could feel his apprehension mounting, throbbing in the space behind his eyes.

"They sank the yacht."

"The yacht?"

"The *Global III*, you know?"

"Yes, Sterling, I'm familiar with it. When was this?"

"Today," Holbrook replied. "I mean, about an hour or so after the bastards shot up my office. Police were still here when we got the word."

"What happened to the *Global III*, exactly?" Napier felt his blood pressure begin to spike, producing a buzz in his ears. He'd loved that frigging boat.

"The captain—what's his name?"

"Greg Donovan."

"That's it. He says two men showed up in customs uniforms, with paperwork for a surprise inspection. Once aboard, they stuck guns in his face and made him take it out a mile or two from the marina."

"And?"

"There was some shooting, out at sea. They killed one of the crew—I don't recall his name—and made the rest jump overboard. They must've had explosives no one saw. We'll never really know, I guess. Long story short, they blew the yacht up and it sank."

"May I assume they didn't go down with the ship?" Napier inquired.

"Go down…? Oh, I see what you mean. They used the motor launch and left it at the dock. Police are checking it for finger-prints, but they're not very hopeful."

"I'd imagine not." Napier felt numb.

"There was a message, too."

"What kind of message?" Napier asked.

"As they were passing in the launch, they slowed down long enough to have a word with Donovan."

"I'm waiting, Sterl."

"Um, well...one of them said, 'Tell Napier not to play with fire.' Or words to that effect."

Napier's head was throbbing now. He could count his own pulse just by closing his eyes and hearing it thump in his ears. There was a migraine coming, sure as hell.

"These men who sank the *Global III*," he said, proud of his level tone. "What did they look like, Sterling?"

"Donovan says white guys, like American or European. One who talked the most sounded as if he had a British accent."

"And the captain didn't think this all a trifle odd, for two Israeli customs officers?"

"I asked him that, myself!" Holbrook sounded excited by his own genius. "He said it didn't register, what with the uniforms and the official-looking paperwork."

"Which we can now assume were fake," Napier remarked.

"I guess so. Sure."

"You guess so? Tell me, Sterling, what steps have you taken to correct the situation?"

"Uh, well, I thought job one was getting hold of you."

"And you were right, Sterling." He heard a faint sigh of relief at the Israeli end of the connection. "Now I'm up to speed, we need to find out who these shooters are and deal with them effectively. I take for granted that they were also involved in the last incident, with our friend."

"You mean—"

"No names!" Napier reminded him. "This line's supposed to be secure, but still..."

"Sorry!"

"It's not a problem, Sterling. Just stay cool. You know who to contact and what must be done."

"I'll take care of it, Arn."

"There was never a doubt in my mind."

"You'll be telling the others?"

"I think that's wise, don't you?"

"Of course! I only meant—"

"I'll handle it."

"All right."

"You know the men to contact on this other matter, Sterling?"

"Yes. I'll get in touch with them, first thing."

"It might not hurt to offer a reward."

"That's good. I'll see to it."

"Make it enticing, not extravagant."

"Half-million?"

"Why split hairs? A million's easier to visualize."

"Okay. It's done."

"And keep me posted, will you?"

"Absolutely."

"Fine. Goodbye."

Napier resisted an urge to rip his telephone from the wall and hurl it out the nearest window. Such behavior was unseemly, and he didn't need Saudi police at *his* door, while the problems multiplied in Tel Aviv.

The others wouldn't like this, but they had to know. He might need help from both of them before the mess was finally resolved.

Frowning, he lifted the receiver and began to dial long-distance, already rehearsing his portrayal of the facts. A little grease, a little steel.

With any luck, it might not be the end of everything.

Tel Aviv

BOLAN WAS CHANGING out of his customs uniform and back into civvies when the cell phone shrilled for attention. He grabbed it midway through the second high-pitched ring.

"Hello?"

"We have a problem, I'm afraid." Rebecca Mindel's voice was strained. Bolan hoped part of it, at least, was due to the cell phone.

"What's happened?"

"Not this way," she said. "We need to meet."

That wasn't good. "All right," he said. "You have a place in mind?"

"The safehouse?" she suggested.

"We're not finished yet," he told her.

"We should talk before you do anything else." She hesitated for a moment, then added, "It has to do with Uncle Yakov."

"Twenty minutes," Bolan told her.

"I may be a little longer, coming from the airport."

"Fine."

She severed the connection first and left him wondering what could have happened on the short run to Ben Gurion. If Mindel thought it serious enough to interrupt their scheduled operations, he would trust her judgment—to a point.

"Twenty minutes for what?" McCarter asked. He was already finished dressing, slipping a windbreaker over his SIG-Sauer in its shoulder rig.

"To meet Rebecca at the safehouse," Bolan answered. "Something about Katz."

"Dammit! I should've known he'd try something."

"We don't know what she needs to tell us, yet."

"I've got a tenner says it can't be jolly news."

They made the drive in fifteen minutes, beating several traffic lights before they changed, and waited fifteen more for Mindel to arrive. She came in looking haggard, angry at the world in general and ready to start snapping, but her anger seemed to wilt as she found Bolan and McCarter watching her.

"I won't try sugarcoating it," she said. "He got away. I let him use the washroom at the airport terminal—"

"Oh, Lord!" McCarter groaned.

"And went along to watch the exit, mind you," Mindel flared at him. "One of the soldiers came along and started asking questions while I waited. By the time I checked my watch, he'd knocked out some poor tourist, traded clothes with him and slipped away."

"I don't suppose you mean the soldier," McCarter said.

"No, you ass! My *uncle!*"

"You went after him, of course," Bolan said.

"Yes." She seemed relieved to have the statement phrased respectfully. "But by the time I got outside..." She hesitated, bit her lip, and started fresh. "The hell of it is that I saw him going. God! It was the clothes that threw me off."

"That must have been some outfit," McCarter said. "Are we talking top hat? Tails?"

"You had to be there," Mindel told him.

"Wish I had been."

"So do I!"

"All right, enough," Bolan snapped. "We've got Katz at large somewhere, and I assume he's picked up wheels."

"My people have a line to the police," Mindel said, "but we may not get results for several days, if then. The airport has a long-term parking lot. We won't know whether anything's gone missing out of there until the travelers come back from wherever they've gone and file an auto theft report."

"It just keeps getting better," the Briton commented.

"Okay," Bolan said, trying to defuse the tension between Mindel and McCarter. "We know who he's after, more or less, but finding them without connections he can use may slow Katz. Also, he wasn't packing when he left the airport."

"Packing?" Mindel didn't seem to recognize the slang term.

"Armed," Bolan explained. "He'll want weapons first, before he tries a move on Allah's Lance or Napier's crew."

"He's lost his bloody mind," McCarter said. "This goes so far beyond the basic insubordination that he'll never live it down."

Assuming that he lives, Bolan thought, but he kept the gloomy observation to himself. They all knew what Katz risked by disregarding orders, hunting well-armed and well-organized opponents on his own. Katz knew it, too, but he was willing to risk everything—his life, his job, his friends and family—to pull off one last mission and repay the heavies who'd humiliated him.

"Where do we look?" Mindel asked.

"Around his targets," Bolan said. "He may find them, or it could be the other way around. We need to be there when it happens, either way."

Damascus, Syria

WASIM JABBAR WAS entertaining his third wife when a timid rapping on the bedroom door distracted him. He turned toward the door and barked, "Not now!"

"Wasim," the too familiar voice came back at him, "I must! It's the American."

That left Jabbar confused. "What, here?" he asked.

"The telephone," Salim Zuhayr replied.

"Son of a goat!"

Jabbar drew back and heard Fatima whimper in frustration. Rolling out of bed, he grabbed the tangled sheet and drew it up to hide her perfect body, then retrieved the robe he'd draped across a nearby chair and slipped it on.

Zuhayr stood waiting in the hallway, eyes downcast. "Forgive the interruption, please."

"What does he want, Zuhayr?"

"There's been some kind of problem."

"What, another one?"

"'Wasim's ears only,' I was told."

Americans, Jabbar thought to himself. More trouble than they were worth. If it weren't for all the money they possessed, he thought Americans—and western Europeans, too—would be completely useless.

Jabbar entered the small room that he called his office, motioned for Zuhayr to follow him and raised the telephone receiver he found lying on the clean top of his army surplus desk.

"My friend!" he said, making a sour face at the same time that nearly forced Zuhayr to laugh aloud.

"It's not a social call, Wasim," Arnold Napier stated flatly. "I'm afraid we've had some trouble there, in Tel Aviv."

"More trouble," Jabbar said. "It's always trouble now, with you."

"The last round wasn't mine, as I recall," Napier replied, "but I have reason to believe our problems are connected."

"Yes? What reason might that be?"

"Let's say I'm not a great believer in coincidence. Also, the shooters left a message for me at their second stop."

"You were attacked twice in the city, there?"

"Not me, of course. They scared the hell out of poor Sterling at his office, shot it up quite badly. Can you believe it? Then they went along and sank my boat at the marina."

Under different circumstances, Jabbar might well have laughed in Napier's face, but now he felt a sudden rush of anger, rising from his gut and flaming in his cheeks. "An office? A boat?" he said. "You speak to me of things, after I lost more than a dozen men?"

"And one man in particular, if I recall," Napier reminded him. "I wouldn't be a bit surprised if he was in on what went down with me today."

"You have some evidence of this?"

"A hunch, is all. I've learned to trust them, though. The shooters that were seen today were European or American. One of them had a British accent."

"We lost an Israeli," Jabbar said. "It's not the same."

"I know that, friend. I'm thinking there may be some sort of international collaboration in the works. You follow me?"

Jabbar considered that and didn't like where it was leading him. Of course, his deal with Napier and the rest was such an international collaboration, too. It stood to reason that some of the nations they were targeting might take it badly if they knew what lay in store for them.

Was there a leak? Did he have traitors in the ranks of Allah's Lance? Jabbar wished that the old Jew had been broken, made to talk before he slipped away. As it stood now, he still had no idea whether the man served an Israeli master or someone outside the Middle East.

Someone like Napier, for example?

Where on earth had that come from? Why would the oilman from America do anything to undermine his allies at a crucial point in their cooperative venture? Was it possible—

"What would you have me do?" he asked to dam the flow of paranoid, disturbing thoughts.

"Just what you're doing now," Napier replied. "Keep both eyes open, looking for the one who got away and any friends he might have standing by. We need to clean this up, my friend, before we move ahead."

"I'll see what can be done," Jabbar assured him.

"That's the spirit. Hell, I told the others we could always count on you. It's good to know I wasn't wrong."

The others. Napier reminding him that a betrayal of himself or Global Petroleum would bring the Greek and the Chinese down on him, too. Jabbar hated the feeling that they had him on a leash, but he had walked into the deal with eyes wide-open and he couldn't back out now.

Not while the others lived.

"I'll be in touch," he said.

"That's good to hear. Don't be long, now. Makes me nervous when we're out of touch."

The line went dead and Jabbar cradled the telephone receiver, stricken with a sudden need to wash his hands.

Justice Department, Washington, D.C.

BROGNOLA CLUTCHED the telephone and listened silently, except for nervous fingers of his free hand drumming on the desktop. He could feel his stomach twisting slowly into knots, replacing lunchtime hunger with a dull ache that would carry him through dinner, well into the night.

"She let him walk," Brognola said, when Bolan finished speaking on the other end.

"I don't believe that," Bolan said. "You should've seen her."

"No, I should've seen *him,* getting off a plane in six or seven hours. Now we've got him running wild where you are, doing God knows what."

"We know his targets."

"You know some of them," Brognola corrected. "We don't know what he held back during the debriefing, in anticipation of an order home. We don't know where or when he'll try for them. We don't know where he's picking up equipment. We don't know—"

"I get the point," Bolan said, interrupting him.

"And you don't think she let him slip the leash on purpose?"

"Not a chance."

"Okay, then. What's she done to get him back?"

"We're holding off on that until I had a chance to check with you."

"No contact with Mossad?"

"Not yet."

"You think not yet," Brognola said.

"I have to trust her at some point."

"I'm not so sure." Brognola tasted sour grapes and said, "Scratch that. You're on the scene. I trust your judgment. If you're confident she's playing straight, go with it."

"Right."

"My point is that we need him off the street and out of circulation, stat. He's worse than a loose cannon. If they pick him up again, they'll pull out all the stops. He knows too much to let him talk."

There was a momentary silence on the line, Bolan digesting that. He'd know what Brognola was saying without being told explicitly. In fact, it would've crossed his own mind more than once before he made the transatlantic call. Katz had been in at the beginning of Phoenix Force and Stony Man Farm. He didn't know everything about the stateside operation, granted—only three or four people on earth could honestly make that claim— but he knew enough from his years in the field, and later behind a desk at home base, to blow the whole program sky-high. Public exposure was death to a covert operation, and, all too often, to its frontline agents.

Brognola knew Katz would resist interrogation if the heavies captured him again. He also knew that no one made of flesh and bone could ultimately outlast the techniques employed by modern-day inquisitors. If simple pain proved ineffective, there were drugs to break down inhibitions, loosen tongues—or sent the "patient" screaming through a hellish madhouse that existed only on the inside of his head. If Katz was caught alive a second time, he'd break. There was no question in Brognola's mind.

And he couldn't allow that to occur.

"I know," Bolan said.

"Anyway, I'm hoping it won't come to that," the big Fed told him, not having to explain for Bolan what "that" was. The Farm's field agents didn't carry cyanide or other suicide devices with them in the field, because Brognola trusted them—and because, with the sole exception of Bolan himself, they never worked alone. The men of Phoenix Force and Able Team knew what to do if one of their own was captured and he couldn't be liberated. They took the sanction for granted—and prayed that none of them would ever have to exercise that deadly option.

So far, it hadn't been required.

Brognola was afraid the hunt for Katz might be a first.

"He'll figure that we have the airports covered," Bolan said. "He didn't have much money with him, so my guess would be he's handicapped on getting new ID or any kind of major hardware."

"Don't forget he has connections over there."

"We're not forgetting anything," Bolan assured him. "Mindel has a better lock on the old friends than we do, since most of them were Mossad or military."

"Don't forget the family."

"They're covered. His daughter's on an archaeological dig in the Sinai peninsula, and Mindel gave her father a heads-up."

"He's the brother?"

"Affirmative."

"No government connection there?"

"Ex-soldier, like everyone else in the country. He's been in retail women's clothes for years."

"Another time, I'd have to riff on that," Brognola said.

"Consider it riffed."

"I ran a check on Napier. He's in Saudi—or he was, three hours ago. That business with the ship may've spooked him."

"Stranger things have happened," Bolan said.

"I doubt he'd head your way, though, with the heat and all."

Implicit in his observation was the fact that Katz couldn't reach Napier without leaving Israel, unless Napier came to him. The last thing that Brognola needed was to have one of his men picked up by the police or military for attempting to assassinate a U.S. oilman on Israeli soil. Granted, Katz might pull it off, but without official support and in his present state— both physical and mental— Brognola wouldn't bet the farm on it.

Except, in a way, he was doing just that.

He was betting Stony Man Farm that Bolan and McCarter could find and restrain their old comrade before he did something irreversible that left them all out in the cold—or worse, hauled before Congress to explain how a covert killing program had been run from Washington for years, without official sanction from the dimwits on Capitol Hill.

"We'll find him," Bolan said.

"Whatever it takes."

And the Executioner agreed. "Whatever it takes."

REBECCA MINDEL HAD never taken easily to failure. Add to that suspicion from her comrades of the moment, both men clearly speculating that she may have failed deliberately, and she burned nonstop with a mixture of embarrassment and rage.

Part of the anger was directed toward her uncle, for humiliating her and leaving her to face suspicion and conflicted loyalties. His selfishness astounded her. Uncle Yakov had clearly known the repercussions that his disappearing act would have for her, and chose to dupe her anyway.

That observation brought her mind back to the second target of her rage: namely, herself. Mindel was unforgiving in assessment of her own performance at the airport, wasting precious time on the young sergeant when she should've blown him off immediately and maintained her focus on the men's room exit. If she'd only glimpsed her uncle in profile, before he had a chance to turn away from her, Mindel was certain she'd have recognized him in his flamboyant disguise.

Too late.

The blame game wouldn't bring her any closer to retrieving her uncle and restoring her own credibility. She saw how Blanski and McCarter watched her now, as if expecting her to break down and confess collusion with her vanished uncle in some grand conspiracy. They had contacts, primarily Americans or contract agents for the CIA, but for the most part, local operations were her venue, via the Mossad. If they mistrusted her, it would be difficult to sell the fact that she was doing everything within her power for the team.

She didn't want her uncle roaming free in Tel Aviv, seeking vengeance, any more than Blanski or McCarter did. At the same time, she had a grudging admiration for his spirit and his dogged perseverance that she couldn't altogether will away. She could conceal it, with an effort, and she had so far. But if it started showing through...

Where would he go?

Intelligence reports placed Arnold Napier in Riyadh, which was—at least in theory—beyond her uncle's reach. Sterling Holbrook, his second in command, had gone to ground after the shooting incident that morning and was "indisposed." She frowned, thinking about the action she had missed that day and where it still might lead. She knew that Blanski and McCarter hadn't finished with their enemies. It wasn't clear how far they'd go to bring down Napier and the rest, but something told her that the tall American was limited only by his imagination and the killing range of his weapons.

There would be more blood, yet, before the game was done. And Mindel wondered how much of it she would have to spill.

One casualty of the operation might turn out to be her own career, if her superiors knew she was holding out on them, censoring the reports she filed. It was a form of self-defense, in Mindel's mind, but she knew her control would take a very different view.

If he found out.

See that he didn't, then, she thought, and turned her mind back to the problem of her uncle. Where he might be found. Which of his several enemies would be the first to die.

She had to find him soon, before her whole life went up in flames.

MCCARTER SAT with two maps spread in front of him. The large-scale map depicted Tel Aviv—its streets, landmarks and suburbs—while the other, drawn to smaller scale but nearly twice as large in size, showed Israel and her hostile neighbors: Jordan, Lebanon and Syria. The country map was marked with symbols that included camps and hideouts linked to Allah's Lance, along with various facilities owned by Global Petroleum.

McCarter still had no idea why Napier or his company would seek alliance with a killer like Wasim Jabbar, but he trusted Katz on the sightings. If nothing else, his abduction and torture proved that much of the case—but it still left the question of *why* at loose ends. Typically speaking, Western oil companies had nothing to gain and everything to lose when violence rocked the Mideast. Personnel and equipment were endangered, production lagged or halted altogether, prices fluctuated erratically. It was a recipe for disaster.

The germ of a dark, brooding thought was about to take root when Bolan returned from speaking to Hal Brognola in Washington. The look on his face told McCarter it hadn't gone well.

"Bad news, then?" he inquired.

"Could be worse. We're not hunting him yet."

"Stress the 'yet,' I presume?"

"You'd be right. And it's official—we can't let them have him again."

"That was never the plan," McCarter said.

"It's assumed that if they get another shot at him, he'll crack."

"I wouldn't bet my life on that."

"We're betting his."

McCarter understood and offered no response. If Katz were captured and they couldn't rescue him immediately, they would be called upon to ensure his silence by other means. The Briton knew the drill and had prepared himself for it from the beginning of his military service, but he didn't have to like it.

Not even a little bit.

McCarter pictured Katz as they'd recently found him, then imagined himself sighting down the barrel of an automatic weapon at his old friend, squeezing off a kill shot. Would it be a mercy in those circumstances, or a pure cold-blooded act of pragmatism? Did it even matter which, if the result was still the same?

"I'll do it if I have to," he told Bolan, settling any doubt that may have stood between them.

"So will I," the Executioner replied.

"I guess that makes us heroes, then."

"It makes us soldiers, nothing more or less."

"That doesn't help, somehow."

"I know. The only way to help is end the game before it comes to that."

"Square one again," McCarter said.

"Not quite. We know more of the players now. It isn't only Allah's Lance."

"I have a feeling we don't know them all."

"Neither does Katz. If we can nail that information first and roll them up, then he'd have no war left to fight."

"He won't be sitting on a bench somewhere and waiting for the bulletin."

"That's right, but we've still got a head start on equipment and mobility. As for intelligence, he doesn't have our resources."

"We don't know who or what he has around here from the good old days."

"Mindel's on top of that."

"You hope so, anyway."

"I don't believe she let Katz skate to spite us," Bolan said.

"Oh, I admit it doesn't make much sense, but families do crazy things sometimes."

"You'll get no argument from me on that. I just don't read her that way," Bolan told him.

"I hope you're right. We hold a poor hand as it is, without an extra joker in the pack."

"If you want me to, I can have Hal request that somebody else from the Mossad take her place."

McCarter thought about it, frowning. "Never mind," he said at last. "Better the devil you already know, eh? The people who know we're here resent us, as it is. No need to make them apoplectic when it won't help, anyway."

"Agreed."

"What's next on the agenda, then?" McCarter asked.

"I'd say we need to shake the opposition up some more, maybe find out who Napier's working with besides Jabbar and Allah's Lance."

"You reckon Global isn't just a corporate logo, then?"

"A company that size," Bolan replied, "doesn't do anything downscale. Whether it's prospecting for oil or puppet governments, they run with the big dogs."

"That sounds like you have some specific curs in mind."

"I wish," Bolan said. "No, the fact is I'm as lost as you are, but I know we won't learn anything sitting around the house and waiting for a call that Katz is in the bag again."

"You think we need to get proactive, then?"

"I do."

McCarter smiled. "It's about bloody time."

8

Yakov Katzenelcnbogen ditched his stolen car at Tel Aviv's Central Railway Station, on Namir Road, and walked a half-mile north before he found another to replace it, in the parking lot of a stylish shopping center. In lieu of stripping wires one-handed, he used the screwdriver blade on his Swiss army knife to crack and key the ignition, thereby saving himself a world of time and aggravation, fumbling underneath the dashboard. The fuel tank, to his great relief, was nearly full.

Katz knew where he was going, but he took his time, observing posted speed limits, taking the long way around to his destination. If the police or Mossad—or both—were hunting him, there was a chance they might anticipate his move and beat Katz to his goal. In that case, he preferred to let them gather and announce themselves, rather than swarming in to take him by surprise while he was doing business.

Rebecca was the key to most of it, he knew. Her reaction to his airport getaway might well determine whether he survived the night at large or wound up in a jail cell or a psychiatric ward. Katz didn't like embarrassing his niece professionally, but she was young and would survive it. In time, she might even forgive him for making her look like a fool.

In the meantime, though, she could make life hard for him if she chose to. Alerting Mossad, the police—even the military— to his situation could put countless eyes on the street in an hour, covering his former haunts and allies, watching bus and railroad terminals, observing auto dealerships and pawnshops—anyplace at all, in fact, where Katz might surface in pursuit of his revenge.

The other side of that, though, was Rebecca's natural instinct for self-preservation. She was on loan from Mossad to help Bolan and McCarter rescue Katz, as a favor from one besieged state to another. Katz had stepped on some important toes in Tel Aviv before he left for the United States, but he was still remembered as a hero of sorts, even among those who wished that he'd never come home. They wouldn't want to kill or seriously damage him—in public, anyway—and Rebecca, for her own sake, might be slow to report his escape.

That word—*escape*—felt odd in his mind and on his tongue. He hadn't been a prisoner in any conventional sense, at least not after Bolan and the others pulled him from the camp of Allah's Lance. His flight from Tel Aviv—gone now, he noted with a glance at his wristwatch—hadn't been taking him to prison or to any other kind of punishment. The worst he would've gotten from Brognola on arrival in the States was probably a terse reminder of his status and assignment at the Farm.

Katz wasn't fleeing, then, as much as going in pursuit of something. Call it justice or revenge, maybe a mixture of the two. It was a job Katz had to do before he earned the right to face himself each morning in the bathroom mirror, knowing that he hadn't let the bastards beat him down.

And in the process, he would find out what the hell his enemies were doing in Israel.

It was a point of professional pride now, despite the repeated orders to stand down and pass the torch to other, younger hands. Katz knew he'd blown it by failing to report his first sighting of Napier and Jabbar together, but that was history now. He knew they were allies and took their illicit collusion for granted, but he still didn't know what they were planning, who would suffer when the plan bore poison fruit.

Israel, of course, Katz thought. It always came back to that with fanatics like Jabbar. The United States might also come in for its share of abuse, despite Napier's role in the plot. In Katz's experience, multinational corporations harbored no great loyalty except to profits, which they stuck in secret bank accounts whenever possible, to dodge taxation in the countries where their offices and CEOs were legal residents. Napier, if questioned, would no doubt proclaim his ardent love for the U.S., but he was just another snake as far as Katz was concerned.

He watched his rearview mirror, making frequent random turns to see if he was being followed. There was no sign of pursuit, no nervous watchers when he pulled into a laundry's parking lot and sat for fifteen minutes in the hot sunshine. At last, when he was satisfied, Katz pulled out with a purpose, heading for Old Jaffa and a contact who wasn't expecting him.

He could've called ahead, but why take chances if the line was being monitored? Katz preferred to find out for himself.

What was the point of living, after all, without a few surprises now and then?

REBECCA MINDEL HAD a list of places where she thought her uncle might turn up, people he might approach for help, or to wreak havoc on them, in the case of enemies. The list was in her head, not written down. Her memory was excellent—if not eidetic, then the next best thing. It served her well, most times, but it could only catalog names and addresses. Predictions of where her Yakov would go were beyond her ability, and the failure frustrated her, compounding Mindel's anger at herself.

She would have to inform her superiors of what had happened, at some point, or risk being counted AWOL when she didn't return from her "loan" to McCarter and Blanski. After confirming her uncle's rescue, she'd been granted two days of "compassionate leave," but she'd already used up nearly eight hours of that. Make it forty remaining, before she had to confess, explain the mess she'd made and beg for assistance in keeping her uncle alive.

Of course, by that time, it might well be too late.

Pushing her Fiat through traffic, testing the speed limit, Mindel ran through the mental list of her uncle's cronies from the old days, mentally plotting their homes and business addresses on the Tel Aviv street map. None of them were likely to betray him, being veteran warriors from another time who valued personal loyalty above anything save their duty to Israel. And with that in mind, the choice came down to a question of priorities.

What would he need in order to remain at large and punish those who had abused him? She assumed that he already had a car, and might have switched vehicles once—or even several times—since he eluded her at Ben Gurion Airport. He wouldn't use a credit card for gasoline, assuming that he even carried one. She knew he had some cash but hadn't taken time to learn how much.

More errors of omission. She had run up a depressing score, and if her uncle died because of Mindel's negligence, she knew she'd never quite forgive herself.

But it wasn't her fault her uncle had decided to play cloak-and-dagger games on his vacation. She hadn't caged and tortured him when he was caught at it; quite the reverse, in fact. Mindel had risked her life to save him then, and she was risking her career right now, because *he* was a stubborn fool, behaving like a willful child.

It helped to redirect her anger for a few brief moments, but the nagging sense of guilt was inescapable. She wouldn't rest until she found her uncle, and if he was dead or gravely injured, she knew part of her would never be the same.

Where to begin?

She could discount another car for now, and focus on his other needs. Money, perhaps. A change of clothes. Someplace to hide between engagements with his enemies.

But most of all, he needed weapons.

Mindel assumed her uncle had learned his lesson in regard to facing his enemies unarmed. The first round of his game had been intended as surveillance, but this time would be different, she knew. Her uncle had a score to settle with the men who had held him captive, and she feared he wouldn't rest until that debt was paid in blood.

Where would he go for military hardware if official arsenals were closed to him? Any of his friends from the old days were likely to have weapons at their homes, for self-protection, but four of the nine on her memorized list had been analysts or otherwise engaged in the nonviolent side of Mossad operations and were thus unlikely to maintain stockpiles of surplus hardware at their homes. Two others were disabled from the injuries they'd suffered on assignments in the field: one had lost both legs when a mine exploded on a covert crossing into Syria; the other had been wounded in a drive-by shooting, paralyzed from the waist down. Lack of mobility barred either one of them from taking part in mercenary operations after their release from the Mossad, suggesting that a private arsenal in either case would be superfluous.

And that left three.

She visualized the city map again, plotting her course of travel to minimize backtracking. Caleb Reis was farthest from her own present position, down in Jaffa. Nahum Herzhaft was closest, with his sporting shop on Pinkas Street, with Asher Kleinman midway in between the two, on Dizengoff. She could drop in on each of them in turn, ask questions, listen to their words and watch for lies in their expressions.

But she might already be too late.

That thought made Mindel change her mind, select another target from her list. Even before the thought was fully formed, she knew she ought to contact Blanski and McCarter for support, but they were off on business of their own.

She had misplaced her uncle, and retrieving him was *her* job, not the Briton's or the American's.

Mindel turned left at the next major intersection, eastbound toward the city's outskirts. She would take a risk and see what happened—for her uncle's sake and for her own.

CALEB REIS HAD joined Mossad about the same time Katz came over from the army, possibly a year behind. They were assigned together for the first time, with two others, on a mission into Jordan, hunting Black September terrorists responsible for several airline hijackings and other incidents that left nearly a hundred persons dead. Most of the victims were Israelis—fourteen of them children on a school bus raked by submachine gun fire—and a response was ordered by the brass in Tel Aviv.

As covert missions went in those days, it was fairly typical. Katz and the others found their targets, took them down and managed to return alive. There had been controversy at the time, Jordanian officials lodging protests with the World Court and United Nations over violation of their sovereign territory, but the raiders didn't care. They'd done their job, and if their names were never etched on any monument, what of it?

"If you're in it for the glory," Reis had once remarked to Katz, "you should have a plastic surgeon fix that face of yours and go to Hollywood."

They'd been fast friends for twenty years, though falling out of regular contact since Katz had left Israel and gone to work with Phoenix Force. Neither was good with written correspondence, and the telephone seemed too impersonal—as well as insecure. Katz knew his old friend hadn't budged from Jaffa, but he wasn't sure what kind of reception to expect in the present circumstances.

Reis had a small house two blocks south of Pasteur, in Old Jaffa. He had married briefly in the 1980s, but it hadn't worked out and he lived alone, tending a backyard garden large enough to meet a wiry bachelor's solitary needs. The house had been sky-blue the last time Katz came calling, but it had been painted pink at some time in the past three years. The front door stood ajar as Katz approached, a screen door keeping out the flies.

He rang the bell and waited. When he was about to ring again, a gruff voice called from somewhere in the house, "I don't buy anything from peddlers."

Through a smile, Katz answered, "I'm not selling anything, you stingy bastard."

The door flew open. "Who the hell do you—? Jehovah's testicles!" Reis bawled. "They've let you go without a keeper, then?"

"Just barely," Katz replied.

Reis automatically reached out for Katz's left hand, pumped it twice and used the grip to pull him through the open doorway. "Too damned hot out there," he said. "You'll want beer, I suppose, and show up bearing none."

"I wouldn't mind a bottle of Goldstar."

"Predictable," Reis said. "What's happened to your face, if you don't mind my asking?"

"And suppose I do mind?"

"Tell me anyway! You can't just turn up after all this time away, looking like you've been through the grinder and expect to get away with it."

"It's not that bad," Katz said.

"You look like shit, my friend. *Old* shit, at that. Now give!"

"Beer first, then talk."

"You and your one-track mind. All right, then, come along."

Katz followed Reis into the kitchen, where his friend pulled two dark bottles of Goldstar beer from the refrigerator. "Want a glass with that?" Reis asked.

"What for?"

Reis grinned. "At least they haven't made a sissy of you, over in the States."

"Not yet."

"They're trying, though? What did I tell you, when you left."

"You said, 'Don't go.'"

"It's still the best advice you ever got," Reis said. "Not that you're smart enough to listen." When they were settled into chairs with a small dining table set between them, Reis drank half his Goldstar in a single gulp and said, "Now, give! I want to know what happened to that lovely face of yours."

Katz told him most of it, omitting names and any reference to his work with Phoenix Force or Stony Man. Reis listened, interrupting half a dozen times to clarify some point or other, interjecting curses here and there for punctuation. When the tale was done, he brought more beer, sat again and asked, "How can I help, old friend?"

"I need some hardware," Katz replied.

"And more than that, it sounds like. I can come with you. We'll kick their asses like the good old days."

"I can't accept your offer," Katz said, "but I thank you for it. Weapons only, for the time being."

"You'll drink my beer and take my guns, but spurn my help?"

"I have no choice, Caleb."

"You always were a stubborn bastard," Reis said, a surprising tremor in his baritone. "All right, then. Let's go have a look downstairs and see what's on the shelf, shall we? I may be able to surprise you, even after all this time."

"WE NEED TO KEEP the heat on Napier," Bolan said. "I have a hunch he's not the only big dog in the ring."

"Agreed," McCarter said, scanning the map spread out before them on the dining table in their safehouse. "What about Jabbar and Allah's Lance, though? Do you think they could enlighten us to what the Global crowd is doing?"

"Maybe," Bolan said, "if we could bag Jabbar himself. I'd question whether his lieutenants know the whole scoop, and their soldiers are the kind who only know where they've been told to go and who they're told to kill."

"And we've got no fix on Jabbar, I take it?"

"None so far," Bolan confirmed.

McCarter's eyes devoured the map, as if the secret might be lurking there. Bolan could almost read his comrade's mind: so many targets and so little time.

"We could rattle them, though, and the oil boys as well," McCarter said "I'd hate to leave anyone feeling neglected."

"And watch out for Katz while we're at it?" Bolan asked. "No problem. All in a day's work."

McCarter looked up from the map then, asking, "Where do you think he's gone?"

"I figure Mindel's right. He'll want some decent heavy-duty hardware on hand before he jumps into the job. She'll touch base with his contacts and see if they've heard from him."

"If they'll admit it," McCarter amended.

"That's her end," Bolan said. "She's got the connections to squeeze them, one way or another, if they're holding out."

"I hope she's up to it."

I hope so too, Bolan thought, but he kept it to himself. "We can't anticipate where Katz will go or what he'll do, beyond the fact that he'll be looking for some payback."

"Too damned many targets," McCarter said. "Even splitting up, I don't fancy our odds of running into him."

"And I don't fancy splitting up right now," Bolan replied. "With Global's holdings in the city, we can cause as much damage at one stop, together, as we could flying solo and hitting Jabbar's low-rent hideouts."

"Agreed."

"With that in mind, I'd recommend an alternating pattern. Make a hit on Global first, then Allah's Lance, and keep it up like that. We can leave word along the way, to shake up the big boys."

"Unless we happen to meet one of them," McCarter added, smiling.

"I could live with that," Bolan affirmed. "Equipment check?"

"I'm there," McCarter said.

They went over the silenced MP-5s, topped off their magazines and checked the spares. Side arms were next, followed by some last-minute sharpening of knives. Their stockpile of grenades had dwindled, but they had enough to see them through a few more days. Bolan didn't expect to use the Galil sniper rifle on this outing, but he packed it anyway, because he hated leaving anything behind.

The safehouse, he considered, might not be all that safe. He didn't know the shadow players on Rebecca Mindel's side, and there was a chance—however remote it might seem—that a corporation with Global's resources might have eyes and ears behind the scenes in Tel Aviv.

Even inside Mossad.

They left the safehouse as they'd found it, looking lived-in but without a trace of evidence to place them in its rooms. Bolan retained a key, and they could come back anytime but for the moment they were well and truly gone. Rebecca Mindel had his cell phone number and McCarter's. She would get in touch if she found something, or even if she didn't. They were still a team, at least in theory, but he couldn't wait around for her to clean up after the fiasco at the airport.

It could be a problem, Bolan knew, if the police and agents of Mossad were mobilized to look for Katz. Mindel had promised to avoid that if she could, but Bolan wasn't sure how far she could proceed on guts alone if she was frightened for her uncle's life. Exposure meant she'd take some kind of hit from her superiors, but she might think it worth the risk to save Katz, if they couldn't find another way.

And, then again, it might already be too late.

There was no reason to suppose they'd know if Katz had already found a nest of enemies and tried to take them out. He could be dead and buried in a shallow desert grave—or locked up in another cell somewhere—without word ever getting back to Tel Aviv.

Frowning, he locked the safehouse door and trailed McCarter to their waiting vehicle. That kind of morbid speculation only made things worse. The antidote was action. It might shake loose vital evidence, or simply leave the opposition reeling in shock.

Either way, it beat hell out of standing still.

KATZ HAD BEEN surprised by the extent of Caleb Reis's private arsenal. He had offered Reis money—the little he had in his pocket, coupled with a later ATM withdrawal or check—but Reis had refused.

"Get the bastards," he'd said. "If you won't let me come with you, at least let my guns tag along."

And so they had. His new hardware included a Browning Mark 3 autoloading pistol with ambidextrous safety, chambered in 9 mm Parabellum; a Beretta SCS-70 assault rifle, barely thirty-two inches long with its folding stock extended, tipping the scales at 8.5 pounds; and a dozen Austrian HG-86 minigrenades, weighing less than half a pound each. Overall, he felt well-equipped to meet his enemies.

Now all Katz had to do was track them down.

He had to start in Tel Aviv, close by; that much was obvious. Leaving the city would increase his risks, and he still didn't know how many people were hunting him, or which side they represented. The farther he traveled from Tel Aviv, the more cash he would need—a problem in itself, since any ATM transaction would leave tracks—and the more likely he was to be spotted.

Cruising the busy streets of Israel's capital, he wondered if Brognola had ordered Bolan and McCarter to stop him. They would surely be aware of his escape, by now. As for their reaction, well, it remained to be seen.

Katz hoped that he wouldn't be forced to deal with Bolan and McCarter in a violent confrontation. There were enemies enough in this city without fighting friends. By the same token, however, he'd already put himself out on a long, shaky limb with his flight from Ben Gurion Airport. A disagreement with Brognola over policy at Stony Man was one thing, but desertion and defiance of an order to stand down was something else entirely.

No, Katz checked himself. He hadn't deserted the cause; rather, he was resisting an order to stand on the sidelines and watch while his friends risked their lives on a mission that started with *him*. A mission that began for Katz with pain and ended with embarrassment.

How could he go back to the Farm and face his colleagues there, knowing that each and every one of them knew every detail of his failure? How could they respect him in the future, when he had no respect for himself? What good was he to the program in his present state, feeling defeated and humiliated?

The only answer Katz could think of was to face the enemy himself, with or without approval from Brognola and the others. He had faith in his ability to carry out the mission, recent events notwithstanding. He was armed now, and prepared for anything. The bastards wouldn't take him by surprise a second time.

And if he failed, if this was his last act on Earth, what better finale could a soldier hope for? Anything was better, he'd decided, than wasting away at a desk, marking days on the calendar like a convict in prison.

Caleb Reis had helped him out with information, as well as small arms. Katz had a list of addresses in and around Tel Aviv where suspected associates of Wasim Jabbar might be found.

They'd evaded arrest to this point by keeping their hands clean in public, aiding the terrorists through covert means, but Katz wasn't concerned with legal niceties.

What he wanted right now was information and revenge, not necessarily in that order. And he wouldn't rest until he had both.

First stop, a pawnshop off Levinski Street, run by a Palestinian named Ahmed Hazril. He was alleged to deal in weapons, though police had never caught him at it.

"Maybe I can do a better job," Katz muttered to himself, and focused on the traffic flowing past him.

One way or another, he was bound to try.

THE MAN'S NAME was Ferran Khalid. He was a lawyer, known to represent outspoken Palestinians when they were hauled into court for violation of various statutes, most often involving proscribed political or paramilitary action. Once identified, in his youth, as a member of the Popular Front for the Liberation of Palestine, Khalid had severed any public ties with revolutionary groups after he graduated from the university and entered law school. Still, there was no doubt among authorities in Israel as to where his loyalties lay.

Most recently, he had defended several bombers linked to Allah's Lance, after a terrorist attack in Ashqelon. Khalid had failed to win acquittal for his clients—that was hopeless, going in—but he had turned their trial into a forum for the views espoused by Wasim Jabbar. These days, his home and office telephones were tapped by the Mossad and Khalid seemed to know it, asking members of his "special" clientele to meet with him on neutral ground, where they could watch for spies and eavesdroppers.

Mindel hadn't scheduled an appointment with Ferran Khalid. She didn't need his legal services, but she intended to have words with him concerning Allah's Lance. If there was anyone in Tel Aviv who might know what Jabbar and Arnold Napier had in common, she believed Khalid to be that man.

And if she solved that portion of the mystery, with any luck, she would be one step closer to her uncle. She might even track him down before he was destroyed.

Khalid's office was located on Derech Hahagana Street, in the Hatikva Quarter. It wasn't a place where Arabs congregated, but she thought his choice was probably no accident. What better way to gall his enemies than to parade before them every day, with clients known to hate them bitterly? Khalid's office also stayed open on the Sabbath, to accommodate his clients and to twist the knife a little, while he had the chance.

Khalid's office occupied half of a subdivided house, what the Americans would call a duplex. He had the east half of the building, with some kind of print shop to the west. Mindel walked in and shut the door behind her, feeling petty satisfaction as the young, attractive Palestinian receptionist glanced up from her typewriter, blinking in surprise.

"I'm here to see Mr. Khalid," Mindel announced before the younger woman had a chance to speak.

"I am afraid—"

"Don't be afraid, child. Show me to him." Mindel flashed her ID card. "Right now."

"Of course. Please come this way."

The receptionist knocked on Khalid's door, then entered, framing her apology before she crossed the threshold. "Mr. Khalid, please excuse me, but—"

"He won't blame you," Mindel said, interrupting as she stepped into the lawyer's private office. "Not while there's a Jew around to blame, at least."

Khalid didn't rise from behind his desk. "Thank you, Leila," he said. "Please finish with those letters, will you?"

Turning coal-black eyes on Mindel's face, he said, "And you are...?"

She moved toward the desk, extending the ID card. Khalid studied it for several seconds, smiling to himself. He shifted in his chair, his left hand slipping out of sight beneath the desk. Mindel tried to imagine how fast she could draw and fire her pistol, if he came out with a gun.

The hand resurfaced, empty. "Please, sit," Khalid offered. "You honor me. It's been some time since the Mossad came calling."

"Then you're overdue," she said.

"Perhaps. I'm sure you think so, anyway."

"What I think doesn't matter at the moment."

"To your business then," he said. "That's good. No wasted time."

"I need some information."

"And you come to me?" The lawyer's smile was dazzling, mocking.

"Yes."

"We call that a fool's errand, Miss Mossad."

"Mindel," she said, correcting him.

"You're all the same to me."

"Would you feel justified if I said, 'Likewise'?"

"I don't justify myself to you," Khalid replied. The smile was gone. "You have a question? Ask it."

"Wasim Jabbar," she said.

"That's not a question. Have they given up on language studies in the Hebrew schools?"

"I need to know his business with Global Petroleum and a man called Arnold Napier."

Khalid blinked at that, whether in guilty knowledge or sheer surprise she couldn't say. "And what would I know of such things?" he asked.

"A great deal, possibly. We can discuss it here, or in a holding cell."

"The truncheons and electrodes." Khalid had retrieved his smile. "One thing about you Zionists—you're always perfectly predictable."

"Are we?" It was Mindel's turn to smile. "Perhaps I should surprise you, then."

"It would be a refreshing change."

"Try this. We'll skip the cells. If you don't tell me what I need to know, I'll kill you here and now."

"That's better," Khalid said, "but I'm afraid you don't convince me."

As he spoke, she heard the door open behind her. Mindel swiveled in her chair to find a pair of Arabs standing on the threshold, both of them with pistols in their hands.

"And now," Ferran Khalid told her, "I think it's *you* who are surprised."

9

The first stop was a washout. Cruising down Levinski Street, they met police roadblocks before they came within two blocks of the pawnshop-cum-arms cache maintained by Ahmed Hazril. Downrange, Bolan could see squad cars and fire trucks, various uniforms milling around while smoke hung thick and acrid in the air.

"Too late?" he said.

McCarter, driving, frowned and glanced across at Bolan. "You don't think...?"

He didn't have to say it. Bolan *did* think Katz might've been there ahead of them, but there was no way he could prove or disprove the hypothesis without interrogating witnesses. That was, assuming there were any left alive.

"It could be anything," he said. "Some kind of feud between the different factions, maybe."

"A coincidence?" McCarter sounded every bit as skeptical as Bolan felt. "You don't believe that."

"Let's do number two," Bolan replied.

"Uh-huh," McCarter said. "I didn't think so."

Bolan thought about it while McCarter drove, concluding that he couldn't outthink Katz or plot his moves in Tel Aviv. That option laid to rest, Bolan was free to focus on the plans they'd sketched out at the safehouse.

The second target was a social club located in the city's Arab quarter, where associates of Allah's Lance were said to congregate. It was raided periodically by Israeli authorities, various suspects hauled away for questioning, but no case had been made so far against the owners of the club themselves. Bolan and his companion, on the other hand, weren't bound by any rules of law.

They found the club, drove past and circled once around the block. A lookout made them on the second pass and ducked inside to warn someone that trouble might be on the way.

"There goes surprise," McCarter said.

"In a neighborhood like this, we couldn't hope for much," Bolan replied.

"Still going with the plan?"

"Unless you have a better one."

"I wish Mindel was here," the Briton said grudgingly.

"They're bound to have some English speakers in the house," Bolan stated.

"You hope so, anyway." McCarter double-parked outside the club and left the engine running. "I could tag along," he said.

"I'd rather have the car here, waiting in one piece, when I come out."

"You'll have that, anyway. How long?"

"Five minutes, tops."

McCarter checked his watch. "I'm counting...now."

Bolan brushed past some dawdlers on the narrow sidewalk, feeling hostile eyes on every side of him as he approached the entrance to the social club. He hadn't stopped to think what he would do if someone simply locked the door. Shoot through the lock? Provoke a riot on the street before he ever got inside?

It didn't matter, since the lookout chose that moment to emerge. The young man blinked at Bolan, frozen like a deer in headlights with the door ajar. Bolan took full advantage of it, shoved him backward, bulling through, and let the door swing shut behind him.

Wasting no time, Bolan produced the silenced MP-5 and shoved its muzzle in the young man's startled face. "Wasim Jabbar," he said.

The lookout blinked at him, cross-eyed from staring at the gun, then shook his head—a swift, emphatic negative.

"Not here?" Bolan asked. "Let's just ask around, shall we?"

He spun the young man and was shoving him in the direction of a curtained doorway to the main club proper, when a blur of motion on his left made Bolan turn. The young man's backup had been lurking in a cubby hole of sorts, coffin-size, perhaps designed specifically for ambushes. The lurker had some kind of wavy-bladed dagger poised to strike, but Bolan wasn't letting him connect.

A 3-round burst from Bolan's SMG ripped through the blade man's chest and slammed him back into his niche, a real-life coffin now. Before the dead man slumped into a crouch, Bolan swung back to face the lookout and propelled him through the beaded curtain.

Business obviously wasn't great during the daylight hours. Bolan counted nine men seated here and there, at small round tables, mismatched coffee cups in front of them. Devout Muslims shunned liquor, so the club wasn't a bar, per se. Nine pairs of eyes pinned Bolan as he cleared the threshold, forewarned by the spotter, waiting to find out what he'd do next.

For starters, Bolan pushed his captive out into the middle of the room, thus freeing up his field of fire. "Wasim Jabbar," he said again. "I want him. Arnold Napier wants him. If you know him, pass the word. There's no way out."

Nobody moved, so Bolan broke their trance. He sprayed the walls and ceiling with his MP-5, the muffled rounds more startling for their lack of sound before impact. He took out ceiling fixtures, shattered glass, sent artwork plummeting from wall hooks. Somewhere in the midst of it the club went dark, as if someone had thrown a master switch.

And it was time to leave.

Bolan retreated through the foyer, heard a rush of feet behind him and used up the last rounds in his magazine hosing the darkness where a beaded curtain hung between him and his enemies. Someone cried out in pain, the rest retreating in a rush as Bolan gained the sidewalk, tucked his weapon out of sight and jogged back to the waiting car.

McCarter had the vehicle in motion before Bolan's door slammed behind him. "Warm reception?" asked the Briton.

"Nothing I couldn't handle."

"Planting seeds, eh?"

"Sowing discontent," the Executioner replied. "Find me another garden plot."

REBECCA MINDEL WAS DIZZY from the heat and lack of air by the time the car stopped and her kidnappers switched off the engine. She heard doors slamming, as if from a distance, then tracked them by the muffled sounds of footsteps on gravel, circling around the vehicle. When one of them opened the trunk she sucked in a great breath, though the rough burlap hood kept much air from her face.

She didn't resist as they lifted her out of the trunk, none too gently at that. It could've been worse—and it would be, she thought, once they got her inside. She could try a break now, but her legs were unsteady, hands cuffed behind her back, and the hood left her blind.

Those were poor prospects for a getaway, and so she let them guide her over pavement, through a doorway and along some kind of corridor, until they reached a door that needed keys to open it.

The building had no air-conditioning, no fans in operation at the moment, but it still beat riding in a smelly car trunk. Mindel stood and waited for the door to be unlocked, feeling the men around her, guessing distances, deciding there was nothing to be gained by lashing out at them with kicks, when they could simply beat her down or shoot her where she stood.

Inside the room that seemed to be their destination, someone finally removed the hood she'd worn since moments after she was captured in the lawyer's office. Blinking at the light, Mindel counted three men in front of her, feeling at least one more behind. The only one she recognized among them was the mouthpiece, Ferran Khalid.

"You've made a nasty slipup, Counselor," she said. "Kidnapping means disbarment for a start, before you go away for twenty years to life."

"I'd be concerned," Khalid replied, "if there was any risk of prosecution. Since you'll simply disappear, however, I'm not worried in the least."

"Proving that you're a foolish man, in case we hadn't got the point already."

"I admire your nerve," the lawyer said. "I shall be interested to see how long it lasts."

"Uncuff me, and we'll see how long *you* last."

"I do my fighting in the courtroom," Khalid said. "Well, most of it, at least."

"Defending terrorists."

"I think of them as freedom fighters, but no matter. We're not here to argue broad points of philosophy."

"Why are we here?" As if I didn't know, she thought.

"To find out what you know about Global Petroleum and Allah's Lance," he said. "The same thing you inquired of me, but in reverse this time. It makes an interesting change for Palestinians to question the Mossad."

"You'll learn nothing from me," Mindel assured him.

Khalid smiled at that. "By all means, please resist. I would be disappointed if you cracked too soon and spoiled the entertainment. In the end, though, I assure you that you'll beg to tell me everything you know and even make up fairy tales to satisfy my curiosity."

"We'll see," she said, with more bravado than she felt.

"Indeed." Half turning toward the short man on his left, Khalid said, "Amer, we require a chair."

The Arab left, returning moments later with a straight-backed wooden chair that had no arms. Its seat was shiny from the countless backsides that had polished it through years of use. Amer set the chair in front of Mindel with a mocking smile, then backed away.

"We shall require you to disrobe before you sit," Khalid informed her. "If you'd rather not participate, of course, we can undress you."

Mindel kept her face impassive. "I can't reach the buttons with these cuffs on," she reminded him.

Khalid considered that, frowning, then nodded to the man who stood behind her. Mindel waited while the unseen Arab fumbled at her handcuffs with a key, releasing first one wrist and then the other. Stalling, she took time to flex her fingers, rub her wrists, as if the cuffs had interfered with circulation.

"If you please," the lawyer prodded her.

"My pleasure," Mindel told him—just before she sprang across the space between them, hands outstretched to rake his face like claws.

She never made it, though. Some heavy object slammed into her skull, behind one ear, and in the split second of consciousness remaining Mindel felt as if the concrete floor had opened up to swallow her.

THE PAWNSHOP HAD BEEN easy. Katz had breezed in off the street and lulled Ahmed Hazril's suspicion with a burst of rapid-fire Arabic, pretending he wanted to purchase a musical instrument. The Arab had smiled knowingly, thinking to himself that Jews always loved bargains, assuring Katz that they could almost certainly do business.

The rest was child's play, after Katz had satisfied himself they were alone. He showed the gun, telling Hazril he knew about the pawnbroker's illicit services for Allah's Lance, knocking the smaller man around when he denied it—obviously lying through his teeth.

Hazril knew nothing of the link between Global Petroleum and Wasim Jabbar, of course. He wasn't highly placed enough for that. But he knew other things—names and addresses, contacts and connections, the location of specific training camps across the border, where his weapons were delivered to young comrades in the cause. Before he left the shop, Katz had it all.

And when he left, he'd left the place in flames, Ahmed Hazril long past caring about losses to his inventory. The next stop on his hit list was a private residence. The tenant, one Gamal Girgis, was an accountant who moonlighted as a treasurer for Allah's Lance. As such, Katz reasoned that he might have knowledge of Jabbar's dealings with Arnold Napier and Global Petroleum. If not, well, at the very least, his death would cause some inconvenience to the terrorists. It was another step toward payback, wounding Katz's enemies by any means available.

Revenge wasn't his only motivation, though, not even first on his short list. Katz knew that nothing good could come of a collaboration between Allah's Lance and any major corporation, much less one immersed in Middle Eastern oil. Katz didn't know what the conspiracy entailed, yet, but he meant to find out soon.

Beginning with Gamal Girgis.

The Palestinian accountant had a midsize house off Derech Hashalom, on the east side of Tel Aviv. Katz found an alley in the rear and left his stolen car there, slipping through an unlocked gate to cross Girgis's fenced-in backyard.

So far, the money man was careless, but Katz couldn't take such negligence for granted as he neared the house. He watched the windows for disturbance of the curtains drawn across them and saw nothing. Ditto when he reached the back door and examined it for wires suggesting an alarm. There could be something on the inside, hidden from his gaze, but Katz would have to take that chance.

He tried the knob and found it locked, as he'd expected. There was no dead bolt, however—careless, that—and thirty seconds with the small blade of his pocket knife was all it took to beat the lock. Palming the Mark 3 autoloader, Katz stepped cautiously across the threshold, entering a small utility room with a washer and dryer stacked on his right, pantry space on the left. Ahead of him, lights burned in a kitchen with no one to use them.

Katz eased the back door shut, relieved that no alarm had sounded when he entered. Moving through the kitchen, he heard a sound of voices coming from the far end of a hallway on the other side. When laughter joined the mix, he knew it was a television program. Better yet, if he caught the accountant with his guard down.

Stepping from the lighted kitchen to the hall, Katz glanced in both directions, saw no one, and trailed the noises to his right, closing the distance to a parlor. He was nearly there when something clicked behind him—could it be a door?—and he heard footsteps on the bare wood floor.

Katz turned in time to see the blow coming, from a long

knife in the hand of a young Arab with a snarling face. Instinctively, he fired his Browning from the hip, its first report ear-shattering inside the quiet house. Cursing his failure to request a sound suppressor, Katz saw the bullet strike an inch or two off center, still a solid chest shot that propelled the young man backward and away from him, dropping without a sound of protest from slack lips.

Katz spun and rushed the living room, clearing the hallway just as two men bolted from the sofa there, turning to face him. One was armed and dressed more casually than the other, telling him which was the bodyguard and which the man he'd come to see. Katz didn't know if it was usual for Girgis to have armed guards in his home, and there was no time to consider it just now.

The shooter had his pistol drawn but never got the chance to use it. Katz fired twice, still moving, one round drilling through the Arab's cheek, the other opening his throat. The man went down, blood spurting from his wounds, while Girgis stood and gaped at him, as if about to scream.

"Don't make a sound," Katz cautioned him. "We're leaving now, before your neighbors make a fuss. We'll get acquainted on the drive."

MCCARTER'S MOUTH was dry, making him wish for a cold Coke. It wouldn't be that hard to find one, even in the Yad Eliahu district—Coke was everywhere—but he had no time to go prospecting for a dispenser or convenience store. In fact, his time was up right about...*now.*

He crossed the street, a short block over from LaGuardia, still wondering why any street in Tel Aviv was named for an Italian mayor of New York City. If they'd called it Ed Koch Boulevard, he would've understood. LaGuardia remained a riddle, but McCarter put it out of mind as he approached a midsize office building on the north side of the street.

McCarter breezed in like he owned the place, passing the information desk without a second glance. He hoped Bolan hadn't been intercepted on the rear approach. If they were synchronized, his comrade should be entering the building's service elevator even as McCarter stepped aboard the lobby lift and pressed a button for the seventh floor.

It was the top floor of the building, occupied entirely by a firm called Paradigm Synthetics. McCarter didn't have a clue what Paradigm produced, but Stony Man had pegged it as a wholly owned subsidiary of Global Petroleum, and that made it fair game for a visit, as Bolan and McCarter played connect-the-dots.

McCarter wasn't dressed for the Israeli weather, but his lightweight raincoat hid the MP-5 SD-3 submachine gun slung beneath his right arm, accessed through a pocket he'd slit open on that side. McCarter didn't know if there'd be killing in the Paradigm Synthetics offices, but he was ready if it came to that—or if they simply had to trash the place as an example to the drones.

Emerging from the elevator, he saw Bolan at the far end of the hall. A balding man in polyester was attempting to explain why Bolan had to be lost, inviting him to get back in the service elevator and select another floor. His last mistake was reaching out for Bolan's arm, a move that put him on the floor two seconds later, facedown in a crumpled heap.

McCarter scanned the hall and waited for the Executioner to join him. Bolan took the point as they pushed through a door of frosted glass, into the office suite's main waiting room. The Briton was surprised to see a solitary male receptionist, his desk planted dead-center in a room that could've easily accommodated six or seven more. File cabinets ranged along three walls suggested that the space was meant for storage, rather than receiving visitors. The middle-aged receptionist's expression validated that suspicion at a glance.

"I'm guessing they don't get too many walk-in customers," he commented.

"Here's a chance to make a difference," Bolan said, and drew his pistol as he stepped up to the desk.

He told the seated man, "We need to see the manager."

The man behind the desk made no objection. Leaning toward Bolan, he keyed the intercom and said, "Two gentlemen to see you, Mr. Bright."

McCarter watched the man's right hand slip out of sight beneath his desk and knew they had a problem. He was ready, taking up the trigger slack on his SMG when a door opened behind the receptionist and three men with weapons spilled into the room. As if they had rehearsed the move, the three fanned out, while the receptionist kicked backward in his chair and swung a pistol into view.

McCarter shot the seated man, a close-range burst of Parabellum manglers driving him backward, chair and all, until the nearest filing cabinet stopped him dead. By that time, Bolan had engaged the others, dropping one of them and swiveling to bring the others under fire.

McCarter's submachine gun stuttered with a sound like ripping canvas, taking down one of the shooters as he tried to sight on Bolan, spinning him and slamming him against the door from which he had emerged. Bolan squeezed off a double tap to drop the last one where he stood, a wild round from the dying gunner's pistol plowing up a strip of carpet as he fell.

They found the manager beneath his desk in the second private office that they checked. He was unarmed and offered no resistance as they dragged him out into the light.

"We have a message for your boss," McCarter said.

"M-m-my boss?"

"No games," Bolan instructed him. "If you can't get in touch with Napier, you're no good to us at all."

"I can! I'll call him now!"

"Wait till we're gone," McCarter said.

"All right! I will!"

"Tell him his deal with Allah's Lance is falling through," Bolan stated. "Do you think you can remember that?"

The trembling man repeated it verbatim. Twice.

"Call Napier first," McCarter said, "then the police. Got it?"

"I swear!"

They left him kneeling in the ruins of his dignity and took the service elevator down. If anyone had heard the gunfire on the seventh floor, it didn't show as they emerged and walked back to their car.

"Next stop?" McCarter asked.

"Let's turn it up a notch," Bolan replied. "We need to hear from someone Napier trusts enough to share his plans."

"The number two?"

"Why not?" Bolan was almost smiling as he said, "Let's find out if he's had a chance to change his underwear."

WASIM JABBAR HATED coming to Tel Aviv. On one level, it sickened him to walk the streets surrounded by his enemies, the people who had dispossessed his ancestors in 1948 and driven them to live in desert camps or chased them out of Palestine completely. Every moment spent in Tel Aviv reminded him that he hadn't yet done enough to rid the land of Zionists and lead his people back to their homeland.

The other problem with a trip to the Israeli capital was physical security. Jabbar was at or near the top of every Wanted list in Israel, hunted constantly by agents empowered to kill him on sight. Mossad had placed a bounty on his head years earlier, but so far they'd had no luck in arranging his demise. So far, he had survived two bombings, an attempted kidnapping, a drive-by shooting—maybe not Israelis that time; he was never sure—and an attempt by an enticing whore who had been paid by his enemies to slit his throat while he lay sleeping, after sex. The bitch's aim was bad. Though wounded, he'd been able to disarm her and apply the blade in ways she'd never dreamed of in her wildest nightmares. The other attempts had cost lives, friends and soldiers, while sparing Jabbar to pursue his work.

Despite all that, Jabbar didn't believe he was invincible. The whore had come too close to killing him for any such illusion to survive. He *was* convinced, though, that God had some great purpose for him to fulfill, whether through combat or by martyrdom at some point in the future. Either way, although he still observed the rules of strict security and wore disguises any time he traveled through Jerusalem or Tel Aviv, Jabbar believed his days were numbered and his enemies wouldn't be granted power to derail God's design.

Or maybe that was nonsense, but at least it gave him peace of mind.

He had come to Tel Aviv that afternoon after receiving word that one of his opponents had been captured. It didn't surprise him that the hostage was a woman. The Israelis let their females join the army, serve in combat, even occupy positions of importance in Mossad and the police force. They'd allowed a woman to command their country for five years, in the early 1970s, and she had proved more ruthless in suppression of the Palestinian cause than her male predecessors.

All the more reason, Jabbar told himself, to obey the Koran's injunction that females had to be kept subordinate, securely in their place. Who could predict what other travesties of natural law might ensue if God's rule was disobeyed?

The hostage was confined in a house on the Tel Aviv outskirts, east of the city. Jabbar's driver found it without incident, parking in back and stepping out to open his master's door. Jabbar greeted his welcoming committee and resisted an urge to scratch the fake scar glued across his left cheek.

Inside the safehouse he was offered tea or coffee—both declined—then ushered to the room where Khalid and the others had attempted to interrogate their prisoner. Jabbar was startled to behold a certain dignity about her, even naked, after all that she had suffered, taped and handcuffed to a simple wooden chair.

He stepped around in front of her, stooping until their eyes met, hers a dim, pain-weary gaze. "You've been courageous," he congratulated her. "Your stamina is most impressive. But it's time for you to tell us everything."

"In hell," she answered, barely whispering.

"I thought you knew," he answered, smiling. "You're already there."

STERLING HOLBROOK WAS nervous. He considered that a normal situation, after nearly having been shot in his office by a

sniper, but he still didn't like it. Subordinates expected
the man in charge than ducking and hiding like a gun
mal. He should be taking charge, doing something proactiv
murder attempts were beyond his experience—at least they had
been, until that morning—and Holbrook didn't know what else
to do besides cooperating with authorities.

In fact, he'd been specifically commanded to do nothing else.
Napier had left no doubts on that score: any bungling efforts to
investigate the shooting or retaliate in any way would be the kiss
of death to Holbrook's lucrative career. Napier had taken pains
to remind him that he was an assistant, not a field commander.
That made him a glorified gofer, but what could Holbrook do
about it? Napier called the shots—in this case, both figuratively
and literally.

"I'll take care of it, Sterl," he had vowed on the phone from
Riyadh. "I'll be there by sundown. Just relax."

That was good advice, except for one small hitch—Holbrook
couldn't stop hearing the gunfire, couldn't stop seeing the blood
splashed on carpet and walls from the men who'd been killed in
his office.

Make that former office. His first order of business, after talking to the cops and doubling security around the Global offices
downtown, had been to boot a regional vice president for mar-
keting out of his windowless office, claiming the space as his own
for the remainder of his stay in Tel Aviv. Holbrook had thought
of sleeping there, having a bed brought up from God knew where
and squeezed into the office, but he was acutely conscious of appearances. Security precautions were one thing; a frank display
of cowardice simply would never fly.

With that in mind, he would be going back to the apartment
Global kept in Tel Aviv for visiting executives, departing within
twenty minutes under heavy guard. The shooters didn't make him
feel self-conscious; quite the opposite, in fact. Great men often
traveled with bodyguards, particularly after threats or actual attempts upon their lives. The guards gave him a kind of macho

status, Holbrook thought, but it would've been more convincing if he could forget the image of himself screaming for help, curled up beneath his desk.

He hoped Napier was ruthless with the bastards who had done this to him, if and when they were identified and run to ground. Holbrook wasn't a violent man, in ordinary circumstances, but he would've loved to watch the sniper punished for humiliating him in front of his employees.

And perhaps he would've found the nerve to lend a hand himself. Perhaps.

A soft knock on the office door distracted him from bloody daydreams. "What?"

"The car's downstairs, sir."

"Right. Okay. I'm coming."

One more glance around the unfamiliar office, to make sure nothing was left behind, and Holbrook went to join his bodyguards. Four of them walked him to the elevator, cramming in around him like well-armed sardines. They rode down to street level and emerged into the lobby, where another pair of hardmen in dark glasses and dark suits stood watch. All six surrounded Holbrook on the short walk to his limousine, two climbing in behind him, while the other four jogged to a second car parked just behind the stretch. The limo's driver had a shotgun rider at his side, to keep him company.

They pulled out from the curb, slowly at first, accelerating as the limo made room for itself in the afternoon traffic. Holbrook left the driver to it, thankful to be going anywhere right now, away from the office that had suddenly become a crime scene. Watching the storefronts slide past, he had a sudden thought.

"Is this glass bulletproof?" he asked, addressing no one in particular.

"Yes, sir," one of the shooters said.

"We're armored all around," another reassured him.

The limo had made several turns before he noticed that they were no longer headed north, toward the apartment block where Global rented space. Holbrook assumed the driver was pursuing some evasive pattern, watching out for tails, but one of his armed escorts didn't seem to think so.

"Driver! This is the wrong way," he said.

The front-seat passenger swiveled to face them, smiling crookedly. "That all depends on where you want to go," he said.

Holbrook had half a second between recognition of the pistol in the stranger's hand and the first shot. It spattered him with something warm and wet, but he was physically unharmed. A second shot took out his other bodyguard and dumped the man facedown in Holbrook's lap, blood spilling from a head wound onto Holbrook's slacks.

"My God!"

"Relax, gov," said the gunman, still smiling. "We only want to have a private word."

10

Losing the Global oilman's backup bodyguards required some fancy driving and some pinpoint marksmanship, but Bolan and McCarter pulled it off. A sharp turn down a narrow street, a sudden stop, and by the time Holbrook's hired shooters recognized the trap, their car had lost two tires, its radiator spouting coolant from a dozen bullet holes. They still got off a few shots as the limousine departed, but its armored glass and bodywork deflected the incoming rounds.

They ditched the limo in an upscale neighborhood and transferred Holbrook to a less obtrusive vehicle for the last portion of his journey. Bolan didn't want to use the Mossad safehouse, just in case the question-answer game got rowdy, so they drove into the desert, several miles outside the city.

"I don't know who you are or what you want," Holbrook was saying, as McCarter dragged him from the car, "but I can pay you. Well, I mean the company can pay you. It's no problem. Within reason, naturally."

"And what do you consider reasonable?" Bolan asked.

Holbrook blinked at him, sweating through his shirt and tailored jacket in the unrelenting desert heat. "I...I wouldn't know," he said. "I've never been kidnapped before."

"Today's a bargain for you, then," McCarter said. "We don't want money. Only information."

"Sorry?"

"Don't be sorry yet," Bolan advised. "Save that for if you disappoint us."

"I don't understand." Despite his words and evident confusion, Bolan saw a cunning light in Holbrook's eyes, could almost hear gears shifting in his head.

"You work for Arnold Napier," McCarter said.

"I work with him, yes."

"In fact," Bolan said, "you're his number two."

"My title is vice president in charge of operations," Holbrook said. "Worldwide, of course, the company has ten or twelve vice presidents. I wouldn't say—"

"False modesty won't help you now," Bolan interrupted him. "If you know nothing, you're worth nothing."

Holbrook swallowed hard and answered, "Tell me what you want to know."

"Tell us about your firm's connection with Wasim Jabbar," McCarter demanded. "We want to know about your boss's cozy deal with Allah's Lance."

Holbrook blinked rapidly. "I'm not sure—"

Bolan drew and fired his pistol in a single fluid motion. His first bullet raised a spurt of dust between the oilman's feet and made him jump. "Pick right or left," he told Holbrook.

"Say what?"

"Next time you lie, it costs a kneecap. Your choice: right or left?"

"For God's sake!"

"Best to leave religion out of it," McCarter said. "You know the way it always mucks things up, here in the Holy Land."

"All right! Jesus! I mean—"

"Allah's Lance," Bolan reminded him. "Wasim Jabbar."

"I guess you know, if I give you what you want, I'm dead."

"We know what happens if you don't," McCarter said.

"Okay. Screw it. You want it from the top? It goes back eighteen months or so."

"Just an abbreviated version," Bolan replied. "Clock's ticking."

"Right. Well, as you know, Global has interests all over the world, connections with a wide variety of firms and governments. We're mainly oil—it makes the world go 'round, you know?—but not exclusively. Good business sense will tell you that the more oil we control, the more profits we make. Somewhere along the way, Arnold and some of his associates in other spheres cooked up a plan to make it happen, while expanding markets in the East."

"Which markets did you have in mind, specifically?" McCarter asked.

"China," Holbrook replied.

"You haven't sold to them before?" Bolan inquired.

"Nothing compared to this. We're talking virtual monopoly. Most-favored status, at the very least. Of course, that means we need a guaranteed supply and huge reserves."

"Beyond what you have now," McCarter said.

"Beyond what we can trust right now," Holbrook agreed.

"And how does Allah's Lance play into this?" asked Bolan.

"Simple give and take," the oilman said. "There's not a country in the region that would shed a tear if Israel disappeared tomorrow. Am I right? Some of them talk peace now, because the U.S. has been leaning on them, but you scratch a Muslim Arab and you'll find an anti-Zionist. Trust me."

"Which helps you...how, again?" McCarter asked.

"If we help tip the scales against Israel, it puts us in the driver's seat next time oil contracts are negotiated. Hell, we might just bypass OPEC altogether, if they're grateful enough."

"And the surplus goes to China," Bolan said.

"Bingo."

"You know this much, you must have names."

"A couple," Holbrook said.

"We're not unreasonable," McCarter told him. "All we want is everything you know."

"A character named Lin Mak has been handling the negotiations out of Hong Kong. I can't tell you much about him. I only met him once, in Switzerland."

"One name?" McCarter asked. "That's it?"

"Well, there's Andrastus," Holbrook said.

"He doesn't sound Chinese."

"Try Greek."

"*Christos* Andrastus?" Bolan asked. "The shipping guy?"

"We have another winner."

"So, who else is in this stew?" McCarter asked.

"Top players, that's the lot. If Arnold has a second string on tap, it's news to me."

"I'd say we're done here, then," the Executioner remarked.

Holbrook swallowed, watching the gun in Bolan's hand, and said, "Let's not be hasty, gentlemen. I might have something left to trade."

"Such as?" McCarter prodded him.

"Maybe a friend of yours, from the Mossad. Does that ring any bells?" When neither of them answered, Holbrook shrugged. "Okay, then. My mistake. You don't mind if she buys the farm, go on and fire away."

THE FLIGHT from Riyadh, into Tel Aviv, was simplified by use of Global's private jet. Commercial flights were problematic, with so much time wasted on security, and Arnold Napier despised the cramped quarters found even in first class. He had erased all memories of flying coach, the remnants of a time when he hadn't been wealthy, when he was subordinate to others and beholden to their whims.

The bad old days.

They might return, in spades, if Napier failed to carry off his grand design, but he had no real fear of failure at the moment. There were obstacles, of course—and one of them required him to observe the action in Tel Aviv from closer range than he would've preferred otherwise, but he still had a sense of control. He still held the critical strings, and his touch was as deft as ever.

He was still the master of his game.

The latest breakthrough might be vital, and it was another reason Napier had changed his plans for sitting out the trouble in Riyadh. Jabbar's men had somehow contrived to capture one of their tormentors, who apparently was part of the Mossad. Napier had been skeptical when they told him about the old man, trying to imagine a one-armed secret agent skulking through the streets of Tel Aviv, but this time there was apparently documentation. Risks aside, Napier wanted to find out firsthand what was happening, scope out the threat to everything he'd worked for in the past two years.

He wouldn't take a hand in the interrogation, naturally. It would most likely be completed by the time he landed, anyway. But part of him still whispered that it might be educational to watch.

A new experience, perchance.

The built-in telephone beside his elbow shrilled as Napier sipped a double shot of sixteen-year-old Bushmills Irish whiskey. He picked up on the second ring, taking his own sweet time.

"Napier," he said.

"Um, Mr. Napier, this is Don Sheehan, your district manager in Tel Aviv."

Napier made the connection in a heartbeat, picturing a forty-something bachelor, slightly overweight, with thinning sandy hair above an oval face.

"I'm heading your way as we speak, Don," he said affably.

"Yes, sir. I understood you might be. That's, um, why I'm calling, sir."

"Is there a problem, Don?" Another problem, that would be. Napier could feel the muscles in his neck and underneath his jaw begin to clench involuntarily.

"Well, yes, sir. I'm afraid there's been more trouble."

"And is there a reason I'm not hearing this from Mr. Holbrook, Don?"

"Yes, sir. That is, I mean, the trouble has to do with Mr. Holbrook, sir."

A conscious effort was required for Napier to relax his stranglehold on the receiver. "Can you be a bit more lucid, Don?" he asked.

"Yes, sir. I'm sorry, sir. Um, it appears that Mr. Holbrook has been kidnapped, sir."

"When you say it appears—"

"They've definitely snatched him, sir. No doubt about it. Killed two of his bodyguards and shot the second car to shit. I beg your pardon, sir."

"I've heard the word before, Don. Do we know who did this thing?"

"No, sir. The police are working on it, but we've had no calls, ransom demands or anything like that. So far, I mean."

"Are any of the bodyguards still breathing?"

"Yes, sir. Four of them came through without a scratch," Sheehan replied. "It's just their car got—"

"Shot to shit. I understand. Can you do something for me, Don?"

"Yes, sir!"

"I want those lucky bastards waiting for me at the airport when I land. I'll have some questions for them."

"Yes, sir. They'll be there."

"Just one more thing, Don."

"Yes, sir?"

"When you pick out my security detail, I don't want anybody who's afraid to catch a bullet on the list."

"No, sir!"

Napier replaced the telephone receiver without any pleasantries in parting. He had much to think about, and barely half an hour left before he touched down in the middle of a war zone, where his best-laid plans were being shot to shit.

GAMAL GIRGIS LOOKED sickly and disoriented when Katz let him out of the trunk. It took the accountant a moment to stand on his own, stamping his left foot several times and grimacing as if the leg had gone to sleep.

"You don't like pins and needles?" Katz inquired. "It could be worse than that, you know."

"What do you want from me?" Girgis demanded.

"I'll stop short of asking for your soul," Katz said, "since you already sold it when you went to work for Allah's Lance."

"I don't know you," the accountant stated. "Who are you to kidnap and insult me?"

"I'm a patriot of Israel who will not stand by and see my people murdered," Katz replied.

"Your precious people stole this land in 1948. The British helped them, signing over deeds for property they had no right to claim. There'll be no peace as long as any Zionists remain in Palestine."

"You're wrong, my friend." Katz drew the Browning from his belt and held it down against his thigh. "You may find peace this very day."

"You mean to kill me, then?"

"I'm searching for a reason not to," Katz replied. "Perhaps you'll help me think of one."

"I have a family."

"So did all the Jews your friends have murdered. All of them had families who mourn them."

"I've killed no one! I'm just a bookkeeper. I've never even fired a gun."

"You count the bullets, though," Katz said. "You make sure all of them are paid for in advance."

"That's nonsense!" Girgis protested. "I have played no part in any violence."

"Why were there gunmen in your home today?" Katz asked.

"My bodyguards!"

"Since when do honest bookkeepers need bodyguards?"

"We live in troubled times. They were supposed to keep me safe from—"

"Jews like me?" Katz finished for him, smiling wickedly. "They let you down."

"What do you want of me?" Girgis asked once again.

"Your blood," Katz said, "unless you have something more interesting to offer."

"Information!" the accountant blurted. "I know things!"

"About Global Petroleum? About a man called Arnold Napier?"

Katz had never seen an Arab pale before, but Girgis nearly managed it. "You ask too much," he answered, sounding hopeless.

"Too much for your life?"

"I'm dead in any case, if I speak of these things."

"Your friends won't hear from me what we've discussed," Katz said.

"They'll find out anyway."

"All right, then. As you wish." He cocked the Browning pistol with his thumb and raised it into line with the accountant's face.

"No! Wait!" Girgis held both hands out, as if their flesh could stop a bullet.

"I don't have much time," Katz said, holding the pistol steady on his target.

"I don't know any of their plans," Girgis said, cringing, "but I do know where the money comes from. I know where it goes."

"I'm listening," Katz said. He dropped the pistol to his side again, but left it cocked.

"China and Greece!" Girgis informed him, smiling as if that said everything.

"Explain yourself," Katz snapped.

"Some of the money goes to China. Some of the money goes to Greece. More stays with Allah's Lance."

"Where does it come from?"

"Swiss accounts, the Cayman Islands, the Bahamas. Global Petroleum has many banks. Some even comes from the United States itself, but not so much."

"Why Greece and China?" Katz inquired.

"For that, I need the promise of my life."

"You have it."

"In Hong Kong, the payments go to Lin Yuan Mak. In Greece, to shipping lines owned by Christos Andrastus."

Katz had never heard of Mak, but anyone who'd ever read a newspaper would recognize Christos Andrastus, self-made billionaire. "His ships carry the oil, I take it?"

Girgis shrugged. "Again, I'm just a bookkeeper. If you want names of companies that have received the payments—"

"Never mind," Katz said. He didn't have the time or wherewithal to visit Greece, much less Hong Kong. Those portions of the network would be left for others. Katz knew he'd be lucky to wrap up the loose ends he'd already found in Tel Aviv before—

Before what?

He ducked the silent question and returned his full attention to Gamal Girgis. "Napier," he said. "Where can I find him now?"

"Wasim might know. As for myself—"

"And where's Wasim?" asked Katz.

"He'll be in Tel Aviv tonight."

"I'll need an address."

Shoulders slumping, Girgis gave him one. "I was supposed to meet him there tonight."

"I'll give him your regards," Katz said, and raised the pistol.

"Wait! You promised me!"

Katz shot him twice and left him where he fell.

"I lied," he said, and turned back toward the car.

Washington, D.C.

BROGNOLA LISTENED to the latest grim report from Tel Aviv, not interrupting Bolan as he spoke, framing a list of questions in his mind.

"You're sure they have Mindel?" he asked when Bolan took a break.

"As sure as I can be," the Executioner replied. "Holbrook's description was a fair match and he had her name, apparently from her ID. Also, she's out of touch—four hours and counting now. No response from her cell phone or pager."

Four hours, Brognola thought. It could be a lifetime, under torture. How long did it take to squeeze a trigger and dig a shallow grave?

"Have you touched base with the Mossad?" Brognola asked.

"That's more your end," Bolan replied. "They wouldn't know me. Anyway, I take for granted that the lady was in contact with her keepers."

"We don't know the schedule, though. They might not miss her for a day or two, if then."

"I had a thought on that," Bolan said.

"I'm all ears."

"Since Napier's coming in tonight, it couldn't hurt to ask about a trade," Bolan went on.

Mindel for Sterling Holbrook, sure. Brognola frowned, considering the list of felonies involved in the operation so far, with no tangible result. Exposure of any phase could spark an international incident, Mossad collaboration notwithstanding. At the very least, it would mean gross embarrassment for the United States. At worst...

Brognola thought about his job, his pension, and he knew that didn't even start to cover it. Two of his best soldiers—both of them also his trusted friends—were risking everything they had to help another member of the team who obviously didn't want their help. The body count was rising, and Brognola drew small solace from the fact that none of those chewed up so far were allies.

"What if Napier doesn't want to trade?" Brognola asked.

"For his vice president in charge of operations?" Bolan paused, considering. "It's possible, but I suspect he'll want a chance to silence Holbrook, even so. Smart money says he'll buy a meet and try to clean house in the process."

"That means two against—how many?"

"No predictions on that score," Bolan replied. "It may depend on whether he trusts Global talent or falls back on Allah's Lance."

"Jabbar," Brognola said. "No luck on tracing him, I guess?"

"Not yet. We've left some wake-up calls. So far, he's in the wind."

"Most likely sitting out the game in Syria or Lebanon," Brognola said. "Where's that ruthless Israeli efficiency when you need it?"

"They can't hit everybody," Bolan said.

"Same goes for you guys," Brognola reminded his old friend. "Don't spread yourselves too thin out there."

"We do with what we have."

"If you want to wait a day or so," Brognola said, "I can round up the rest of Phoenix Force and put them on a military flight to Saudi. They've been on my case for updates every day."

Bolan declared what Brognola already knew. "No time for that. We stall another day, I figure Mindel's done."

"Your call," Brognola said. "I won't try second-guessing you on this one. What about our other friend?"

"There've been a few things on the local news that could be

linked," Bolan replied. "Two hits on subjects linked to Allah's Lance are closest to the mark. I don't know where he's going with it, yet."

"You think he knows about Mindel?" Brognola asked.

"I don't see how he could."

"Or Napier coming in?"

Bolan was silent for a moment, thinking. "Maybe, if he squeezed someone who's in the know. Too soon to tell."

And by the time we know for sure, Brognola thought, it will be too damned late to head him off.

"Okay," he said. "You've got the ball. Reach out if I can help in any way."

"Will do," Bolan replied and broke the link.

Brognola cradled the receiver, then addressed it in a muted tone. "Stay frosty, guy," he said. "And try like hell to stay alive."

WASIM JABBAR WAS never truly comfortable in Tel Aviv. For all the good disguises did, too many soldiers and policemen knew his face; a small army of traitors and informers occupied the city, any one of whom would gladly sell him out for cash or favors, possibly dismissal of a pending charge. He wouldn't know the trap was set until it closed around him—by which time it would already be too late.

Jabbar had no illusion that the Zionists would try to capture him alive. They hated him too much for that, and while Israel rarely invoked its death penalty for "exceptional and extreme" cases, quick-trigger commandos more than made up the difference with executions of suspects "resisting arrest."

They would have a grim fight on their hands if they came for Jabbar, but he hoped to avoid that. Arnold Napier had scheduled the meeting, providing his personal guarantee of security—whatever that was worth, these days—and Jabbar would trust him, to a point.

As long as he had men and guns behind him for support.

The meeting place was a private home off Namir Road, not

far from the Eretz Israel Museum and Planetarium. Jabbar didn't know who owned the house, nor did he care. Presumably it was one of Napier's subordinates, grown rich from the trade in black gold. Valets were waiting to take the cars as Jabbar and his people got out, a butler of sorts standing by to show them inside.

Arnold Napier met them in the parlor, beaming smiles as he shook Jabbar's hand and ignored the others, leaving his people to offer them food and drink. Jabbar and his chief aide, Salim Zuhayr, trailed Napier down a hallway to a library of sorts, books shelved from floor to ceiling on all sides. "Some wine?" he asked.

"God forbids it," Zuhayr replied.

"Ah. My mistake. Shall we get down to business, then?"

They sat around a glass-topped coffee table, sinking into low-slung chairs with too much padding. Napier wasted no time getting to the point. "You're probably aware that we've had further...incidents...since the Israeli spy escaped your custody."

"The Jew was liberated by commandos," Jabbar said. "And yes, I am aware of other losses. Some of them were mine."

"This afternoon," Napier went on, "a sniper tried to kill my first vice president in downtown Tel Aviv. Two other men were killed. A short time later, gunmen struck at one of our subsidiaries, also in the city. They left four more corpses—and a message. Shall I tell you what it was?"

"Should it concern me?" Jabbar asked.

"Yes, indeed. They said—and I believe I'm quoting, now—they said my deal with Allah's Lance is falling through. You understand the phrase?"

"It means to fail," Jabbar replied.

"That is correct. Which leaves two questions foremost in my mind. The first—how did these strangers know about our business in the first place? And second—why would they suggest that it has failed?"

"I have no answer to the first question," Jabbar answered. "As to the second, Allah's Lance has given you no reason to suspect betrayal."

"None that I'm aware of," Napier said.

Jabbar could feel Salim Zuhayr crane forward in his chair. He raised a hand to stop Zuhayr from saying anything. "There is no reason we should trust each other," he told Napier, "beyond the limits of our common interest. I have no regard for the United States, but I have pledged myself to *you* and your associates, as long as you fulfill your part of our arrangement."

Napier spent a moment staring at Jabbar before he said, "We must determine what these strangers know and how they got their information. While we're on the subject, we already have another problem."

"Oh?"

"They've kidnapped Sterling Holbrook," Napier said. "First thing, he's almost shot, then someone commandeers his limousine and carries him away. It's quite fantastic."

"If it's true," Jabbar replied.

"You think I'm lying?" Napier didn't seem to take offense.

"I think you may be misinformed. Suppose our unknown enemies desired to kill Holbrook. They missed a chance this morning. Why come back and capture him alive, when it would mean less risk to shoot him on the street?"

"You think he's turned?"

Jabbar could only shrug. "Such things are not unknown. It would explain the information leak, at least."

"It would explain a great deal," Napier said, frowning.

"There have been no demands?"

"Not yet."

"Then I suggest we wait," Jabbar replied. "Unless he's dead already, you'll hear something from them soon."

"I'm glad we had this chance to talk," said Napier. "Are you sure you wouldn't like some wine?"

MCCARTER SPENT a full half hour field stripping and cleaning his weapons, killing time while Bolan spoke to Hal Brognola in Washington and reached out to arrange their next move. He had drawn baby-sitting duty with their hostage, making sure Holbrook stayed quiet and serene, waiting for Bolan to return and tell him that the plan was good to go.

And once the wheels were set in motion, there would be no turning back.

They were headed for trouble, he knew, on a scale beyond anything they'd faced so far in this mission, and McCarter had his doubts about the outcome. Still, couldn't turn his back on Bolan—or Rebecca Mindel, for that matter, even though the present spot of bother was her fault. Damned stupid of her, going off and getting picked up by Jabbar's gorillas while she scoured the city for her missing uncle.

Katz.

All this came back to him, in fact, for mucking with the bloody Arabs when he was supposed to be on holiday. As if that wasn't bad enough, he'd paid them back for saving him by skipping out again and trying to even the score on his own. And now their odds of finding him in Tel Aviv—or finding him alive, at any rate—were nil, at least before they settled this unhappy business with his niece and Sterling Holbrook.

They had returned to the safehouse after grilling Holbrook in the desert, for the simple reason that they had nowhere else to keep him. At the moment, he was handcuffed to a bed frame in the smaller of the two bedrooms available. The captive wasn't gagged, but he'd been warned about the penalties for making any noise in an attempt to rouse the neighbors. McCarter had fired a silenced round from his MP-5 into the mattress, an inch or two from Holbrook's thigh, to emphasize how swift and final punishment for any breach of safehouse etiquette could be. It worked, because he'd made no sound since Bolan left the house to make his calls.

McCarter finished reassembling the SMG and fed a freshly

loaded magazine into the receiver, drawing the bolt to chamber a 9 mm Parabellum round. He set the piece for 3-round bursts, then switched on the safety and started on his P-220 pistol. He could've done the job within five minutes, but he stretched it out: no point in rushing until Bolan returned with some word on their next move.

McCarter could almost see it now: a prisoner exchange with the pair of them outnumbered five or ten to one, their opposition waiting for the chance to blaze away and finish them. The hell of it was, that even knowing what the enemy had on his mind, no countermeasures could be planned until they got a look at the terrain.

And that was where the strategy came in.

Napier and his associates were bound to know the city and environs better than Bolan or McCarter, since Global kept offices there and Wasim Jabbar's Palestinians would've scouted countless targets in advance of their guerrilla raids. Bolan could pick a site for the exchange, but would have no decent opportunity to scout it out in depth, including various triangulation exercises, searching for covert approaches on the sewer route, and so forth. They were even limited in their ability to show up early and stake out the place, since Tel Aviv's police would be alert to any sign of Sterling Holbrook on the streets.

McCarter hated flying blind, but he would do what had to be done and make the best of it.

Assuming there was anything to make of it at all.

He wished the other men of Phoenix Force were there to help, but that would only make them more conspicuous. He didn't fancy drawing fire from the police before they even had a chance to meet with Napier's crew and rescue Katz's niece.

Thinking of Mindel drew his mind to thoughts of what she might be suffering, but McCarter nipped it in the bud. He had no room for pity in his reckoning, just now. Not when he faced a struggle to the death against an enemy of unknown strength and capabilities.

He needed to be cold and hard, devoid of sympathy or any

other human weakness when the killing started. He needed to be empty at the point of battle.

Emptiness would make it that much easier to cut down his adversaries without a second thought—and second thoughts could get a soldier killed.

Whatever else went down this night, David McCarter planned on coming out of it alive.

11

The cell phone's number was a closely guarded secret, known to fewer than two dozen friends or close associates in business. Arnold Napier had it set to vibrate, since he loathed the thought of shrill sounds emanating from his person, and he felt it shudder through the satin lining of his tailored jacket, pressed against his chest.

"Excuse me for a moment, won't you?" Napier felt Wasim Jabbar and his companion watching as he took the cell phone from his pocket, opened it and raised it to his ear. He thought the interruption might help put the Palestinians more firmly in their proper place. "Hello?"

"I'm reaching out for Arnold Napier," a deep voice said.

"Speaking."

He didn't recognize the voice, which meant he didn't know the caller. As to what *that* meant, a stranger calling on his private line in Tel Aviv, of all places, Napier could only guess. He felt his pulse quicken, hoping it was the call that he'd been waiting for.

"We have some business to conduct," the caller said.

"I never deal with strangers. Possibly, if we were introduced—"

"What's in a name?"

"I can't help being curious. This number is unlisted," Napier said.

"I got it from your number two."

"How *is* Sterling?"

"He's had a stressful day."

"Ah, well, who hasn't?" Napier kept it casual. He was assisted in the effort by the fact that he cared little whether Sterling Holbrook lived or died.

"He needs your help," the caller said.

"Is this about money?" Half turning, Napier smiled at the two Palestinians. "Because I have to tell you, Global has a strict noransom policy."

"I wasn't thinking money," the stranger said.

"Oh?"

"I understand you recently made contact with a friend of mine."

Napier hadn't survived this long by stepping into traps, or by speaking too freely on the telephone. "With a company this large," he said, "you must understand I don't know everyone around me."

"Something tells me you could find her if you tried."

"A lady, is it?"

"I suspect she's having second thoughts about Global's recruiting pitch."

"It's possible, of course. We try to keep our people happy, but you can't please everyone. Some have a rougher time than others."

"Like your friend Holbrook."

"A case in point," Napier replied.

"Maybe we ought to meet," the caller said. "Exchange thoughts on the subject, so to speak."

"Sounds like a plan. Just let me check my calendar and see—"

"Make it tonight. The expiration date on your pal Sterling's coming up."

"How colorful. Tonight it is. Shall I select the venue," Napier asked, "or do you have a time and place in mind?"

"I'll let you make the call."

"Considerate *and* generous. You're quite a catch. Just let me think." He had a place in mind, but dragged it out. "There's a facility due east of Tel Aviv, about ten miles. It's an experimental treatment plant for, well, I'm sure you'd find the details tedious. Shall we say midnight, for the sake of drama?"

"What about the night shift?" the caller asked.

"They're about to get an unexpected half day off, with pay."

"Midnight," the stranger said.

"Oh, wait! No threats or warnings? You've forgotten to advise me that I shouldn't speak to the authorities."

"I never thought you would," the caller said, and broke the link.

Napier folded his cell phone and returned it to his pocket. "We're in business," he informed Jabbar.

"The kidnappers?"

"They want a prisoner exchange."

"The woman for Holbrook," Zuhayr remarked.

"Unless you're holding someone else we haven't talked about," Napier replied. "We're meeting at the waste disposal plant, midnight."

Salim Zuhayr craned forward in his padded chair. "You cannot let the woman go!" he said. "She is Mossad, our mortal enemy. We can learn much from her."

"You've learned exactly squat so far, from what I understand," Napier retorted. He basked in the heat of Zuhayr's rage for a moment before adding, "You don't need to fret about setting her free, though."

Jabbar caught it first, his full lips twitching into the suggestion of a smile. "You have a plan," he said.

"I always have a plan," Napier assured the ruling lord of Allah's Lance. "There'll be no prisoner exchange tonight, or at any other time."

"A trap, instead?"

"I'm glad to see we're on the same page," Napier said. "I'd like to borrow some of your guerrillas for the evening, just in case our opposition has more men and guns than I suspect."

"Of course," Jabbar replied. "Zuhayr will supervise the operation personally."

Zuhayr blinked at that but said nothing, easing back in his chair as if movement were painful. Napier turned on his best high-wattage smile and said, "That's better still. Perfect, I'd say."

"About your friend—"

"What friend is that?"

"Your Mr. Holbrook," Jabbar said. "He may be placed at risk."

"Oh, him." Napier made a dismissive gesture with one hand. "Don't let it worry you. Vice presidents have always been expendable."

"HARD LUCK, this going out of town," McCarter said, when they were five miles east of Tel Aviv. The city lights still blazed behind him, reddening the night sky, washing out all but the brightest stars.

"Better than fighting in the city, with police around the corner."

"Maybe. We haven't got much hope for a diversion out here in the middle of the desert, though."

"Unless we make our own," the Executioner replied.

"You have something in mind?" McCarter asked.

"Nothing concrete until we've seen the place."

"Some kind of treatment plant, you said?"

"What I was told. We'll need to have a look around."

McCarter locked eyes with their captive in the rearview mirror. "What about you, then?" he asked. "You've seen this place, I reckon."

"I was out here once," Holbrook replied, not sounding pleased about it. "It's experimental. Hasn't turned a profit yet."

"Experimental how?" Bolan asked.

"We take dirty oil and look for ways to clean it up."

"You mean like recycling?" McCarter asked.

"Basically. The thought was, if we could collect used motor oil and purify it inexpensively—"

"Then you could turn around and sell it twice," McCarter said.

"Why stop at twice?" Bolan suggested.

"Anyway," Holbrook said, "we've found ways to clean the oil, but so far nothing cheap enough to turn a decent profit. I suspect the plant was more a make-work project for Israelis than anything else, to curry favor with the government."

"While you and Napier work behind the scenes to knock them off," McCarter said. "That's pretty slick."

"It wasn't *my* idea," Holbrook protested.

"But you went along to keep those nice, fat paychecks rolling in," Bolan said. "Not to mention stock options."

"Hey, I'm a businessman, all right? Sue me."

"Tonight, you're bait," McCarter said.

That silenced Holbrook, which was an improvement from McCarter's point of view. The man had added little to their concrete knowledge of the killing ground, and hearing from him grated on McCarter's nerves.

"How far?" Bolan asked, when they'd driven for a few more silent moments.

"Just about five miles, if Napier had the distance right."

"A plant like that, we ought to have some warning," Bolan said.

"I'll kill the lights and start to look for side roads when we're two miles short," McCarter said. There was a risk in driving dark along the open highway, even with a moon three nights past full to light the way. The good news was that he could spot headlights when they were far enough away, approaching from the front or rear, to switch on his own lights or veer off the road and thus avoid a confrontation with police or soldiers on routine patrol.

The last thing that McCarter wanted now was to attract attention from a pack of uniforms. He knew Bolan's unwritten policy about not firing on lawmen, and while McCarter didn't share his comrade's squeamishness in that regard across the board, he knew that any sort of contact with authorities would blow their meet with Napier and their only chance to free Rebecca Mindel.

Which assumed, of course, that she was still alive.

McCarter, for his part, wouldn't have bet a week's pay on the odds of her survival, but he could be wrong. Napier and company might want their bait alive and kicking for the showdown they had engineered, but it was far from guaranteed. Once he and Bolan made their way into the kill zone, Mindel's health would be superfluous to their opponents. She should've served her purpose by that time, transformed from an asset into a liability.

McCarter wished he knew how many guns would be arrayed against them. Long odds were all right, but apprehension worked on nerves and jeopardized his concentration. The advantage of surprise was often critical in combat, and McCarter wasn't sure what they could do in terms of balancing the scales. He wouldn't know, in fact, until they reached the battleground and studied it.

The dashboard clock showed him that it was nearly half-past eight—call it three and a half hours before their scheduled meeting with the enemy. Would Arnold Napier come in person for the confrontation? McCarter hoped so, but he wasn't counting on it. Men like Napier lived by delegating authority and by letting others take the blame for failure, when it came. So far, he couldn't even guarantee that Mindel would be present for the party they were throwing in her honor.

"Time," he said, with one last glance at the odometer, and switched off the headlights.

REBECCA MINDEL'S clothing had been shredded, more or less, after her ill-conceived attempt to blind Ferran Khalid. The clothes her captors laid before her now consisted of a denim shirt and jeans, a pair of black men's stockings and the shoes she'd worn when she was captured. They provided nothing in the way of underwear, and stood around her smirking as one of the goons unlocked her handcuffs, then produced a knife and slit the tape that bound her ankles to the wooden chair's front legs.

"Get dressed," one of the men commanded. Even with her left eye swollen nearly shut, Mindel recognized Salim Zuhayr at a glance.

"Where are you taking me?" she asked.

"No questions!" Zuhayr's voice was tense, more from anxiety than anger, if Mindel was any judge.

She took her time dressing, ignoring her audience, trying not to grimace as rough denim aggravated her various wounds. The shirt showed blood spots, front and back, before she had it fully buttoned. When she sat again, to put on the socks and tie her shoes, the jeans chafed painfully at cuts and burns.

When she was finished, Mindel stood, pleased that she didn't stagger from the effort or the pain. She offered no resistance when her hands were cuffed behind her back once more. Surrounded, with a gunman clinging to her arms on either side, Mindel retraced her steps from earlier that day, along the corridor and back outside, where she found four sedans lined up and waiting. Zuhayr grabbed her roughly and drew Mindel toward the sec-

ond car in line. One of his flunkies opened the left-rear door and
Zuhayr pushed her inside, following close behind her, while a
gunman squeezed in on the right. Two others sat in front, while
thirteen more—she'd counted them painstakingly—were packed
into the three remaining vehicles.

It was too many for an execution party, she decided, but the
thought brought Mindel no relief. Where were they taking her,
and why? It was a point of honor not to ask, and she was relatively certain that Zuhayr wouldn't have told her anyway. She felt
relief at being spared further interrogation for the moment, but
she feared it was a temporary respite, and that her abductors
might have something worse in store for her upon arrival at their
unknown destination.

Mindel considered her options and came up with nothing to
encourage her. Unarmed, without the use of her hands, the best
she could do was start kicking Zuhayr and the gunmen around
her, but to what effect? Weakened as she was, surrounded in a
moving vehicle, even if she managed to disable all four of them,
she would only succeed in crashing or stalling the car, where-
upon the rest of the team would rush in to assist their comrades.
By contrast, if she waited to see where they were going, she
might find an opportunity to run—but where? To what end?

On the best day of her life, Mindel could never have outrun
a bullet.

She was trapped, as surely as if they had left her taped and
handcuffed to the straight-backed chair.

She thought of Blanski and McCarter, then of her uncle. What
could any of them do to help her now? Her companions might
know she was missing, as opposed to simply searching Tel Aviv
for her uncle, but they couldn't know she had been captured
without tapping sources inside Allah's Lance. As for her uncle,
bent on personal revenge, it seemed impossible that he could
know about her plight.

So much for wishful thinking, then. She couldn't count on any
outside help, and there was precious little prospect of escaping
on her own. At least she hadn't spilled her guts and jeopardized
the others or revealed the secrets of her craft to Khalid's tortur-

ers. It had been tempting, and Mindel had no doubt she'd have broken down eventually, but she took grim pride in her resistance.

Failing to escape, she thought, at least a new location might provide some opportunity to end her life and cheat the bastards out of any further sport. If that turned out to be her only exit from the nightmare of the past few hours, so be it.

She could handle that.

In fact, right now, it sounded like a fine idea.

THE ADDRESS he'd obtained from Gamal Girgis led Katz to a house on Tel Aviv's northern outskirts. It stood apart from neighbors in a quarter where every fourth or fifth house was abandoned or listed for sale—not a slum, so much as a kind of urban no-man's-land it seemed. Katz parked his stolen car at the rear of a vacant house three doors from his target, taking all his weapons with him as he moved through the shadows.

If he could catch Wasim Jabbar and take him down, it just might be enough. Not perfect—not a resolution of the terrorist's alliance with Global Petroleum—but at least a wrench tossed in the works.

And if he didn't find Jabbar, then what?

Try again.

Katz came at the house from behind, clutching his Beretta assault rifle, ready to fire one-handed at the first sign of a threat. He'd seen one car parked in front of the house on his first pass, a dim light burning within, but he couldn't interpret the signs without going inside.

There was an awkward moment at the back door, when he had to let go of his rifle to try the doorknob. Katz was startled when it turned, bracing himself for the clamor of an alarm, but there was no sound as he pushed the door open on well-oiled hinges, revealing a modern if sparsely furnished kitchen. Tightening his grip on the shoulder-slung rifle, Katz pushed the door shut with his right elbow, moving deeper into the house.

Light emanated from a bedroom to his left, as Katz emerged from the kitchen. It was dim light, on the order of a shaded bedside lamp. The bedroom door was open, nothing to obstruct his progress as he passed by other rooms, doors closed, trailing a murmur of voices.

From the threshold, Katz saw a young Arab stretched out on the bed, lying on his back, arms raised and crossed behind his head. The youth was naked to the waist, the sheets covering his lower body not so much draped as mounded above him, revealing in outline the form of his partner, head bobbing in the midst of undercover work that had put a wide smile on the young Arab's face.

Katz spoiled the party when he said, in Arabic, "It's time to rise and shine."

Beneath the sheets, the second figure froze, then cautiously revealed itself. The second face Katz saw was thin, dark, bearded. He couldn't tell if the young men were more appalled at being caught in flagrante delicto or at having an armed stranger surprise them in Jabbar's safehouse.

"Such goings on," Katz said, keeping them covered as he stepped into the bedroom. "What would Allah say?"

The clean-shaven youth was first to find his voice. "What does a Jew know of the one true god?" he challenged.

"More than you," Katz said. "I've known Him longer, and unless our holy books are both mistaken, you two are in trouble."

"What do you want?" the smooth-faced youth demanded.

"Just your boss. Give me Wasim and you can go back to your little games."

Katz hadn't meant it as a provocation, necessarily, but his words galvanized the youth on top. Forgetting his embarrassment, he lunged across his partner's naked body toward the nightstand, where a pistol lay beside the room's one lamp.

It was a bold attempt, but still too little and too late. Katz barely had to aim, trusting his muscle memory from countless practice sessions, skirmishes, pitched battles. Squeezing off two rounds in semiauto mode, he saw the first shot strike his man between the shoulder blades, an inch left of the spine, before round two drilled the back of the young Arab's skull. Impact propelled him off the bed, slamming his face into a corner of the nightstand, smearing it with blood before he slithered to the floor.

"It's just the two of us," Katz told the gaping survivor. "Shall we talk, or are you in a rush to join your little friend?"

"Wasim! You want Wasim?"

"I do."

"He's gone," the young man said. "He took the others with him, to exchange the woman for another prisoner."

A faint alarm bell started clanging in the back of Katz's mind. "What woman?" he demanded.

"From Mossad. I wasn't told her name."

A sick feeling had settled in the pit of Katz's stomach. "But you saw her, yes?"

"I did."

"A woman in her early thirties, dark hair cut to shoulder length, without much makeup on her face. Five-six or seven and perhaps 130 pounds?"

"You know her, then?" the Arab asked.

"One final answer for your life," Katz said, moving a long step closer to the bed. "Where and when is this trade supposed to take place?"

"Midnight," the young man told him. He went on to give directions: ten miles east of town, some kind of factory or plant he'd never seen.

"You've told the truth?" Katz asked. "That's all you know?"

"I swear!"

"Then go to Allah," Katz replied, and shot him once between the eyes.

He left the death house running, back through silent darkened yards to reach his car. Squealing away, Katz prayed that no police would try to intercept him.

He was late already, and he had to beat the clock.

"YOU NEEDN'T THINK your friends can help you," Salim Zuhayr stated. He felt the woman watching him, but she couldn't respond. His men had gagged her, on his order, slapping a piece of duct tape on her lower face. "They won't live long enough to set you free."

Zuhayr felt strong and confident. It was an honor that Jabbar had trusted him to spring the trap without supervision. Zuhayr had also considered the alternative explanation—namely, that

Wasim preferred not to risk his own life in such fashion, but rejected it because it hurt his ego.

And because it troubled him.

Beneath the confidence, Zuhayr was conscious that he still had no idea how many adversaries might be coming to the prisoner exchange. He didn't know how many were involved in the raid on their Syrian compound or the different strikes around Tel Aviv. The uncertainty rankled, threatening to spoil his moment, prompting Zuhayr to taunt his captive as a form of compensation.

"First a one-armed grandfather, and now a woman," he said, sneering. "Is Mossad so desperate for agents these days?"

The woman's eyes narrowed in anger, and Zuhayr had no doubt that she'd have rushed him if she weren't handcuffed to a standing pipe. The baggy denim men's clothes were incongruous, and they couldn't erase the image in his mind of how the woman looked, naked and bound, when he'd first seen her. Given time and opportunity, Zuhayr might've enjoyed interrogating her himself, but now he wouldn't have the chance.

He had a job to do. Wasim was counting on him.

Zuhayr glanced at his watch and frowned. Nine-thirty. There was ample time for him to tour the plant, make sure his men were all in place, prepared to spring the trap. The woman wasn't strong enough to bend or break the cuffs, and there was nothing within reach that she could use to pick the locks.

Still...

"Tarik!"

At his call, a young man armed with a Kalashnikov assault rifle came running, snapping to a fair approximation of attention as he stood before Zuhayr. "Yes, sir?"

"Stay here and watch the woman while I check the others. She's secure for now, but stay beyond her reach, no matter what she says or does. You understand?"

"Yes, sir!"

"If by some chance the handcuffs fail, shoot her immediately in the legs. You hear me, Tarik? In the legs only."

"Yes, sir."

"If she dies on your watch, you die."

The young man blinked at that but offered no protest. Like all members of Allah's Lance, he was accustomed to swift, harsh discipline.

Zuhayr felt better when he'd put distance between himself and the Israeli agent. There was something in her eyes that troubled him, as beaten down and helpless as she was. Something that told Zuhayr she'd gladly rip his throat out with her teeth, if given half a chance.

Zuhayr took his time patrolling the waste-oil treatment plant. In addition to his eight remaining gunmen, there were half a dozen mercenary types supplied by Arnold Napier. Zuhayr wasn't surprised to find that a multinational corporation like Global Petroleum had killers on its payroll; indeed, he would've been amazed if it hadn't. In his experience, all giant companies were killers, in one fashion or another. Some worked peasants to death in sweat factories for a bare subsistence wage; others leveled rain forests, sending commando teams ahead of the bull-dozers to rout or slaughter native tribes; the worst poured deadly toxins into the air, soil and water, threatening all of mankind.

Salim Zuhayr was generally oblivious to such matters, believing as he did that he was marked for early death as a crusader for God, but he amused himself from time to time by noting the hypocrisy of wealthy, influential men. Their lies and double-dealing reinforced Zuhayr's own sense of righteousness and sanctified his war against Israel.

Making his rounds, checking each rifleman in turn and making sure the gunners understood their tasks, Zuhayr convinced himself that this time, failure was impossible.

He would succeed, because the grim alternative was death.

BOLAN CROUCHED in shadow, waiting for the Palestinian on foot patrol to pass by. He remained motionless as the man slipped from view, letting the sound of boot heels crunching gravel fade with distance. Only then, when he was sure he had the darkness to himself, did Bolan make another move.

He'd come this far without encountering resistance, but he knew the enemy was here, staked out and waiting for a target to reveal itself. He didn't have a head count yet and couldn't guess the enemy's standing order—whether they'd been told to kill on sight or wait for a prearranged signal—but Bolan hadn't lived this long by following an adversary's rules of play. The other side might call the game, but Bolan made up the rules as he went along.

Like now.

McCarter waited in the darkness, some three-quarters of a mile beyond the open front gate of the Global waste-oil treatment plant. On Bolan's signal, he would deliver their hostage for the exchange, but not in the way their opponents had planned. Whatever happened after that would be determined by some incalculable formula that factored planning, skill, blind luck and fate.

Before that happened, though, Bolan still had some work to do, preparing for the meet. He edged forward, moving between two massive waste-oil tanks until he could lean out and track the mobile sentry on his rounds. It wasn't difficult, because the man had no idea that he was being watched. He moved with confidence as he circled the compound, stopping at first one point, then another and another, on around the circuit.

Checking in with soldiers, right.

Bolan counted the stops, noting where his mark ducked inside a shed or outbuilding, where he climbed ladders or stood waving from the ground to snipers perched on scaffolding and catwalks overhead. Eleven times he stopped, while Bolan watched, before returning to a kind of blockhouse on the west side of the compound. Bolan timed it, guessing that the captain of the guard had likely checked on two or three more gunmen, at the very least, before Bolan had marked his progress. Call it fifteen shooters, to be on the safe side, and there could be more inside the blockhouse with their leader.

With Rebecca Mindel.

He could think of nowhere else the woman might be hidden—if, in fact, she was alive and present for the prisoner exchange. It would be difficult, but not impossible, to run the game without her. Napier's men could use a stand-in but it seemed unlikely, in the circumstances. They would probably go through the motions of exchanging hostages in earnest, then attack when they were satisfied all targets had been counted, marked and zeroed in.

Bolan, meanwhile, was marking targets of his own. He couldn't take them all from his position on the south side of the compound, but two were positioned within range of his silenced MP-5, at least four others reachable with the Galil sniper rifle Bolan carried slung across his back. When the killing started, the soldier would be ready with a few surprises of his own for those who thought they'd laid the perfect trap.

When the killing started.

Twelve minutes and counting, by Bolan's watch. The posted snipers would be waiting, watching for their targets on the road that served the plant, and Bolan didn't plan on disappointing them. He would deliver Sterling Holbrook as agreed, though not exactly as the watchers might expect.

He made one last scan of the compound, noting subtle movement from a couple of the shooters, thankful that they weren't accustomed to long waits before a kill. Patience and stillness were a sniper's primary virtues. Without ample helpings of both, he lived on borrowed time and survived by pure dumb luck.

And Bolan's enemies were running out of luck.

He palmed the cell phone, keyed McCarter's number on speed dial and heard his comrade's voice midway through the first ring. "Ready," McCarter said.

"Roger," Bolan replied. "Let's rock."

12

"Let's roll," McCarter said, grinning fiercely in the darkness. He was crouched behind the driver's seat, the muzzle of his silent SMG pressed to the back of Sterling Holbrook's skull.

"You mean, in there?" Holbrook asked.

"And why not? Your friends are waiting for you."

"Where will you be?" Holbrook asked him.

"Never far away," McCarter said. "Don't fret yourself on that score."

"But—"

"Move out! We're wasting time."

With obvious reluctance, Holbrook twisted the ignition key and put the car in gear. He almost stalled it, lifting off the clutch too quickly, but he saved it and the car began to roll.

"Bad form," McCarter said.

"I don't do lots of driving," Holbrook said, a tremor in his voice.

They were two hundred yards from the plant's open gates when McCarter said, "Turn on the headlights."

Holbrook fumbled at the dashboard for a moment, cursing under his breath, then found the switch and pressed it. Sudden beams of light carved tunnels through the desert darkness, lighting up the plant's tall chain-link fence with curls of razor wire on top. A few lights burned inside the compound, but not many. It was clear Napier had shut down the place for the night, to let them have some privacy.

"Faster!" McCarter said.

"All right!"

"You want to see your mates again, you shouldn't dawdle."

Holbrook snorted, a bitter sound. "You think I have friends here?"

"That's what we're going to find out."

"Okay, then. You want speed, I'll give you speed."

The shift was smoother this time, coming up to third from second. McCarter's left hand found the inside handle of the door beside him and he flicked a glance in that direction, double-checking to make sure he hadn't locked it by mistake. He didn't fancy dying like some juvenile delinquent in a James Dean movie, fumbling with his door latch in the final seconds of a chicken run.

"Where do I stop?" Holbrook called back to him, his voice whipped by wind streaming through the open windows.

"Anywhere you like, inside the wire," McCarter said. "You'll want to let them know it's you, though, just in case they're feeling trigger-happy."

Holbrook glanced back at McCarter from the rearview mirror, then pressed one hand down on the button to sound the car's horn. They were still fifty yards from the gate, but he wanted insurance. At forty yards he found the high-beam switch and started flashing the headlights, making doubly sure the welcoming committee couldn't miss him.

Up ahead, McCarter glimpsed three figures crossing open ground, inside the fence. They seemed to be emerging from a kind of blockhouse, set off center to the left or north side of the open gates. McCarter thought one of them was a woman, but he couldn't swear to it.

At thirty yards, Holbrook was craning out the open window on his side, shouting, "It's me! Don't shoot! I'm Sterling Holbrook! Hold your fire!"

Good luck, McCarter thought, tightening his grip on the door handle as they sped toward the gate. Any second now, as soon as they crossed that invisible line...

McCarter threw himself from the car just as Holbrook began to decelerate. They were still doing fifty or better, and the shock of impact jarred him, even when he tucked and rolled the way he'd learned in jump school, with the SAS. Still rolling when the gunfire started, he didn't hear any rounds snapping close by as he sprang to his feet and ran for the cover of the nearest building.

Behind him, the car was taking hits and he could hear Holbrook screaming in vain for a cease-fire. Above McCarter, on a catwalk overhead, an automatic weapon suddenly cut loose in his direction, bullets kicking up dust as he raced for cover. The Briton returned fire without aiming, a short burst from his MP-5 that sent Parabellum rounds clattering around on metal stairs and railings. Someone cursed up there, in English, but the firing cut off long enough for McCarter to find cover.

He was inside the compound.

Now the trick would be to stay alive.

SALIM ZUHAYR RETREATED toward the plant's blockhouse office complex, dragging the handcuffed Israeli agent behind her. She struggled, but weakly, and he had Tarik to prod her with his rifle if she faltered in her stride. Between them, they could handle one woman.

As for the rest...

Zuhayr wasn't concerned with Sterling Holbrook, dead now in the bullet-riddled car as it continued taking hits. The American's death had been approved at the highest levels, a "sacrifice" on behalf of the cause. In fact, it delighted Zuhayr to see Holbrook slumped in the driver's seat, head thrown back as bullets pummeled his limp form. The Arab's one regret was that he hadn't joined in the chorus of firing that snuffed out the oilman's last spark of despicable life.

At the moment, though, he had other concerns, such as counting the guns ranged against him and wiping out the faceless men who wielded them, before he suffered any further losses.

One enemy, at least, had made his way inside the plant. Zuhayr had seen him leap from the moving car as it passed through the gates, leaving Holbrook to die alone. It was a clever move, and Napier's gunman on the catwalk nearest to the enemy had thus far failed to bring him down.

They stumbled into cover, the Israeli woman ramming Zuhayr with one shoulder as if by accident, glaring at him with her battered face as Tarik yanked her back and away. Zuhayr considered killing her at once, had thumbed the hammer on his pistol back to fire, when caution stayed his hand.

The bitch might still be useful if the battle somehow turned against him. He couldn't conceive that happening, but recent days had taught Zuhayr that anything was possible.

"Be careful," he advised her, speaking through clenched teeth. "I won't need you much longer."

"But you need me now," she answered back defiantly.

He struck her with an open hand, jolting her backward. Tarik caught her by one arm to hold her upright. "I need you alive," Zuhayr reminded her, "but your kneecaps are expendable."

It pleased Zuhayr to see her cringe as he raised the pistol knee-high, pretending to sight down the slide. An explosion outside wiped the smile from his face as he turned on Tarik. "Bring her! Any more resistance, shoot her in the legs."

"Yes, sir!" Tarik's eyes brightened at the prospect.

Zuhayr led the way deeper inside the warren of tiny offices, plucking a compact two-way radio from his belt as he went. Thumbing down the red transmitter button, he barked into the mouthpiece, "Status report! All stations!"

The radio hissed static at him for a moment, before the first answer came back. "I'm busy here, dammit!" an American voice rasped from the receiver—one of Napier's men, punctuating his rude comment with a burst of automatic fire.

Of the sixteen snipers he had deployed, three others answered Zuhayr on command, all Palestinians. From the volume of fire still audible outside, he knew there were more than four shooters alive, but he couldn't guess how many unless he obtained full reports.

Seething, Zuhayr keyed the transmitter again, snarling, "Report at once!"

The response came this time from another American. "Fuck off, will you? Or grab a piece and join the fucking party!"

Tempted to fling his radio across the room, Zuhayr restrained himself, remembering that he might need it later. Instead, he turned his wrath on Tarik, startling the young Palestinian.

"Take this one back and cuff her to the pipes again," he said, "then join me in the compound. Remember what I said if she resists."

"Kneecaps," Tarik replied, turning to leave.

"Wait, there!" Zuhayr approached Tarik, holding his pistol out, butt-first. "Give me your rifle. This is all you'll need to deal with her."

Tarik knew better than to hesitate. He gave Zuhayr his folding-stock Kalashnikov and took the pistol in return. Scowling, he turned and shoved the woman in front of him, down the short hall to the utility room with its stout standing pipes.

Zuhayr stared after them for a moment, then turned and retraced his steps toward the front of the building. It was time he joined the battle and discovered what was happening. With any luck, he might be privileged to meet one of his enemies and cut the bastard down.

A little blood, he thought, would do a great deal to improve his mood.

BOLAN WAS LINING UP a target when a hot round sparked the fuel cascading from a ruptured tank and set the car on fire, with Sterling Holbrook slumped behind the wheel. He was stone-dead already, wouldn't feel a thing, and Bolan didn't spare the guy a second thought. As much as anyone, he could've pulled the plug or blown a whistle when the deal was made between Global and Allah's Lance, but he'd preferred to ride the gravy train—and they'd been known to crash from time to time.

Like now.

Ashes to ashes, right.

His first mark was a huddled shadow in the Galil Sniper's six-power field of vision, but sometimes a shadow was enough. Bolan made the acquisition, stroked the rifle's trigger once and watched his adversary topple from the catwalk, half a clumsy somersault completed prior to impact with the earth.

By the time number one hit the ground, Bolan had already fixed his crosshairs on another target, this one sheltered in the recessed doorway of what seemed to be a common lavatory. Working from the shooter's muzzle-flash, Bolan picked out his profile, dropped his sights six inches to the point where neck and shoulders met and sent another round hurtling downrange at 2,650 feet per second.

The projectile was a military round, full-metal jacket, and it drilled the sniper's neck in something like a microsecond, shearing through the jugular and the carotid artery before it clipped his spine and dropped him like a puppet with its strings cut, helpless to resist the pull of gravity. If not an instant kill, it was the next best thing. The shooter would bleed out within two minutes, three at the outside, and in the meantime he was paralyzed.

A sudden burst of firing on his flank brought Bolan's head around in time to see McCarter dueling with a catwalk gunner near two standing oil tanks, on the north side of the compound. Bolan left the Phoenix Force warrior to it, swinging back to bring his third mark under fire—only to find the man was gone.

It wasn't unusual for snipers to shift positions in the middle of a firefight; in fact, it was routine. As targets moved about a battlefield, shooters sought to improve their fields of fire without undue exposure to the enemy.

He shrugged it off and shifted to acquire his fourth target, but that shooter was missing, too. Before the first alarm bell had a chance to sound in Bolan's mind, he registered a muzzle-flash in his peripheral vision and a bullet scored the cinder block beside his face, stinging his ear and scalp with shards of concrete.

Bolan recoiled, slinging the sniper rifle and unlimbering his SMG. A burst of automatic fire followed that first probing round, but he had found cover now, the slugs rattling harmlessly past overhead. He didn't waste time cursing luck or fate for letting his opponents spot him. They were obviously trained professionals, but were they good enough to match the Executioner?

Time to find out.

A rush of footsteps told him that the enemy was coming. Bolan waited, dropping from a crouch to belly-down on rough pavement. It would require only a shove with boots and elbows to reveal himself and face his adversary.

Now!

He cleared the corner, angling with the MP-5, in time to see two gunners charging toward him, armed with folding-stock Kalashnikovs and firing as they came.

YAKOV KATZENELENBOGEN heard the sounds of battle from a mile away. It was impossible to miss the gunfire crackling on a clear, cool desert night beneath the moon and stars. He couldn't see the muzzle-flashes yet, but there was enough ambient light for him to switch his headlights off and cover his approach.

Too late, the small voice in his mind chanted. *Too late!*

"I'm *not* too late," he argued with himself, then cracked a rueful smile. If Bolan or the rest of them could see him now, they wouldn't need a doctor's vote to recommend him for a mental disability discharge.

To hell with it.

Whether he reached the battleground in time to help his niece or not, the fight would be ongoing. He could still avenge her and wreak bloody havoc with the bastards who had snatched her in the first place. The same bastards who had caged and tortured him, and who were plotting even now against Israel.

Katz stood on the accelerator, racing toward the plant where something—it appeared to be a car—had just burst into flames. He saw the secondary detonation of its fuel tank, heard the hollow boom of it across the desert flats, and wondered if his friends could feel the heat of that consuming fire.

It's my fault they're here, Katz thought. *My fault Rebecca's here.*

And to that self-reproach, no answer. It was true.

He had a chance to wipe away those debts, if the three of them weren't dead already. Failing that, Katz had an opportunity to mix his blood with theirs and kill as many of the enemy as a one-handed ex-commando could manage, before they cut him down. Wages of sin, he thought—the sin in this case being stubborn pride. And even now, regretting what his hubris might have cost those closest to him in the world, Katz couldn't let it go.

He had a war to fight, and if it was his last one, he could still go out in style.

The compound's gates were standing open. Katz drove through them, cranking hard left on the steering wheel as automatic weapons found the range and started peppering his vehicle. The windshield shattered first, spilling its pebbled safety glass into his lap. Unable to return fire while his one hand gripped the steering wheel, Katz cursed his enemies and gunned the car across a stretch of open ground, swerving at last behind a massive storage tank.

He hit the brakes and bailed out, pausing long enough to goose the accelerator one last time when he was clear. The car rolled on, a moving target as it cleared the north side of the storage tank and started taking hits again. Katz didn't know how long it would deceive his enemies, but he wasted no time in doubling back to search for targets of his own.

Careful, he thought. It wouldn't do for him to fire on muzzle-flashes randomly, with Bolan and McCarter somewhere in the middle of the fight. They wouldn't know he had arrived to join them, and Katz knew full well the dangers posed by friendly fire. He hadn't come this far to shoot his friends, or have them shoot him in return.

Katz was rounding the south side of the storage tank when he heard a new outbreak of firing behind him, coupled with the sound of bullets striking metal. More hits on the car, telling the warrior that his short-term ruse had been successful. By the time they realized that there was no one in the car, he should be—

The other man was there before Katz knew it or had time to raise his weapon. They collided, both men staggered by the impact, reeling back a pace or two from each other.

"Shit!" The taller man swiped at his bloody nose, where Katz's forehead had connected. Recognition—or, to be precise, a *lack* of recognition—registered a heartbeat later and he cursed again, raising the Colt Commando carbine into target acquisition.

Katz was quicker, squeezing off a burst from his Beretta autorifle at a range so short he literally didn't need to aim. The 5.56 mm rounds tore through the gunman's chest and put him down without a whimper, thrashing briefly on the deck before his life ran out through ragged exit wounds.

Katz took another moment to compose himself, then went to find his niece.

To find the war.

REBECCA MINDEL STRAINED against the handcuffs, trying to be unobtrusive even as the steel drew blood. It wouldn't help, she realized. The cuffs were too damned tight for any kind of lubricant to make a difference. Without a key...

She eyed the young Arab who'd been left to guard her in Zuhayr's absence and found him standing with his back turned to her, watching the door and the hallway beyond. He flinched at each new sound of gunfire from the outer compound, clutching his pistol so tightly that his knuckles blanched.

The handcuff key was in his left-rear pocket, where Mindel had seen him put it after he unfastened one cuff and then tethered her to the upright pipe, all the while grinding his handgun into her stomach with bruising force to forestall any resistance. There was a chance that she could take it from him, even now, if she could lure him close enough.

"You don't think he's coming back, do you?" she asked in Arabic.

The young man turned to face her, scowling. He despised her as a Jew and as an agent of Mossad, but Mindel knew she'd hooked him when he asked her, "Who?"

"Salim Zuhayr. Why do you think he left you here and took your weapon?"

"I have this," he said, and held the pistol up for her to see, electing to ignore the first part of her question.

"That won't stop them, Tarik."

He blinked in surprise at her use of his name, forgetting that Zuhayr had summoned him in Mindel's presence. "Won't stop who?" he asked.

"My friends," she said. "They've come for me, and you won't

hold them in this feeble trap. They'll find us here together and they'll kill you, after one good look at me."

"I never struck you!" he protested.

"How will they know that? One look at my face, Tarik. They won't be in a mood to talk, after they've finished with the rest outside. What's one more body in the scheme of things? Zuhayr knows that. He's left you here to die for him."

"Liar!"

"Don't get me wrong," she said, smiling despite the pain of split and swollen lips. "I'm not suggesting you should run away. Wait here and die, by all means. I look forward to it."

"That's all any of you care about," he said, sneering. "Dead Palestinians and stolen land."

"I don't own any land myself," Mindel replied. "As for the other part, I've killed my share of terrorists. Some of your friends, maybe—or family."

It was a risky game she'd chosen, but the only way to bring him within reach that she could think of was to goad him, prod him into striking her. She didn't think he'd shoot her in cold blood, but anything was possible. If she'd misjudged him—or if he came closer and she failed to overpower him—the next few moments might be all the time she had on Earth.

"Jews killed my father," Tarik said.

"I'm not surprised. Was he a part of Allah's Lance?"

"Fatah."

"Worse yet," she said. "It was before my time, of course, but I won't grieve for him. What's one less peasant murderer?"

"You bitch!"

He rushed at her, raising the pistol in his right hand—not to fire, but rather as a bludgeon. Mindel clutched the standing pipe in both hands, braced herself against the coming pain and lashed out with her left foot in a roundhouse kick, as Tarik came in range.

She'd waited long enough to catch him on the right side of his head, behind the ear, and pitch him *forward* with a sharp cry of surprise. The pistol struck her shoulder, then his sweaty face was next to hers and Mindel lunged to bite him, burying her teeth in the side of his neck while her legs scissored up and around him, catching his waist.

It was an ugly parody of sex, the young man's pelvis bucking against hers, arms flailing as she gnawed his throat, shaking her head to open up the wound. His pistol struck her skull a glancing blow but she ignored it, tasting salty blood as he began to squeal.

Another moment. Deeper. Deeper.

Mindel drew back, smeared with blood, recoiling from his fists but clinging tightly with her legs around his waste. If Tarik broke away from her and staggered out of reach to die, she'd never reach the handcuff key. It would be difficult and painful even so, if he fell dead between her thighs—but not impossible.

Blood pumped from Tarik's severed artery with every heartbeat. By the time he understood how badly he was injured, it was too late for the youth to save himself. He struck out blindly at Rebecca, empty-handed now, but he was losing strength too rapidly to do much damage. Finally his legs buckled and he collapsed, his blood-slick face pressed tight against her groin.

She held him for another moment, making sure. When there were no more heartbeats, no more crimson geysers, she began maneuvering his flaccid body, nudging it around until her hand could worm its way inside the left-rear pocket of his denim pants.

The key was there.

As Mindel palmed it, she was conscious of the hot tears streaming down her face, washing the stranger's blood away.

MCCARTER CAUGHT the sniper coming down a flight of metal stairs and shot his legs from under him, a short burst from his submachine gun taking out both of his adversary's knees. The wounded man pitched forward with a yelping cry and slithered down the last ten feet of stairway on his face.

The shooter lost his automatic rifle in the fall, but he was digging for another weapon, reaching underneath his jacket, when McCarter stepped out from beneath the stairs and put a silenced round between his ears. The loser made a little huffing sound and then collapsed, gun hand pinned underneath him by deadweight.

McCarter stepped around him, scooping up the Colt Commando that his enemy had lost when he went down. It was a cut-down version of the classic M-16 A-2 assault rifle, smaller even than the M-4 carbine with its sliding butt and 10-inch barrel. Only six inches longer than McCarter's SMG, the Commando had twice the effective range and greater stopping power with its 5.56 mm tumbling projectiles. He relieved the still-warm corpse of three spare magazines and stuffed them in his pockets, moving on.

McCarter hadn't glimpsed Rebecca Mindel—if in fact it *was* Rebecca—since his first rush toward the compound gates, with Sterling Holbrook in the driver's seat. She'd been dragged away by her captors, but where had they gone? Now that battle was joined, how could he hope to find her?

McCarter tried to get his bearings, starting at the compound's open gate and scanning toward the flaming pile of scrap that was his former vehicle, with Sterling Holbrook roasting at the wheel. He knew the car had swerved a bit before it blew, which meant the blockhouse that he'd seen Rebecca being dragged toward had to be...*there!*

McCarter had his fix, but crossing fifty yards of open ground while automatic weapons swept it clean was something else. He'd have to work his way around that no-man's-land, and even then he'd be under the gun the whole damned way.

Clutching the captured Colt Commando, submachine gun slung across his back, McCarter broke from cover, firing short bursts toward the nearest sniper's nest as he began his grim advance.

THE GUNNERS rushing Bolan had his range, but they were firing high, whether to pin him down or thinking he would meet them standing up, he couldn't say. It made no difference to the end result, as Bolan's MP-5 spewed silenced rounds that cut their legs from under them and brought them tumbling down.

One of the shooters dropped his rifle as he fell, the other clinging tightly to his weapon. Bolan finished off the stubborn gunner first, putting a short burst through his scalp at point-blank range, then tracked across to find the other scrabbling desperately for his Kalashnikov.

Too late.

A 3-round burst put out the fumbling shooter's lights, and Bolan wriggled back around the corner before any others could find the range. In fact, he caught a break, no more immediate incoming fire, and he used the respite to plan his next move.

The key was movement. Bolan couldn't win the fight from where he stood, assuming it was winnable. He couldn't count on any more of Napier's men to seek him out, particularly if they'd seen the last two fall. He'd have to seek them out, and hope McCarter would do likewise in his sector of the compound, whittling down the odds.

Bolan left the Galil slung as he moved out, trusting his SMG to answer any close-range challenges. He was circling behind the blockhouse that sheltered him, trying to flank his next mark, when a bullet-riddled sedan lurched into view, coasting to a halt some forty yards away, behind one of the plant's large storage tanks. He didn't recognize the vehicle, couldn't place it even without the dozens of bullet holes scarring its body and paint job. No occupants were visible, but he supposed they could be huddled down below the windowsills—or dead already, from the way the car was shot to hell. At least two different weapons kept raking the hulk even now, blasting away until its fuel tank sparked, then detonated, drenching the sedan in liquid flame.

Bolan had no idea who might've barged into the game this late, and from the look of it he wasn't likely to find out. X rays and dental charts would be required to ID anyone extracted from that blazing funeral pyre, assuming the authorities were interested enough to try. In any case, the occupants could neither help nor hinder Bolan's mission, so he pushed them out of mind and focused once more on his living enemies.

And one of them was visible above him, to his left, moving along a catwalk bolted to the steel skin of the nearest storage tank. The shooter was reloading a Kalashnikov assault rifle and checking out the car he'd helped destroy, watching it closely, as if he expected some invincible opponent to emerge and shrug off the flames, spoiling for a fight.

Bolan took advantage of the shooter's distraction, squeezing off a burst that staggered his target, then sent him tumbling over the catwalk's waist-high railing. The gunner fell without making a sound prior to impact, striking the gravel with a crunch of breaking bones.

How many left?

Bolan had dealt with five, so far, which left an estimated ten to fifteen shooters spotted here and there around the compound. From the sound of it, most of them were engaged in strafing targets, whether living or imaginary, and he hoped McCarter wasn't pinned down by the storm of automatic fire.

The Executioner forgot about the burning car, his latest kill and concentrated on the next one. In a firefight, self-congratulation was a short step from a body bag. No kill rated high-fives unless it was the last kill, wrapping up the fight.

And Bolan hadn't reached that point. Not yet.

He still had places to go, people to kill—and maybe, if his luck held out, a life to save.

13

Salim Zuhayr hugged the shadows, making his way around the plant by fits and starts. He had gone out to check his men, find out how they were dealing with the enemy, but all he saw was chaos. Several of his guns had fallen silent, and he couldn't tell if the shooters had shifted position or if they'd been knocked out of action by enemy fire. The more he saw, the more Zuhayr was sure of one thing: he was better off behind closed doors and stout brick walls.

But getting back to where he'd started from now proved to be a risky proposition in itself.

Zuhayr had never been accused of cowardice, except by some Israeli journalists, but neither was he one to throw his life away by reckless action. He judged that it was nearly certain death to move across the compound openly, as much at risk from friendly fire as from the guns of enemies he couldn't see.

Where were they? How many had come to save the woman? All this shooting, and he still had no idea what sort of force was ranged against him. He'd glimpsed one man leaping from the first car through the gate, before a storm of fire ripped through it, Sterling Holbrook dead in seconds flat behind the wheel. Zuhayr hoped others had been trapped inside the car, but he couldn't be sure.

And what about the second car that came in shortly after, running with its lights off? He had fired a few rounds into that one himself, for all the good it did. Both cars were disabled and burning now, the invaders on foot, but for all the sound and fury in the compound he still couldn't say how many survived or where they'd gone to ground.

There was virtue in movement, Zuhayr thought, doing something, as opposed to standing still and waiting for the enemy to show himself. If nothing else, he could return to the office block and deal with the woman. She might still serve him as a bargaining chip, if his adversaries wanted her alive. Failing that, he could be rid of her for good, secure in the knowledge that at least one of his enemies was dead.

The plant wasn't designed for stealth, but Zuhayr did his best to avoid being shot on the run. Recessed doorways provided fair cover, but the gaps between buildings were perilous, each one a potential sniper's lair. His destination lay within a hundred yards, but each step of the journey placed Salim Zuhayr at risk. He was reminded of his early training as a teenager, in Syria, when his instructors from Fatah and Black September fired live rounds and sometimes killed the green recruits by accident, while they were crawling underneath fat coils of concertina wire.

Zuhayr had managed to survive those trials and all that followed, when the live rounds had been fired by Zionists, Americans, even the British SAS. He made his mind up to survive this, too, if by sheer will alone.

A stray round hit the wall above Zuhayr's head as he emerged from the alleyway between two buildings. It set him running, ducking and dodging all the way, until he'd covered nearly half the distance to the office block. Zuhayr found shelter for a moment in the common lavatory. He waited while a few more rounds pocked the concrete outside, then risked a cautious glance to see if it was clear. When no one fired on him, Zuhayr emerged and made another dash along the line of buildings, passing through a pall of smoke that drifted from the nearby burning vehicle.

The smell of Sterling Holbrook roasting didn't faze Zuhayr. He'd smelled worse things before—the aftermath of Israeli rocket and artillery attacks on refugee camps, or the reek of death after a bombing that he'd planned and helped to carry out himself.

There was nothing new or surprising in the stench of death.

At last he reached the office block and ducked inside, closing the door behind him. He moved down the hallway toward the rear office, calling Tarik's name, but receiving no answer. In another moment, he knew why.

The bitch was gone. She had escaped somehow and left a corpse behind. Tarik lay huddled on the floor, blood pooled and smeared around him, draining from a raw wound on the right side of his neck. Zuhayr didn't examine it or pause to wonder how the handcuffed prisoner had overpowered him. Instead, he cursed and kicked the limp body, glancing around for his pistol.

It was gone. Of course.

Furious and frightened all at once, Zuhayr set off to track down the woman and finish her before it was too late.

KATZ KNELT beside the body of the second man he'd killed since entering the compound, taking a moment to study the thin, startled face. This one clearly wasn't American, a swarthy son of the desert who'd barely reached his twenties and would never see beyond them now.

Too bad, Katz thought. His enemy had picked the losing side and paid the price, as hundreds—thousands—paid each day, around the world. Katz knew the young man would've called himself a freedom fighter, rather than a terrorist. It made no difference either way, once he was dead.

Katz rose and left the corpse behind. Death held no fascination for him anymore, and precious little poignancy. He hadn't wept for anyone, blood kin included, in more years than he could honestly recall. He wondered now if he had tears saved for Rebecca, should he find her dead.

He'd killed the Arab in a narrow passageway between two carbon-copy buildings. It wasn't an alley in the strict sense, but as dark and claustrophobic in its way as any Katz had seen. It held the scorched-meat smell of bodies burning, mixed with acrid fumes of gasoline. Firelight announced his progress toward the burning car he'd passed on entering the compound, flames retreating now to gnaw on rubber, carpeting and vinyl after the accelerant had burned away.

Less firelight meant less risk as he emerged from hiding, checking every nearby shadow first before he made the move. Guns were still going off in the compound, one almost directly overhead, but Katz couldn't match the muzzle-flashes to their targets. For all he knew, the snipers were dueling with each other—or he might find Bolan and McCarter lying dead, around the next corner.

One way to find out.

Katz kept moving, finger on the trigger of his Beretta assault rifle, its muzzle resting lightly on the stub of his right wrist. Katz missed the mechanical hand he sometimes wore, but there'd been no way to retrieve it from his luggage when he fled the airport, or to replace it afterward. As always in the past, he would get by with what he had.

Or maybe not.

The next doorway he approached was labeled Administration in English and Arabic, with the English on top. That meant offices, perhaps some utility storage, and Katz had just resigned himself to search them when a Palestinian emerged, glancing both ways, then turning left and moving away at a rapid pace.

Katz recognized Salim Zuhayr, second in command of Allah's Lance, and made a judgment on the spot to follow him. He would lose time—and lose his man—if he veered off to search the office building now, and something told Katz that he wouldn't find Rebecca there. Zuhayr should know where she was hidden, though.

Katz dogged the Arab's footsteps like a shadow as he moved across the killing ground.

A SHORT BURST from McCarter's captured rifle ripped across his target's chest and sent the shooter cartwheeling through space, a drop of twenty feet or more between his perch atop the oil tank and the flat, unyielding ground below. That first step was a killer, but the rifleman was dead before he hit the ground and never felt a thing.

McCarter had stopped counting with his fourth kill of the night, since he had no idea how many shooters he was facing anyway. The plant was crawling with them, but he knew their numbers had been whittled down, because the volume of defensive fire had markedly decreased. It seemed to him that barely half as many guns were firing now, as when he rolled in through the compound's gate, but it was premature to count the others out. At least a few of them were dead, he knew, but others could be lying back and waiting for a target to present itself, saving their ammunition for a certain kill.

McCarter also had to pick and choose his targets carefully. He was constrained from using frag grenades, for instance, since he didn't want to set the plant on fire and didn't know where Mindel was concealed. McCarter couldn't even swear that she was still alive, but he would act on that presumption until it was proved otherwise.

And in the meantime, he had snipers to eliminate.

They weren't all clumsy, as McCarter learned when he emerged from cover, looking for another mark. He glimpsed the muzzle-flash, winking from a rooftop to his right, and *felt* more than heard the bullet sizzling past his face. He recoiled, cursing, and doubled back the way he'd come, hoping to flank the sniper and take him by surprise.

It wasn't far, no more than fifty yards, which made McCarter wonder how the rifleman had missed. Excitement, maybe, or a trick of shadow and firelight? What mattered now was that he *had* missed, and McCarter had a second chance.

A door swung open on the back side of a laboratory building as McCarter rounded the corner. It framed a dark face, and McCarter fired into the startled eyes on reflex, spraying the room beyond with blood and brains. He made a hasty check, unwilling to leave shooters at his back, but spotted no one else inside. Dismissing the dead man, he moved on toward the next building in line.

At last he stood behind the boxlike structure, staring at a metal ladder bolted to the wall. For all McCarter knew, the shooter could be waiting for him, lining up the shot to drill him when he showed himself. It was the only way to reach his adversary, though, unless the gunman showed himself.

Scratch that. There was one other way.

McCarter checked the place again. Like all the other buildings he had seen so far, it was constructed of cinder blocks and wouldn't burn unless somebody drenched the walls with gasoline. The flat roof made a decent sniper's perch, and it was probably constructed well enough to soak up part of an explosion without bringing down the house.

Maybe.

McCarter palmed a frag grenade and pulled the pin. He didn't bother estimating where the sniper had been standing when he fired his last shot moments earlier. If he had any brains at all, the shooter would've moved since then, to guard against return fire.

No. McCarter wanted maximum shrapnel dispersal, which meant dropping the grenade as close as possible to dead center. With that in mind, he made some hasty calculations, wished himself luck and let fly with a looping overhand pitch. The green egg wobbled out of sight, still rising when it disappeared, McCarter counting off the seconds in his mind.

He heard a muffled curse and thump of running feet before the blast. A human figure vaulted from the rooftop, trailing smoke behind it, and touched down a dozen yards or so from where McCarter stood. He stood above the shooter, noting that both legs were twisted at peculiar angles and the gunman's empty hands were twitching spastically.

"Do you speak English?" McCarter asked.

"Ye-ye-yes."

"I think your back's broken, maybe your neck. Don't worry, though. With modern medicine, you could go on for years like this."

"Finish it!"

"I'd like to help you, but I'm busy looking for a friend of mine. Maybe you've seen her?"

"Woman?"

"That's a decent guess," McCarter said.

"A-a-administration b-b-block."

McCarter had a rough idea of where that was. "You don't mind waiting here, in case you're wrong and we have need to talk again?"

"I s-s-swear. Last time I saw."

"Okay, then. Fair enough." McCarter put a silenced round between the crippled sniper's eyes and moved off toward the plant's administration building, watching out for shooters as he went.

THE DOOR LABELED Administration stood ajar when Bolan reached it. Ready with his SMG, he toed it farther open, checking out the corridor that stretched away from him, with offices on either side. The building wasn't large, no more than two hundred square feet subdivided into boxlike cubicles, but it was next on his list of places to check for Rebecca Mindel.

The offices were empty, none of them revealing any major disarray. Some of the plant's white-collar workers were tidier than others, but the place didn't have that ravaged and picked-over look so often found in the wake of battle. Bolan passed through quickly, making his way toward the storage space in back and found the dead man there.

He'd been a Palestinian, early twenties if that, and he'd died badly, thrashing about in blood that spilled from a ragged neck wound. Make that a *bite* wound, from the look of it, and Bolan had to think about that for a moment, scanning the storage room for further clues, until he saw the discarded handcuffs.

It began to make sense then, in a savage kind of way. A prisoner—presumably Mindel—had managed to escape after disabling her keeper by the only means available. Bolan couldn't begin to guess how she'd gotten him within striking range, the sequence of events unreadable, but bloody footprints of a woman's size led from the slaughterhouse, back toward the doorway he'd just entered.

Gone, he thought. But where?

The dead man had no weapon; Mindel would've taken it along for self-protection. As to where she'd gone, he didn't have a clue, but it meant further searching through the plant until he had exhausted every possibility.

Or until Bolan found her dead.

Escaping from her cell wasn't the same thing as escaping from the compound. Every opposition gunner still alive would likely know her face and do his level best to bring her down on sight. Napier and his confederates had clearly never meant to let her go. Their ruthless sacrifice of Sterling Holbrook proved that point beyond the shadow of a doubt.

He made a final scan and saw more crimson footprints, closer to the exit. Someone else—a man—had come in after the blood-letting and surveyed the scene, his footsteps smearing Mindel's, picking up blood from her tracks in a waffle pattern character-istic of certain boot soles, taking it back toward the door and the hallway beyond.

Another watcher, then. Perhaps sent to relieve the dead man, or simply checking in to confirm the hostage was secure. A su-perior, in all likelihood. He'd viewed the carnage and retreated, seeing there was no more to be done.

Seeking the woman, right.

Bolan followed those smeared and fading footprints back to-ward the exit, emerging into smoky darkness and the sound of scattered gunfire. Some of the compound's defenders, at least, were still holding their own.

Too late, he heard the subtle movement on his left and spun to meet it, staring down the muzzle of a submachine gun pointed at his face.

"You beat me to it," McCarter said. "Where's our damsel in distress?"

"She took a hike," Bolan replied, "with someone on her tail."

"You're off to find her, then?"

"It crossed my mind."

"Right. I guess I'll tag along."

REBECCA MINDEL DIDN'T know where she was going at the mo-ment, but she would've ranked her odds of getting there alive at slim to none. She was the only woman in the compound, thus more obvious to hostile shooters even from a distance, and she didn't have a clue where she could hide, even if she escaped the plant.

The desert offered refuge, and she might try walking back to Tel Aviv, but she'd be no match for her adversaries if they tried to hunt her down. Now that she had a chance to move about, her in-juries were making themselves known, and while she hadn't been disabled, neither was she up to par. Even on her best day, Mindel was willing to admit that Salim Zuhayr's guerrillas were better trained in desert tracking and evasion—skills that weren't greatly valued when Mossad trained agents to conduct its secret war.

And how would she get out?

They'd come in cars, but where were the vehicles now? The only car she'd seen since her escape had been a smoking hulk abandoned near the compound's gate, which did her no damned good at all.

Where were the rest?

She hesitated in the space between two buildings, breathing through her open mouth to minimize the irritation and the risk of sneezing caused by smoky air and gasoline fumes. Gunfire echoed around the plant, but there were fewer weapons now than when Zuhayr had dragged her out to meet her would-be rescuers. The shooting gave her hope, encouraging Mindel to think that Blanski and McCarter were alive, although she knew that it proved no such thing.

The cars. Focus!

She'd come from the west side of the plant and had seen nothing there, although she'd failed to check behind the tanks and buildings. For the moment, she decided to keep moving eastward, then correct her oversight if she survived to reach the easternmost perimeter. If she could find a vehicle and get it started, Mindel thought she'd have a fighting chance. On foot...

She wasted no time thinking of that long run through the desert, hunted like an animal by men with automatic weapons. Slipping out of cover, Mindel moved as quietly and quickly as she could across the drab, dark fronts of buildings laid out in a row facing the fence, almost as if the plant had been a model or a movie set. Most of the gunfire seemed to emanate from roofs and catwalks overhead, the snipers picking high ground for a better sweep—but where were their targets?

The thought had barely taken form when Mindel saw a man emerging from a doorway just in front of her, no more than ten or fifteen feet away. She knew immediately that he was a Palestinian, and thus one of her enemies. She offered up a silent prayer that he would miss her, turn the other way and go about his business, but the heavens turned a deaf ear to her plea. The young man saw her, blinked and then began to raise his automatic rifle.

Mindel shot him in the chest, then once more as he toppled over backward, to be certain he was dead or dying. Making an advantage of misfortune, she bent down to seize the dead man's weapon, only then aware of footsteps closing from behind her.

Mindel tried to turn and fire, the pistol cocked and ready in her hand, but it was already too late. A gun barrel whipped down, across her skull, and she collapsed atop the young man she had slain.

KATZ SAW IT ALL. He was too far behind Salim Zuhayr to intervene, the angle wrong for firing at the Arab without risk of bullets flying past or through him to strike Rebecca. Neither could he call a warning to her as she faced the younger gunman, for fear of distracting her and spoiling her aim, perhaps causing her death. The moment she bent to claim the dead man's rifle, Zuhayr rushing forward and swinging his own like a bludgeon, Katz swallowed his outcry and rushed in to help.

Too late.

Zuhayr heard him coming, glanced back and cut loose with a wild burst of automatic fire before Katz could use his own weapon. Without an alley or a doorway to conceal him, Katz did the next best thing, dropping prone on the pavement, grunting with the impact, angling his Beretta for a killing shot.

Again, Zuhayr was faster, squeezing off another burst that rattled overhead, inches from lethal impact, forcing Katz to kiss the sidewalk. He returned fire automatically, firing high to spare Rebecca, knowing even as he pulled the trigger that it was too high, too far off target. When he raised his eyes again, Zuhayr was crouching on the pavement with Rebecca held in front of him, a human shield.

Katz saw that she was conscious, although obviously stunned. Blood streamed across her face from a fresh scalp wound, masking older injuries, more painful to look at. Blind rage suffused his being, but Katz choked it down, channeling his hatred of Salim Zuhayr into the focus of a laser beam before it carried him away.

Rebecca's life was in his own hands now, as much as in Zuhayr's. Katz was determined not to let her down again.

"You should've stayed away, old man," the Palestinian called out to Katz.

"I have unfinished business."

"We can finish it right now."

"I didn't bring a skirt to hide behind," Katz jeered.

"You care about this one?" Zuhayr demanded.

Katz did his best to make the lie sincere. "I've never seen her in my life," he said. "You want to take her with you when you die, it's fine with me."

Zuhayr blinked twice at that, startled, then frowned. "You're lying," he retorted. "That's no great surprise. Jews always lie."

"You want the truth? I mean to kill you. Hide behind one woman or a thousand, if you like. It's all the same to me."

"You think that killing me will help your country?" Zuhayr asked. "It won't."

"I'm not here on behalf of Israel," Katz informed his enemy. "It's personal."

The truth, this time.

"Leave now," the Arab said, "and I will let you live."

"No deal. Whatever else happens tonight, you die."

Zuhayr stood up, an awkward process, since he had to keep Rebecca well in front of him, ducking his head to peer across her shoulder. When he straightened at last, the Arab kept his face pressed cheek-to-cheek beside Rebecca's, kissing-close.

Katz matched Zuhayr's movements to a point, stopping when he knelt in profile to the Arab and his hostage, balancing the Beretta's short barrel across his right forearm. He didn't try to zero in a mark. It would've been too obvious and might've forced his adversary's hand.

It struck Katz that the sounds of random gunfire from the plant at large had ceased. He couldn't process what that meant in concrete terms, but part of him remained alert for sounds of enemies approaching from his blind side, while the bulk of his attention focused on Rebecca and Zuhayr. His eyes locked with Rebecca's for a heartbeat, understanding flashed between them, and it was as if they had agreed the man who held her couldn't be permitted to escape.

"You're wasting time, old man," the Arab said. "Why don't you fire, if she means nothing to you?"

"You want to die," Katz said, "I'll do my best to help."

Rebecca chose that instant to react, lifting both feet, knees bent and rising toward her chest. Although Zuhayr had one arm wrapped around her body, he was dragged off balance by the sudden shift in weight, unable to support her in his grasp. As he began to topple forward, Katz squeezed off a single round that clipped the Arab's left shoulder and propelled him backward, cursing, while the woman tumbled from his grasp.

Their guns went off together then, both hammering in unison, Rebecca crawling underneath the interlocking streams of fire. Katz felt Zuhayr's rounds cutting into him, the pain eclipsing anything he'd felt before, but he held firm on the Beretta's trigger, pouring 5.56 mm slugs into the dancing puppet his adversary had become.

They fell almost together, both guns empty, sprawling in the midst of blood and bright, hot brass. Katz saw Salim Zuhayr twitch once, twice, then relax in death.

I'm done, he thought, slowly toppling onto his back.

THE HALF-DOZEN surviving shooters had collected for a kind of banzai charge, apparently believing they could overrun two enemies with little problem. Maybe they'd communicated via radios or cell phones. Bolan wasn't sure; more to the point, he didn't give a damn.

The enemy charged in a skirmish line that was intended to trap Bolan and McCarter in the lavatory and exterminate them, but it didn't quite work out that way.

For one thing, once they took their fight into the open, Bolan and McCarter were at liberty to use grenades. They each lobbed one—Bolan to the right, McCarter to the left—as their enemies came rushing toward them, firing on the run. The runners either didn't notice, or they were committed out of desperation to a final showdown at the plant.

Which was exactly what they got.

The frag grenades went off with less than half a second in between their detonations, fire and shrapnel winnowing the hostile ranks. Four men burst through the pall of smoke, and one of those was limping badly, teeth clenched tight around the pain that radiated from his mangled leg.

Still, they kept firing, moving closer. There would be no quarter given, and they asked for none. They meant to kill, or die in the attempt.

The Executioner was happy to oblige.

He used his SMG, McCarter likewise, sweeping right and left across the skirmish line with Parabellum rounds that tore through flesh and fabric, shattered bone on impact, taking vital organs out of play. The shooters went down, one by one, and Bolan fancied that the last one almost looked relieved.

Bolan was moving out to double-check the dead, when yet another burst of autofire reverberated through the plant. Two weapons dueling, by the sound of it, and punctuated by a woman's anguished cry.

They hadn't far to run, before they found Rebecca Mindel kneeling in a pool of blood, cradling her uncle in her lap. A few strides distant lay the crumpled body of another Palestinian. The last.

"He's dying," Mindel said. Her left hand rested lightly on the bloody ruin of Katz's chest.

"She's right," Katz stated, surprising all of them. His eyes blinked once at Bolan, then moved on to find McCarter at his side. "You're late."

"Hung up in traffic," McCarter told him, sounding like a man with something in his throat.

"Don't try to talk right now," Bolan advised.

"There won't be any later," Katz replied. And then, "It isn't finished yet. You know that?"

"We know that," Bolan confirmed.

"Napier...and others."

"We're on top of it," McCarter told him.

"Oil for China...graves for Israel...money for the middleman."

"Rest now, Uncle." Mindel was weeping softly.

"You finish it!" Katz said, his breathing labored now, a tortured wheeze that came as much from fissures in his chest as from his lips. "I'll haunt you if you don't."

"We'll finish it," the Executioner promised.

Katz smiled at that.

And then he died.

Epilogue

There was no need to fly the body home; Katz was already there. Mindel took charge of the arrangements, omitting the memorial service. Katz was buried on a sun-drenched morning at Tel Aviv's Tumpeldor Cemetery. He was in good company, surrounded by early Zionist leaders and Israeli politicians from past generations, dating back to the cemetery's establishment in 1903, but Katz would've been proudest to lie beside his only son, killed years earlier in action with the Israeli army.

No announcement of his death was published in the press. Mossad arranged for the police investigation to be casual, discreet and swiftly closed. The death of U.S. oilman Sterling Holbrook was attributed to Allah's Lance, a ransom scheme gone wrong. Salim Zuhayr's demise was celebrated as a victory, but grim reprisals by his living comrades were predicted in the press.

Sharon, Katz's daughter, was on the way, but had been delayed by bad weather. Fund-raising for her employers had taken her to Paris.

There was no rabbi present at the graveside, as a creaking winch lowered the casket out of sight. Katz hadn't been religious, in the sense of one who studied scripture and devoted his waking hours to solemn prayer. He had believed in something, nonetheless, and at the end had given up his life to make it real.

Mindel waited until the gravediggers were scraping sandy soil into the hole before she spoke. "I hope you'll keep your word," she said.

"How's that?" Bolan asked. He knew what was coming and he dreaded it, but there was no avoiding the inevitable.

"You told him we'd finish it. A promise to a dying man. A dying *friend*."

McCarter took his cue. "That's *we* as in the two of us," he said. "There's nothing left to do in Tel Aviv, unless you've got someone with balls enough to take on this Global outfit and bring the lot of them to book."

"My people won't do that," she answered.

"There's a bloody shock."

"Would yours?" she challenged him.

McCarter's smile was cynical. "You mean that lot in London? Not a chance. They'd need to hear Saddam Hussein himself was sitting on the board, before they'd move against a multinational that size—and even then they'd likely mind their manners, saying, 'please' and 'thank you very much.'"

"We're not so different, then."

"Thing is," McCarter said, "I haven't worked for that crowd in a while. We have a different way of doing things."

"That's what I'm counting on," Mindel replied.

"You're still not listening. You have no part in what comes next."

"He was my uncle!"

"All the more reason you shouldn't be involved," Bolan said.

She turned on him. "It's just a bit late to be talking ethics, don't you think?"

"I'm not concerned with ethics," Bolan said. "Survival's what I had in mind."

"You don't think I can handle it?"

"You did a bang-up job the first time 'round," McCarter said, "but we may not have time to rescue you again."

"You bas—"

"Enough!" The sound of Bolan's voice cut through their bickering. They had retreated from the graveside to a section of the cemetery where they had no audience. The sun beat down on them, relentless even at that hour of the morning. Bolan thought there should've been cloud cover, maybe even rain for the occasion, then dismissed the whimsical idea.

"Mossad wanted an end to it when we got Katz back from the Lance," Bolan reminded her.

"They've had a change of heart," Mindel replied.

"Why's that?"

"I told them what we know, so far. They seem to think it's in the nation's best interest that Napier and his scheme be stopped."

"Say, that's good news," McCarter interjected, nudging Bolan. "You and I can go home and rest easy now."

"Maybe you should," Mindel retorted. "Yes, why don't you do exactly that?"

"We have our orders," Bolan said.

"And I have mine." There was a tremor in her voice, sounding like equal parts of grief and anger. "With or without you, justice will be done. Israel will be protected."

"There may be more at stake than Israel," McCarter suggested.

"All the more reason to see it through."

"You are a stubborn—"

"Bitch? Is that what you're about to say?"

"It wasn't," McCarter said, "but if that's the label you prefer—"

"I said, *enough!*" They both turned eyes toward Bolan, reading anger in his face. "This nonsense is a luxury we can't afford. We don't have time for schoolyard games."

McCarter frowned. "When you say *we*—"

Bolan ignored him for the moment. "Our primary targets are already scattered far and wide. There's one in Hong Kong, one in Greece, and no one seems to know where Napier or Jabbar have gone to ground. Among them, they've got soldiers, several billion dollars, and, just maybe, the official sanction of the Chinese government. I think we've got enough to chew on as it is, without biting each other in the ass."

"The three of us," McCarter said.

"Maybe some wings," Bolan replied. "I'm reaching out for Jack."

"So, we're agreed then?" Mindel asked.

"Not yet," Bolan replied.

"What do you mean?"

"I need it understood that this remains official business, all the way. If all you want is vengeance for your uncle, then you're out. My people have already spoken to your brass, and that's official."

Mindel's posture stiffened, but she didn't argue. "Certainly. Agreed, by all means."

"Wait. There's more."

"I'm listening," she said.

"We'll call it bad luck that the heavies picked you up this time, but we won't play that scene again."

"I don't intend—"

"No one intends to be a prisoner," he said, cutting her off. "I'm laying out the facts of life. Get bagged again, we cut our losses and move on. The same holds true for every member of the team."

"I understand," she told him, eyes burning into his. "When do we start?"

"You read my mind," McCarter echoed.

Bolan glanced back toward his old friend's grave and answered, "How about right now?"

* * * * *

The heart-stopping action concludes in
Mack Bolan
RETALIATION
available now.

James Axler
Outlanders®

MAD GOD'S WRATH

The survivors of the oldest moon colony have been revived from cryostasis and brought to Cerberus Redoubt, leaving behind an enemy in deep, frozen sleep. But betrayal and treachery bring the rebel stronghold under seige by the resurrected demon king of a lost world. With a prize hostage in tow to lure Kane and his fellow warriors, he retreats to the uncharted planet of mystery and impossibility for a final act of madness.

Available February 2004 at your favorite retail outlet.

Or order your copy now by sending your name, address, zip or postal code, along with a check or money order (please do not send cash) for $6.50 for each book ordered ($7.99 in Canada), plus 75¢ postage and handling ($1.00 in Canada), payable to Gold Eagle Books, to:

In the U.S.	In Canada
Gold Eagle Books	Gold Eagle Books
3010 Walden Avenue	P.O. Box 636
P.O. Box 9077	Fort Erie, Ontario
Buffalo, NY 14269-9077	L2A 5X3

Please specify book title with your order.
Canadian residents add applicable federal and provincial taxes.

GOUT28

TAKE 'EM FREE

2 action-packed novels plus a mystery bonus

NO RISK
NO OBLIGATION TO BUY